# ROBERT B. PARKER'S
# BUZZ KILL

For a comprehensive title list and a preview of upcoming books, visit PRH.com/RobertBParker or Facebook.com /RobertBParkerAuthor.

# ROBERT B. PARKER'S
# BUZZ KILL

## A SUNNY RANDALL NOVEL

# ALISON GAYLIN

G. P. PUTNAM'S SONS
New York

**PUTNAM**
— EST. 1838 —

G. P. PUTNAM'S SONS
*Publishers Since 1838*
An imprint of Penguin Random House LLC
penguinrandomhouse.com

Library of Congress Cataloging-in-Publication Data

Names: Gaylin, Alison, author.
Title: Robert B. Parker's buzz kill / Alison Gaylin.
Other titles: Buzz kill
Description: New York : G. P. Putnam's Sons, 2024.
Identifiers: LCCN 2024009345 (print) | LCCN 2024009346 (ebook) |
ISBN 9780593715642 (hardcover) | ISBN 9780593715659 (e-pub)
Subjects: LCGFT: Detective and mystery fiction. | Novels.
Classification: LCC PS3607.A9858 R633 2024 (print) |
LCC PS3607.A9858 (ebook) | DDC 813/.6—dc23/eng/20240311
LC record available at https://lccn.loc.gov/2024009345
LC ebook record available at https://lccn.loc.gov/2024009346
p.        cm.

Printed in the United States of America
1st Printing

Interior art by YARUNIV Studio/Shutterstock

## ROBERT B. PARKER'S
# BUZZ KILL

# ONE

I never thought I'd say this," I told Richie, "but I love New Jersey."

Richie grinned. "All you've seen of it is my apartment."

He was correct, if a little generous. I'd seen the kitchen, because my dog, Rosie, had insisted. And then the bedroom, which was where we currently were, lying on our backs in the pink glow of a glorious December sunset, having just caught our breath. The ocean view from the bedroom window was spectacular, and the bed itself was heaven, the sheets a fine Egyptian cotton and with a ridiculously high thread count, bought by Richie especially for this occasion, "because I know you like that fancy stuff." But if I was going to be honest, the rest of Richie's apartment was a blur. "I've seen and experienced the best that the Garden State has to offer," I said.

"Can't dispute that," Richie said.

Rosie nosed open the bedroom door and scuttled in, her claws clacking on the parquet wood floor. She jumped up on the bed and burrowed between us until her big bull terrier head was under both of our pillows, her lower half sticking out, tail wagging. The perfect family portrait. I'd have snapped a selfie so I could paint it later, but I didn't want to ruin the mood.

"I've missed you, Sunny," Richie said.

I gave him sad eyes. "You've only missed me for my dog."

Rosie knew the word *dog*. On cue, she pulled her head out from the pillows and licked Richie's cheek. He smiled, scratching her behind the ear. "It is a pretty sweet package deal," he said.

It had been nearly five months since I'd been in the same room as my ex-husband. The last time he'd seen me in bed, it had been a hospital bed, and I'd been recovering from stab wounds after a run-in with a psychopath.

And so, for two people who had decided to try to make a go at . . . something . . . we had a lot of catching up to do. Physically speaking, we'd accomplished that mission, but that was no surprise. Nonverbal communication had always been our strong suit. The problem was talking. Figuring out what, exactly, this "something" was.

The one constant throughout our very long and complicated relationship was this: Richie was the one who wanted to put his foot on the gas, while I was content to keep the gearshift in park for as long as I possibly could. It had been the reason we'd divorced—and the reason he'd remarried, had a kid, and divorced again. And it had been the reason I'd gone into analysis.

But things change. People change. Even me. Once you hit a certain age, a long absence can affect you in ways you never expected it to.

"Rosie's missed you, too," I said.

Richie and I had been in touch via phone and the occasional Zoom chat since his big move down the shore (get me, talking like a Jersey girl). But our busy schedules had prevented us from seeing each other until now. On Richie's end, it was starting a new job as general manager of Candy's Room—a bar/restaurant that advertised itself as being "the number-one destination for the world's greatest Springsteen tribute bands"— as well as working out a joint custody schedule for his son, Richard Jr., in a whole new state.

For me, it was the fame I'd acquired as the result of a high-profile case I'd solved—which involved a couple Instagram influencers, as well as the aforementioned run-in with said psychopath. With the Boston press swarming my apartment building and calling me nonstop following my release from the hospital, I'd finally relented, giving an exclusive interview to Tom Gorman, a sweet *Globe* columnist I'd dated for about a minute the previous year. No sparks. (I'd left my heart, as it seemed, in New Jersey.) But professionally speaking, the interview had changed my life. It went viral, landing me with more work than I knew what to do with. Other than Thanksgiving, this was my first free weekend since July. So at long last,

I'd packed a bag, grabbed Rosie, and taken the four-and-a-half-hour drive to Richie's apartment.

So far, the reunion had been better than I'd dreamed it would be. And I have excellent dreams. Ask my shrink. She's blushed more than once—and believe me, she's not a blusher.

I rolled over onto my side and ran a hand through Richie's dark hair, inhaling his clean, familiar scent. Rosie licked my hand and flipped onto her back so I could rub her belly. *I could be happy here*, I thought. *Maybe.*

"You ever miss Boston?" I said.

"Yes and no."

"Meaning . . ."

"I don't miss owning the saloon. I don't miss the traffic. I don't miss all the baggage that comes with people knowing who my dad is. But I do miss my dad. I miss the regulars at the saloon. I miss being able to get a decent lobster roll. I miss the lights on the harbor at sunset. I also miss the Bloody Marys at the Russell House and . . . you know . . ."

"Spike?"

"Sure," he said and smiled. "I miss Spike."

I smiled back. "And Rosie."

"We already covered that." Richie kissed my hand. Rosie snuggled between us, and I felt hopeful and confused and nervous and content, all those conflicting emotions rushing back, the way they always did when I was with Richie after a long absence or even a short one. And I could tell he was feeling the same. *It seems like you understand each other*, my shrink, Susan Silverman, had told me during my last visit.

*We do,* I'd replied. *We always have. But does that mean we belong together?*

*That's a question only you can answer,* she had said, which hardly seemed fair, considering how much time and money I'd invested in her over the years.

I asked Richie how his son was enjoying his new school. He said he loved it. I asked him about work, and he said he couldn't complain. He asked me about my work, and I told him that I couldn't complain, either. Then I let him know that I'd turned down multiple offers from Bill Welch, a multimillionaire who wanted me to "discreetly" track down his wayward son, Dylan—the CEO of an energy drink company called Gonzo and, as a side note, a total douchebag. (I'd dealt with Dylan back in July, and in my humble opinion, he was better off missing.)

"How much did Welch offer you to find his son?" Richie asked.

"Not enough to cancel my weekend plans."

Richie looked at me in a way that could have melted the polar ice caps. "As your weekend plans, I'd like to show my appreciation."

We kissed. We kissed some more. Things progressed. And then, when we were catching our breath for the second time, Richie asked the million-dollar question.

"Sunny," he said. "Where do we go from here?"

I gazed deep into his eyes and gave him a blinding cop-out of a smile. "How about out to dinner?"

"I was thinking the same thing," Richie said. He looked

relieved. Or maybe I was just projecting. Another question for my therapist, I supposed.

After we were dressed and outside and he'd locked the door behind us, Richie slipped his arm around my waist. "You know what?" he said.

"What?"

"I wouldn't mind having you nearby for more than just a weekend."

"You say that now, but I only just got here."

"I know."

"You could be really annoyed with me in forty-eight hours."

"I'm willing to take that risk."

I rested my head on his shoulder, the palm of my hand against the back of his coat. It felt terrifyingly comfortable. "I'll think about it," I said.

Richie kissed my forehead. He pulled me closer. "That's good enough for me."

# TWO

I spent an extra day down the shore. It meant I had to leave on Monday before dawn to get home, shower, change, and go back to my office at a reasonable hour, but it was worth it. I loved Asbury Park in December—the windswept beach, the absolute quietness of it, the Christmas tree Richie and I passed every day during our long walks by the water—a scraggly pine bedecked with painted seashells. I loved the cold, the way it made us huddle together, and the fact that the Jersey Shore's population thinned by more than half during the offseason, making it possible to get a table at any restaurant we wanted, no matter the time.

And the sunsets. Always, the sunsets.

By the time Rosie and I got back to my apartment, I was

already deeply homesick for New Jersey. I listened to Spring-steen on Spotify as I got ready for work—changing out of my comfy sweats and into a Brunello Cucinelli sweater dress—replaying scenes from the weekend in my mind. I thought about everything Richie and I had said to each other—and every-thing we didn't say. Beyond that brief exchange outside his apartment, we'd never gotten around to answering the dreaded "Where do we go from here?" question. But maybe that was for the best. When it came to relationships, I'd never done well with road maps. It was better to take things one day at a time. And on this particular day, at this particular time, anything felt possible—even moving away from Boston.

Once I was dressed and Rosie was fed, I stretched a canvas. After work, I planned to paint the view from Richie's bedroom.

"What do you think, Rosie?" I said as I eyed the blank white cloth. "Winters on the Jersey Shore? Summers? The whole year?"

Rosie barked.

"You're right," I said. "It might be difficult to move in with Richie right away with his son there every other week. I mean . . . Richard Junior is great, but am I ready to be a stepmom?"

Rosie barked again.

"Find a place of my own down there? That could be very ex-pensive, Rosie. Especially if I want to keep this loft."

She followed me into the kitchen. I tossed her a treat and thanked her for listening.

My phone dinged. It was a reminder that, at five p.m., I had an appointment with Susan Silverman. It couldn't have come at a better time.

When I arrived at work at ten a.m., my new-ish reception-ist, Blake James, was sitting at his desk, taking a selfie. Once an influencer with hundreds of thousands of followers, Blake had deleted his Instagram account four months ago following a family tragedy. But in his case, apparently, old hab-its died hard.

"Morning, Blake," I said as I walked in.

"Morning," he said. "I was just trying to get a look at this . . . this wound."

"What wound?"

"This one." He pointed to his jaw. "I cut myself shaving this morning. I think it might be infected."

"I don't see anything."

"You sure?"

I moved closer. From this distance, I could make out a tiny scratch in Blake's otherwise flawless skin. "It doesn't look in-fected," I said. "Does it hurt?"

"No."

"Then it's probably not."

Blake's face relaxed. I was used to this. Blake was a very young twenty-two. He'd grown up mostly without a mother and had been through a lot of trauma within the past year.

And so, as muscular and self-assured as he appeared on the surface, he was continuously showing me his ouchies. "Thank you, Sunny," he said.

"Don't mention it."

He put down his phone. "How was your weekend?"

"Fantastic."

"Did Rosie have fun?"

"She did."

"I wish you'd brought her in. I miss her."

"She was pretty tired this morning," I said. "But I'll bring her in tomorrow."

"Cool," Blake said. He loved Rosie. I appreciated that. I also understood his need for a job, and, following the uptick in business, my need for a receptionist. But still, it was hard getting used to anyone in my office every day—especially on those mornings when I wasn't in the mood to talk. Blake was always in the mood to talk. Always.

"I made coffee," Blake said. "It's really good. I saw this TikTok where a girl put a teaspoon of nutmeg and a teaspoon of cinnamon in with the grounds. She said it makes the coffee less bitter, so I tried that and it worked. You want some?"

"Maybe later," I said. "Thanks." I started toward my office.

"Oh, I almost forgot," Blake said. "You have a customer . . . Sorry. Client," he said. "I'm still learning this private investigator lingo."

"Potential client? Because I haven't taken on anybody new."

"Right. Potential," he said. "Anyway, she's in your office."

"I don't remember scheduling any meetings."

"Yeah, it wasn't on the calendar. But she said it was urgent."

"Who is she?"

"Dylan's mom."

"Dylan Welch?"

"Yeah."

"I said no to his father."

"His mom said 'no' wasn't an acceptable answer."

I let out a long, draining sigh.

"Rich people," Blake said. "Am I right?"

"Why did you let her in?"

Blake's cheeks reddened. He picked at a nail. "You know how pushy Bill Welch was?"

"Yeah?"

"How he kept having his assistant call about his son over and over again after you said no and recommended other PIs, and how he sent you all those emails telling you that the names you sent were unacceptable, and we were both like, 'What the hell is his problem?' Remember all that?"

"I remember, Blake," I said. "It was a week ago."

"Well, his wife, Mrs. Welch. Lydia."

"Yeah?"

"She's worse."

On cue, the door to my office opened. A tall blond woman stepped out, sporting head-to-toe Chanel, a fresh blowout, huge but tasteful diamond stud earrings, and a look on her face like she wanted to speak to the manager—and rip her limb from limb if she didn't get her way.

Blake shuddered, noticeably.

"Lydia Welch?" I said to the woman.

"Sunny Randall," she said. "We need to talk."

# THREE

Before today, I'd seen Lydia Welch only once, and that wasn't even in person. I'd seen her in a family photo that she'd shared on Facebook five years ago, taken at the Welch summer home in Nantucket on the Fourth of July.

Surrounded by her loved ones, Lydia had struck me as laid back, relaxed, and very down-to-earth, especially for someone in her tax bracket. It just goes to show how misleading social media can be. Granted, she was on vacation in the picture—and clearly in a much better mood. But the Lydia Welch I encountered in my office could have easily pulled a set of quietly elegant brass knuckles out of her Birkin bag and knocked Facebook Lydia senseless.

I asked Blake to bring us two cups of his coffee, and he practically sprinted out of the room.

Lydia Welch and I spent about a minute getting situated—me behind my desk and Lydia on one of the two comfortable leather client chairs I'd bought about a month ago, when I'd spent my newfound surplus on an office renovation.

Then, for what felt like a few hours but was probably around a minute, the two of us just sat there. There was a lot of throat clearing on my part, a few well-placed glares on hers. For someone who had led with "We need to talk," Mrs. Welch was distinctly nonverbal. It felt like a power play to me. Whoever cracked first and spoke lost.

I lost.

"Mrs. Welch. If this is about your son, I'm afraid I can't help you."

"Of course it's about my son," she said. "Yes, you *can* help me find him. And you *will*."

"I already told your husband, I'm not the right person for the job."

"I read the *Globe* article," Lydia Welch said. "You're the best out there. That makes you the right person."

"I'm flattered," I said. "But the truth is, Mrs. Welch, Dylan hates me."

"That's ridiculous."

"Oh, no, it isn't."

"Why?"

"Well, for one thing, I insulted him."

"You're not the first."

"I drew a gun on him."

"A misunderstanding."

"I caused him serious bodily injury."

"You called an ambulance afterward." She smiled sweetly. "That was kind."

Blake returned with our coffees, along with a cream pitcher and a sugar bowl, all on a tray. He placed it on my desk. "Is there anything else you'd like?"

"Privacy." Lydia glared at him. Blake's face flushed and a look crept into his eyes, as if he'd discovered another ouchie. "Okey dokey."

"Thank you very much, Blake," I said as he left.

Lydia stirred cream into her coffee. I sipped mine. Blake was right. It was very good.

"That assistant of yours. I recognize him."

"He used to advertise Dylan's product on his Instagram account," I said.

"Gonzo," she said.

"Yes."

"We gave Dylan that company, you know," she said. "He told us he had an idea for an energy drink with twice the caffeine of the strongest blend on the market and twenty-two essential vitamins. Bill and I gave him the start-up money. He'd failed with the dating app, but he desperately wanted to be an entrepreneur. I convinced Bill to provide the funds. I thought Gonzo was a catchy name."

I looked at Lydia. It was pretty clear she'd been the force behind her husband's persistent calls and emails. "I'm not a fan of energy drinks," I said, "but it seems like a popular brand."

"It is." She swallowed her coffee. "Especially in the past two quarters. Not because of Dylan, though."

"No?"

"The COO—an old college friend of his—does all the work."

"Oh."

"Just like the dating app and every other new toy we've ever given him, he got bored with it," she said. "Your assistant probably takes his job more seriously than Dylan has ever taken anything. Even Harvard. Dylan went to Harvard, you know."

"Yes, I know." In fact, I'd heard all about his Harvard years from Teresa Leone—his girlfriend at that time. "I understand he wanted to go to film school after graduation," I said, "but his father wouldn't let him."

Lydia Welch rolled her eyes. "First of all, who *doesn't* want to go to film school?"

I shrugged. That was kind of true.

"Second, his father wouldn't let him because he felt it was a stall tactic. And I did, too. Dylan didn't want to make movies. He wanted to spend another two or three years hanging out in Hollywood nightclubs and spending our money."

I nodded. "Okay, but this friend of Dylan's also told me that his father wouldn't give him the backing for the dating app," I said, "and that made him turn to some dicey sources."

"That's partially true," she said. "*I* gave him the money for the dating app. Out of my personal account. When the business failed and I wouldn't bail him out, he did obtain additional funding from Russian gangsters."

*Wow,* I thought. *That's even worse.*

"By the way, this friend of his," she said. "Was this a girl, by any chance? One he was interested in and trying to impress?"

"Yes," I said.

"I knew it," she said. "In any case, it took a lot of finagling on my part, but I found the right lawyers, we paid off the right gangsters. And he was free to disappoint us again and again."

I looked at her for a long while. "This is enlightening," I said. "It doesn't make me want to take this case. But it is enlightening."

Lydia let out a sigh. "Sunny," she said, "you take your job seriously."

"I do."

"I could tell that just from reading that article," she said. "You care about people. You care about families."

"Not all people," I said. "Not all families."

She opened her mouth as if to say something, but drew a sharp breath instead. She seemed to be at a loss for words—unusual for her, I was sure. Surprisingly, it made me feel kind of bad.

"You know, I'm not as great as that article would have you believe," I said.

"Modesty," she said. "Yet another virtue."

"Full disclosure, I used to date the guy who wrote it."

She smiled. "That speaks even more highly of you. An *ex* portraying you that way."

I sighed. "You get your mind set on something, you don't let go, do you?"

"Like a dog with a bone," she said. "It's how I got Bill to propose."

I watched her for a few moments. "I'm assuming you want to offer me more than your husband did."

"Absolutely."

I thought about the second home on the Jersey Shore. "How much more?"

Lydia opened her Birkin bag. She removed a piece of ivory-colored stationery and a Montblanc pen. She wrote a number on the stationery, turned it face down, and slid it across the desk. "I know this is corny," she said.

"I've only ever seen it done in movies."

"Same here," she said. "But some numbers are better off written than said out loud."

I turned the paper over. Looked at the figure—enough for a down payment or at least a year's rent on a very nice, dog-friendly apartment in Asbury Park.

I cleared my throat. "Can I ask you something, Mrs. Welch?"

"Lydia."

"Lydia," I said. "How do you know that Dylan is missing?"

"Pardon?"

"He's a grown man. He leads an active lifestyle. Would it be that out of character for him to take off somewhere for . . . How long has it been?"

"Two weeks."

I exhaled. "That doesn't seem like a very long time."

"Have you ever gone that long without talking to your mother?"

"Yes."

"Truly?"

I cleared my throat. "I do talk to my dad very frequently."

Lydia set her coffee cup back on its saucer. She tucked a lock of shiny hair behind an ear, then folded her hands in her lap—every move of hers perfectly composed, but with a tension beneath the surface, like a smooth white sky just before a storm. "I'm sorry you don't have a good relationship with your mother."

"I didn't say that."

"You didn't have to."

"I suppose not," I said.

"Dylan doesn't have a good relationship with his father," she said. "They're very different personalities. They speak rarely. I don't even think they necessarily trust each other."

I nodded.

She looked at me as though she expected me to contribute to the conversation—to tell her that my mother and I shared a similar dynamic. But I didn't take the bait. My shrink appointment wasn't until five p.m., and I could handle that discussion only once in a day.

"Every child needs at least one parent on their side," she said.

I nodded again.

"Dylan and I have a special connection, Sunny," she said. "I know all about what you generously called his 'active lifestyle,' when what you really meant was the clubbing, the benders, the rehab stays, the escapes from rehab . . ."

"So you understand," I said.

"I understand he isn't perfect," she said. "But that doesn't change our connection. It doesn't stop me from knowing when he needs my help. Like with those Russian gangsters. He didn't have to tell me . . ."

An emotion passed through Lydia's clear blue eyes—a type of ache, as though a part of her had been removed and she needed it back in order to survive. It felt genuine enough to move me. I hated her for that.

I let out a heavy sigh. "Tell me about the last time you spoke to him."

"It was at his place of business."

"DylWel Inc.?"

She smiled. "DylWel is just a website, Sunny," she said. "The dating app was his only other venture."

"So . . . Gonzo."

"Yes," she said. "The corporate offices. We had lunch plans."

"You met him there."

"Yes."

"You went out to lunch."

"No," she said. "He said he wouldn't be able to join me."

"Did he give a reason?"

"No." She drank more coffee, then cradled the cup in her hands. "He didn't look very good."

"How so?"

"He probably looked like he did the last time you saw him."

"Strung out?"

"Yes," she said. "A little."

"Well, he looked a lot strung out when I saw him." *Smelled it, too,* I thought. But I didn't say it.

"He seemed more distracted than anything else," she said. "And he hadn't shaved. I asked if he was okay, and he got angry with me. Said it was none of my business."

I nodded.

"He did say he'd see me soon, though. We have a family brunch at our house the Sunday after Thanksgiving. We prefer it to those big, heavy meals, you know. But that day came and went and Dylan never showed."

"Did he call?"

"He texted Bill."

"What did the text say?"

"'Something came up. Sorry.'"

"That was it?" I said. "The whole text?"

"There was an exclamation point after *sorry.*"

"Did you find it strange that he would text Bill and not you?"

"My son texts his father," she said, "when he's trying to avoid having a meaningful conversation."

"And no word from him since then?"

She shook her head.

"I'm assuming you've checked with the rehabs."

"Yes," she said. "Hospitals, too. I check every morning, first thing."

"Okay. I'm going to need a list of friends, relatives. Work associates. Girlfriends, ex-girlfriends. Enemies. Of course, I'll need all of Dylan's info, too. His home address. If it's a condo or apartment, I'll need the name and number of the manager if you have it."

"This means you're taking the case, yes?"

I rested a hand on the piece of stationery and snuck another look at the number. I needed to make sure it was real. "I'm taking the case." I said it firmly.

She unfastened the Birkin bag again and produced a manila folder, which she handed to me. It said DYLAN on the cover in block letters, and when I opened it up, there was everything I asked for: Lydia's son's info, followed by three printed pages of names, most of them accompanied by phone numbers, emails, and "relation."

"You came prepared for me to say yes," I said.

She extended a manicured hand. I shook it.

"Everyone says yes to me, Sunny," Lydia said. "And so I'm always prepared."

# FOUR

So Lydia Welch made you an offer you couldn't refuse."
Spike was doing his best *Godfather* impersonation, which,
if I was going to be honest, was not all that great.

"I saved the piece of paper she wrote it on," I said. "I may
have it framed."

"Oooh, let me see."

We were having lunch at his restaurant, Spike's—something
we did a lot on workdays. I slipped the ivory stationery out of
my purse and placed it on the table face up.

Spike read the number. He let out a whistle.

I quickly put it back in my purse. "Right?"

"I've killed for less than that."

"To be fair, you've often killed pro bono."

"True. But still."

"I know."

The server came by with our orders—a bleu cheese burger for Spike and a classic Greek salad for me, plus two iced teas. The server's name was Norah and I knew her well. She asked me where Rosie was, a concerned look on her face. I told her Rosie was fine—just taking a personal day.

When she left, Spike asked to see Lydia's offer again, just to make sure he'd read it correctly. I obliged.

"I'm awestruck," Spike said.

"I don't know that I've ever seen you awestruck," I said. "In fact, I don't think I've ever heard you use the word *awestruck*."

"You haven't," he said as I put the stationery back in my purse. "If it wasn't lunchtime on a Monday, I'd break out my best champagne."

"Rain check on the champagne," I said. "And I'm buying."

He raised his glass of iced tea. "To future champagne," he said.

"Future champagne." I clinked my glass with his.

Spike sipped his tea. I took a bite of my salad, thinking about how much champagne I could buy with the sum Lydia Welch had written so casually on that luxe piece of stationery. A life-changing number, to be sure. But the truth was, it wasn't just the money that had made me accept Lydia's offer. It was that lost look in her eyes—the very obvious fact that, despite all she had in this world, she was missing something she needed, and that something was a person. Okay, an asshole of a person. But it wasn't my job to judge the missing.

Spike asked me how the investigation was going so far. I told him that, with Blake's help, I'd called all the names on Lydia's list. And of the few who had deigned to pick up their phones for us—two ex-girlfriends, three former employees from the dating app, a college suitemate, a cousin—none of them had seen Dylan in months, if not years. Blake was emailing the non-answerers, but I didn't have much hope there, either. "Dylan Welch doesn't seem to forge lasting friend-ships," I said.

"I'm sure brief friendships don't happen much for him, either," Spike said.

I nodded. "His mother loves him, though," I said. "That's obvious. When Bill Welch met with me, he seemed . . . I don't know . . . Like someone had put him up to it. But Lydia was sincere."

"You're a sucker for sincerity," Spike said. "You always have been."

"Fortunately, it's a very rare quality," I said.

Spike took another bite of his burger. I went back to my salad. It was quite good. The perfect balance of olives and feta, and the dressing was bright and tangy.

Spike asked if I'd checked with Dylan's bank and credit card providers to see if he'd withdrawn money or put any charges on his cards since he went missing. And I told him the sad truth about Dylan Welch: After a post-college spending spree that resulted in maxed-out cards, close to a million in debt—and massive humiliation for his family—Lydia took it upon herself to oversee all of Dylan's finances.

"He can't withdraw five dollars without the bank alerting Lydia," I said. "He has only one card in his own name. And it has a limit of one thousand dollars."

"The ultimate poor little rich boy," Spike said.

"Yep," I said. "Anyway, Lydia said there's been no activity on any of those accounts since he went missing. So he's either obtaining funds from other sources or . . ." I took a sip of tea. I didn't feel like finishing the sentence.

"So what's next?"

"After lunch, I'm going over to the Gonzo corporate offices," I said. "I figure I'll have more luck talking to people there, and I always do better in person."

"Nobody can hang up on you."

"Exactly."

Spike drank some of his tea. "Speaking of doing better in person . . ." He gave me a meaningful look that I understood instantly.

I rolled my eyes at him. "The weekend was good. Richie's good," I said. "We had fun."

Spike kept looking at me. I knew he was waiting for me to say more. Just like I knew what he meant by "speaking of doing better in person" without his having to explain. When your friendship has lasted longer than most people's marriages—and Spike and mine had, to say the least—you can read each other's minds with an alarming facility.

He took another bite of his burger and stared at me some more. I ate some more of my salad and stared back. He drank his iced tea. I drank mine. The whole time, our gazes stayed locked. It was a game of chicken, albeit one that was, compared to most games of chicken, rather polite and low stakes. All Spike wanted was for me to tell him if my relationship status had changed from complicated to super-complicated.

"Okay, you win," I said finally. "I'm considering moving down the shore."

Spike's eyes widened. "Wow."

"Just for part of the year," I said.

"Get you."

"Get me."

"Which part of the year?"

"Probably winters, weird as that sounds."

Spike took another sip of his iced tea. "It doesn't sound that weird."

"I like it there in the winter."

He nodded. "So you really did have fun with Richie."

"I did."

"And you think you can make it work this time."

"I do."

We ate in silence for several minutes.

"I'm happy for you," Spike said finally. I could tell he'd put a lot of thought into that response. And he was telling the truth. Spike always told the truth. "One question," he said.

"Yes?"

"Are you still going to call me when you need some heads busted?"

"It's a five-hour drive," I said. "You might not be able to get there in time."

"Yeah."

"Maybe you should teach me karate."

Spike gave me a long, appraising look. "Judo," he said. "With those skinny arms, you'd be much better at judo."

# FIVE

I arrived at Gonzo's corporate headquarters at one-thirty p.m. They were located on one of the top floors of the Winthrop Center—a futuristic mirrored skyscraper in the Financial District that also happened to be the fourth tallest building in Boston. Riding the elevator, my ears clicked. I was a little lightheaded as I entered the offices—a feeling that was only heightened by the atmosphere. The waiting area was all white leather and chrome, decorated for the season with a white artificial Christmas tree bedecked in shiny red-and-white Gonzo cans. A giant projection screen took up an entire wall, showing continuous footage of old black-and-white monster movies—*Godzilla*, *King Kong*, *The Wolfman*—all with colorized cans of Gonzo edited in. The design scheme here seemed to be "unpleasant hallucination."

I'd been able to do only the tiniest bit of research on Gonzo's COO, Sky Farley, whom Lydia had described in the "relation" field as Dylan's "longtime chum—WONDERFUL." Sky didn't seem to be on social media—not even LinkedIn. A real hindrance when you're trying to learn about someone.

He did look good on paper—what little paper there was. According to the bio I found on the DylWel website, Sky had graduated from Harvard the same year as Dylan, dual-majoring in biotechnology and data science But instead of doing what Dylan did following graduation—which was basically nothing, other than piling up mountains of debt—Sky had gone straight to NYU's Stern School of Business, where he'd gotten his MBA and worked on Wall Street for a couple years. Online at least, Sky seemed like the ultimate silent partner. The bio wasn't even accompanied by a picture (I couldn't find pictures of him on Harvard's website, either), and if he ever went to ribbon cuttings or press events, he wasn't photographed at them.

Here he was, second-in-command at a high-profile company. The one who did all the work, according to Lydia—but otherwise, an invisible man. For all I knew at this point, Sky Farley could have been as serious and brilliant as his bio implied. Or he could have been the one to have chosen this décor.

I moved toward the reception desk, which was very long and white and had padded leather and chrome detailing at the front to match the furniture in the waiting area. It reminded me of a spaceship's console from some cheesy old TV show, save for the neon GONZO logo flashing obnoxiously from the wall behind it.

Actually, it just said GON. The sign was broken—the *Z* and the *O* missing in action. *Strange,* I thought. Everything else in this hellhole seemed immaculate.

The receptionist was gazing down at her desk as I approached. I assumed it was an effort to avoid the flashing red letters, which reflected off all the chrome in a way that was, at the very least, distracting.

"Not a great place to work if you're prone to seizures," I said to her.

She was dressed in all white with silver jewelry, presumably to match the furniture. It made me worried about her dry-cleaning bills. She looked up, confusion all over her face.

"The sign," I said, pointing to it.

She winced. "Oh. Yes."

I noticed a few glass shards on the floor. "Did it just break?"

The receptionist blinked at me. She was young and bird-like and looked very nervous. I decided she wasn't one for small talk.

"I'd like to speak with Sky Farley, please," I said.

"Do you have an appointment?"

"Not really."

One of her eyelids started to twitch.

I felt like she was on the verge of calling security, so I spoke quickly. "I'm working for Lydia Welch."

She let out a long sigh. Her shoulders relaxed. "Dylan's mom."

"Yes," I said. I opened my purse and took out my PI license. She glanced at it.

"You're the private investigator," she said. "Mrs. Welch called and said you might be coming by."

"Oh, good. I hate having to explain things."

She stole another look at my license. "I hope everything works out, Ms. Randall," she said. "My name is Elspeth, by the way."

She stuck out a delicate hand. I shook it gently. "I'll do my best to find him, Elspeth," I said.

"Find who?"

"Um . . . Dylan?"

"Of course." Elspeth visibly cringed. "Sorry. Crazy day. I'll see if Sky is available." She slipped a Bluetooth into her ear and angled herself away from me, speaking in a tone so low I could barely hear her.

Then she turned around and stood up. "She'll speak to you," she said.

"Wait," I said. "Sky Farley is a she?" I was genuinely shocked—not because I was sexist, of course. It was because I couldn't imagine Dylan Welch successfully working with a woman in any type of capacity—let alone viewing her as a "longtime chum."

I nearly explained that to Elspeth, but as it turned out, I didn't have to. "Sky likes everybody," she said.

She stood up and led me to a long hallway. We walked until we reached a metal detector. It was manned by a hulking security guard who asked me to empty the contents of my purse and place them in a plastic tray. I was surprised by the whole setup, but I did as I was told. When I got around to removing my .38, the guard's eyebrows lifted.

"She's a private investigator," Elspeth told him. "Mrs. Welch hired her to find Dylan."

"Oh." If this guy had any opinion of me or of Lydia or Dylan Welch, it didn't show on his face.

Once we'd made it through the gauntlet and I was zipping up my purse, I turned to Elspeth. "I'm all for office safety," I said. "But if you don't mind my saying, this seems like a *lot*."

"I know," she said. "It's new. We're all getting used to it."

# SIX

Sky Farley's office was everything you'd expect from a corner office on the forty-ninth floor of a skyscraper. The view was arresting. So arresting that I barely noticed the cluster of suits standing at the center of the room, which broke up just as we arrived.

I looked at the group as they passed: two men and a woman, all stony-faced and middle-aged and in various forms of tweed. They did not look at me. They left quickly, their eyes downcast, as though the gleaming blond-wood floor was something deeply fascinating.

"Thanks, Elspeth," said the one remaining woman (girl?), who had to be Sky Farley. I knew from her bio that she was at least twenty-six, but she looked more like a teenager. And as opposed to everyone else I'd seen here, Sky was dressed down, in jeans, red Chucks, and a frayed cable-knit sweater. She wore glasses with thick black frames, her thick brown hair pulled into a messy bun, like some college freshman studying for finals. She made me feel overdressed and overly made up. And tall. Too tall. I towered over her in my two-inch Prada heels.

"Did you want anything?" she asked. "Coffee? Water? Gonzo?"

"No, thank you."

Elspeth left. Sky led me to her enormous desk, which housed a sleek computer with a screen the size of a small billboard. "Have a seat," she said.

I did. "Nice digs," I said.

"Right?" Sky said. "Sometimes I have to pinch myself." She seemed even younger and smaller behind the desk—like a kid exploring her mom's office at Bring Your Daughter to Work Day. "I'm glad Mrs. Welch hired you, Ms. Randall," she said.

"Sunny is fine."

"Sunny." She blushed. In that moment, she weirdly reminded me of Blake. "I've read all about you," Sky said. "It seems like if anybody can find Dylan, you can."

"I'll do my best," I said.

"So what can I tell you about him?"

"Well, first of all, is it unusual for him to just disappear like this?"

"Not really," she said.

"I didn't think so."

"But the thing is, when he does disappear, I usually know where to find him."

"Where's that?"

"My place."

I raised an eyebrow. I couldn't help it.

She blushed again. "Not like that. Jeez."

"Like what, then?"

Sky adjusted her glasses. "I'm his friend."

I wanted to ask her why. I didn't, of course. But she answered the question anyway.

"It's been like that since college, really," she said. "He'd party too hard or get in a fight with a girlfriend or do something idiotic—cheat on a test or whatever . . . He'd show up on my doorstep, then hide at my place until things blew over."

"You never dated him? Not even briefly?"

"I cannot stress to you enough," she said, "how incredibly *not my type* Dylan is."

She rolled her eyes. I laughed. This kid was smart. I liked her.

"It's funny," she said. "I was full scholarship at Harvard. My mom died when I was a kid. I grew up in foster homes. I had nothing. Dylan has always had everything. But we became friends mainly because *I* felt sorry for *him*."

"Why?" I said. "How did you meet?"

"He paid me to write a paper for him," she said. "Trust me, it wasn't my finest hour."

I thought of Lydia Welch, the sum she wrote down for me with her Montblanc pen. "You needed the money," I said. "He was willing to pay a lot."

"Yeah," she said.

"I get it."

"It was more than that, though," she said. "The paper was for a chemistry class, which, as far as the Harvard Science Department goes, was pretty much a bird course."

She started to explain what that meant, but I stopped her. "You could sing your way through it."

"Right!"

She looked impressed. I felt kind of smug. *Down with the young people,* if you will. I'd learned the expression from Blake's sister, who was studying photography at the New School in Manhattan.

"The main reason why I wrote the paper for Dylan was not the money, though," she said. "It was that he seemed so desperate. Like he was incapable of doing this unbelievably easy assignment on his own. And as I've gotten to know him, I've learned that there are very few things he *can* do on his own. I taught him how to pump gas. He was twenty-four years old."

"Silver spoon syndrome."

"Exactly," she said. "I also think it's why he can be so awful to people. Why he has literally no discipline. The way he was raised, he never had to develop those parts of his personality, either."

I thought about my one interaction with him—how I'd warned him off stalking his ex-girlfriend Teresa Leone. Dylan had claimed she was his one true love. But Teresa had told me that, after she broke up with him, Dylan had barraged her with threatening calls, texts, and direct messages. "It's made him a lot of enemies," I said.

"And one friend," she said.

"One very charitable friend," I said.

"Well, Sunny, let's not go overboard." She raised an arm and gestured around her office like a game show model. "I mean . . ."

"Doesn't it bother you, though?" I said. "Doing all the work, while he gets top billing?"

"Absolutely not."

I looked at her. "Come on."

"Look, I'm going to be honest with you," she said. "The company started off the second quarter in serious trouble."

"I didn't know that," I said.

"Well, it's true," she said. "For weeks I was even worried about making payroll. I talked to Mrs. Welch—she's our board chairman, and I think she's sort of amazed we've lasted as long as we have. She told me to give it everything I could to save Gonzo. 'Put your back into it, Sky,' she said. 'Don't let Dylan fail again.'"

"She loaded all that responsibility on your shoulders?"

"Yes."

"How did that make you feel?"

"Grateful," Sky said. "I met with our scientists. They created what I can honestly say is the most appealing energy drink formula out there. I told our marketing team to think outside the box, and they wrangled footage and words from world-class athletes, supermodels, top reality stars . . . some of the best endorsements we've ever had. Our social media people worked overtime to blast Gonzo's name out there—and it worked. It all worked. In the fourth quarter, we've seen larger profit margins than we ever imagined. Our shareholders are thrilled. Do I care if my name's up in lights? Abso-fucking-lutely not."

I smiled. "You have a good work ethic."

"So do you, Sunny," she said. "I mean, what's more important to you—working hard to solve a case or giving interviews afterward?"

"No question," I said. "Interviews."

She blinked at me.

"I'm kidding," I said.

"Thank God," she said.

"I actually hate interviews."

"I'm not even on social media," Sky said.

"I'm not, either, except my dog has an Instagram."

"I think we might be very similar, Sunny," she said.

"I think so, too," I said. Though I wasn't sure as I glanced at her desk. It was a flat landscape. No framed pictures. No vases full of flowers. No paperweights or fake awards or bobble-heads, no silly gifts from friends. If Sky Farley had a social life at all, she didn't like to advertise it.

"What do you want to know?" she said. It felt as though she was reading my mind. "What can I tell you . . . about Dylan?"

I lifted my gaze from her desk. "When was the last time you heard from him?"

"The Sunday after Thanksgiving," she said.

"That's the last time his parents heard from him, too."

"I know. Mrs. Welch told me."

"Was this a phone call you got? A text?"

"Text," she said. "He said he was feeling under the weather, so he wouldn't be at work on Monday. I called him to make sure he was okay."

"How did he sound?"

She shrugged. "Under the weather. But, you know . . . coherent."

"So no red flags at the time."

"I didn't think much about it at all," she said. "But then Tuesday rolled around, and Wednesday. I texted him but didn't get a response. I called. It went straight to voicemail. And his mailbox was full. That's when I started to worry. Dylan is always good about keeping his phone charged and his mailbox free to accept messages, even in rehab, when he can only use it for an hour a day. I spoke to Mrs. Welch. We went to his apartment together. He wasn't there, of course. The doorman said he hadn't seen him in days."

"How did the apartment look?"

"Same as always," she said. "It probably wouldn't surprise you that Dylan is kind of a slob."

"Did you notice anything missing?"

"His phone. Maybe some clothes. I don't know. He has a big wardrobe and his closets are a mess."

"Right. When was the last time you saw him in person?"

"Wednesday before Thanksgiving," she said.

"Did he seem like he was in good spirits?"

"Actually, no," she said. "We had words."

"What happened?"

"He was on something," she said. "I told him to go home and sleep it off and he got angry with me. He never gets angry with me. Told me to stop acting like his mother and went into his office and slammed the door. He was there for the rest of the day. We all left early for the holiday; his door stayed closed."

"He told you to stop acting like his mother."

"Yes."

"I thought they were close, Lydia and Dylan."

"They are," she said. "He probably meant it figuratively."

"Okay."

"Mrs. Welch told me that she and I are the only people who truly understand him," Sky said.

"When did she say that?"

"Today, actually," she said. "When she called to tell me you were coming."

I leaned back in my chair, my gaze shifting to the floor-to-ceiling windows. From this vantage point, the Custom House Tower looked like an expensive toy. Post Office Square was the size of a postage stamp. This gorgeous place, this gorgeous view. It brought new meaning to being "above it all." Who needed fake trophies and bobbleheads when you had all this? Who needed friends who weren't Dylan Welch? Sky had made it clear that Dylan was more than a bottomless wallet to her. But if that's all he'd been, I'd have gotten it a lot more.

"It's strange," Sky said. "Every morning since Dylan's been away, I've gone into his office first thing. I turn on the lights in there and look around—under Dylan's desk, in his closet . . . I almost expect him to be in one of those places, ready to jump out at me." She pulled off her glasses and rubbed her eyes, her cheeks flushing again. "Dylan can be very funny, believe it or not. He would do something like that, just to freak me out." Her eyes glistened. For a moment, she reminded me of Blake again—the Blake I'd met in July. Young and confused and more than a little frightened.

A tear trickled down her cheek. Then another. She plucked a dull gray shoulder bag from the back of her chair, a purse so plain I hadn't noticed it until now—and I always notice purses. She unsnapped the bag and removed a tissue and a compact and dabbed at her eyes. Crying over Dylan Welch. "I'm sorry," she said.

"Don't apologize."

As she examined her face in the small mirror, I stared at the compact. Unlike the purse, it was quite remarkable—vintage Bakelite in a gorgeous jade green with a unique hexagonal shape, the initials *SF* in gold at the center. Monogrammed. It looked to be from the 1950s at the latest, which was very odd, considering Sky's age.

She caught me gaping at it and read my mind. "I'm not a time traveler, if that's what you're wondering," she said.

"I actually was," I said.

"The compact was my mom's," she said. "Her name was Seraphina. It's the only thing I have of hers."

"It's beautiful," I said. "I love the shape."

Carefully, she slipped it back into her purse. "When I'm hurting, I just hold it," she said. "It soothes me."

I nodded.

"Do you have anything like that?"

I thought for a moment. "My dog," I said. "Her name is Rosie."

She put her glasses back on. "Can I see a picture of her?"

I took my phone out of my bag and found a photo of Rosie looking sheepishly at the camera, a soup bone between her paws. I handed it to Sky. As she gazed at the screen, her face melted into a smile. "Thank you," she said.

"Don't mention it."

Once she seemed calmer, I took back my phone and returned to the matter at hand. I asked Sky if Dylan had any meetings scheduled in the coming week. "Distributors? Potential sponsors?" I said. "Maybe he makes rounds at the manufacturing plant?"

She shook her head. "It's a slow time for meet-and-greets—a lot of people on vacation," she said. "As for the factory, it's closed for the month of December."

"The whole month? Why?"

"Maintenance, plus morale," she said. "A month paid leave during the holidays can work wonders."

"I'd imagine."

She smiled. "It was my idea," she said. "The assembly-line people worked double shifts overtime in the fall, just so we could make it happen."

I was impressed. I told her so.

Sky's face lit up. "Thank you," she said. I wasn't sure I'd ever met such a devoted people pleaser, but considering her background—all those foster homes, nothing truly stable in her life—it made sense.

"Do please let me know if you remember anything Dylan might have mentioned, even in passing, about plans for the month," I said. "Anything at all."

"Of course," she said. Then she looked up at me, her eyes big and helpless. "You'll find him," she said. "He's out there. He's fine."

"I wish I could promise you that, but I can't."

"I know that," she said. "I was talking to myself. Or praying. Or something."

"I understand."

We sat quietly for a few moments, Sky's eyes on me, mine on her giant computer screen, an idea taking root in my mind and blooming. "Sky?" I said. "Would you mind showing me Dylan's office?

# SEVEN

Back when my dad was a working cop and I was a worshipful kid constantly pelting him with questions, he told me that every criminal has a secret drawer, and it's an investigator's job to find it and get it open. He didn't mean it literally. The "drawers" in which Phil Randall had poked around and found evidence included storage containers, safes, and, in one instance, an Airstream trailer. Actual drawers, too, though. Since it was before the days of clouds and encrypted emails and disappearing texts, there weren't as many places to hide incriminating things.

*Everybody has a secret drawer. And the funny thing is, Sunny, it's almost always somewhere obvious.*

Sky unlocked Dylan's office and turned on the lights. I looked around. While Sky's workplace was sleek and modern and professional, Dylan's had more of a playroom/man cave vibe. There was a refrigerator, a stocked bar, a ninety-inch mounted TV screen. In the corner of the room stood a life-size model of Frankenstein's monster, a Gonzo can clasped in each hand.

His computer, though, was identical to Sky's.

I asked her to turn it on, and she did. The screensaver was of Dylan at a formal event with a curvy brunette with big, vacant eyes. He wore a blue velvet tux. She wore a skintight white dress, gold hoop earrings, and a chunky watch—a men's Rolex, like the one I'd seen Dylan wear. It could have been the same watch, as his wrists were bare. His date was very tan, with pale blue eyes that seemed to cut through the lens. I glanced at Sky. "Some influencer probably," she said. "I have no idea who."

"I'm taking it he dates a lot of them."

"That's an understatement."

I asked Sky if she knew Dylan's computer password, and she moved over to the desk and typed it in. "Same as mine," she said. "Crimson."

Dylan and his lady friend disappeared, and the screen opened up. "Spend as much time in here as you need," Sky said. "I'll be in my office if you have any questions."

I slipped my phone out of my purse's side pocket and asked for her info. She took it from me, typing her name, email, and number into my contacts.

I thanked her, my focus returning to the screen. On the surface, there didn't seem to be that much to go through. One file was marked GONZO, and when I clicked on it, there was only one document inside: *Marketing Ideas*, created six months ago. I opened it and read through it quickly. It included a brief list called "Top Boston Influencers." Blake was on it. Obviously, it hadn't been updated for a while.

I checked his online history. Predictably, it was mostly porn, the few exceptions being sites where you could buy lingerie and designer car and yacht accessories. I went to Google and checked his recent search history, which consisted of his own name (repeatedly), "benzo side effects," and porn.

He didn't have many photos, but three were of the woman from his screensaver. They were called Bella1, Bella2, and Bella3, and all looked like selfies, one a close-up, the other two in skimpy bikinis. I didn't recall a Bella from Lydia's list, and so I pulled the steno pad out of my purse and wrote down the name, plus "Dylan's screensaver" to make sure I remembered. For good measure, I grabbed my phone and took a picture of the close-up—Bella's hand at the side of her face, those sad, empty eyes of hers aimed at the camera, the same watch and earrings as in the screensaver, long fake nails painted a pale coral to bring out her tan.

There were other images—test photos from Gonzo shoots, pictures of Dylan at Welch Industries gatherings and family get-togethers, always standing close to his mother, his dad somewhere off to the side. In one of the more casual shots, he was also flanked by Sky. Dylan looked relaxed and happy, his blond curls glistening in the sunlight, his head tilted toward his friend. His mother's arm was around his back, the hand grasping Sky's shoulder, holding both of them close—as though she was afraid they might escape. Bill Welch stood to the right of Lydia. His arms hung at his sides.

After I closed the photo folder, I stepped back from the computer and looked at Dylan's desk. Like Sky's, it was black and gleaming, with nothing on top except the computer. It didn't seem like Dylan, whom Sky had called "kind of a slob" and who, from what I knew, was messy in every other possible way.

My gaze traveled down, to the one long drawer at the center of the desk. I heard Dad's voice in my head. *Everybody's got a secret drawer.* I slid it open.

"Wow," I said. It was stuffed to the brim with trash.

I took my phone from my purse and called Sky. She picked up right away. "Have you ever looked in Dylan's desk drawer?" I asked her.

"No?"

"Well, I'm doing that as we speak."

"Is it a mess?"

"Major understatement." I pulled out a wad of receipts, a broken yo-yo, an empty Xanax bottle, the cardboard backing from a legal-size pad of paper, a few crushed Solo cups, the wrapper from one of those giant Hershey bars folded in tenths.

"You should see his closets at home," she said. "He's like Stradlater from *The Catcher in the Rye*. Secret slob. I feel sorry for his cleaning lady."

"As I recall, Stradlater didn't clean his razors, right?" I said. "This is next-level hoarding."

"Oh, really?"

I put Sky on speaker and pulled out a handful of Mardi Gras beads; a used tube of some type of prescription ointment; a ripped, empty wallet; a few spent Sharpies; half a wrapped sandwich from Pret A Manger; five flattened cans of Gonzo. "At least he likes his own product," I said.

"Huh?"

I told her about the cans.

"It's a really good drink."

"I'll take your word for it," I said. "No offense."

"None taken."

"Any idea why he'd want to save the cans? Or, for that matter, any of this stuff?"

"No," she said. "I wish I did."

"It's almost like he's got something buried in here."

It went on like this—me methodically removing items from the drawer and placing them on top of the desk like exhibits from a trial. I was quiet for most of it, but I did tell Sky about the particularly strange finds—the broken David Ortiz bobblehead, the vintage *Playboy*, the uneaten tube of Necco Wafers. When the drawer was close to empty, I reached all the way back and felt something hard and thin and rectangular.

"Hello," I said.

"That sounds like a good hello," Sky said. "Did you find anything that might lead us to him?"

"I did find something." I yanked it out of the drawer and stared at it. "But it's not going to lead us to him."

"What? Why?" Sky said.

"Because it's his phone," I said quietly. "I just found his phone."

# EIGHT

S ky made it into Dylan's office in less than a minute. She
brought a charger with her. When I asked her if it was possible that the phone I found was old or a duplicate, she turned
it over and looked at the case, which was black, with a red
Harvard crest at the center and *DW* written in tiny white letters
in the lower-right corner. "That's his phone," she said. "The one
he uses all the time."

"You're sure," I said.

"Dylan went through a really brief phase when he was
into wearing white nail polish," she said. "Turned out to be
too douchey a look, even for him, but it was during the time
he bought this phone." She pointed to the *DW*. "That's the polish.
I remember him doing that. It was Bottle Poppin' Friday—that's
an office thing that he came up with. A morale-booster. He was
tipsy and wanted to mark his new toy."

"How long ago?"

"About six months," she says. "It's an iPhone 15 Pro Max, and it's titanium. He spent a lot on it. He loves being able to drop it and not make a dent. He takes it everywhere."

"Until now," I said.

"Yeah," she said. "Until now."

Sky plugged the charger into the wall and attached the phone. We waited for it to wake up. It did, finally. But it took a couple minutes.

"Do you know his passcode?" I said.

"No. But I feel like he'd choose something meaningful," she said. "You know, so he can remember it when he's wasted."

"How about something to do with his mom? Her maiden name?"

"Sure. It's Baxter."

"It's the right amount of letters." I tried it. The screen shook. "But not the right word."

"Try Finley." She spelled it out. "That was his dog when he was a kid. A toy poodle. He still talks about him."

I typed it in. It didn't work, either.

Sky told me that Cortland was the name of his family's beloved summer estate in Nantucket. "It's Dylan's favorite place in the world," she said. "He even named his yacht after it." I typed in as many letters that fit. But again, no dice.

We gave it a rest for a few minutes so the screen wouldn't lock up, both of us quiet, thinking. If Dylan bought the phone six months ago, I realized, he would have had it for a month or less when he and I had experienced our unpleasant encounter.

So maybe the key wasn't in choosing a name that had always been meaningful to him, but one that had been meaningful to him when he set up this phone.

"Teresa." I thought of the name, said it out loud, and typed it in, all at the same time. It worked.

Sky's eyes widened. "You know Dylan better than I do."

"It was just a hunch."

I looked at his voicemails first. They'd all been deleted.

"Can you recover them?" Sky said.

"Not me personally," I said. "But I have friends in the BPD who might be able to help."

She winced. "I'd rather not involve the police," she said. "Mrs. Welch feels the same."

"Why?"

"We're both worried about Dylan," she said. "A lot of the things he's gotten involved in . . . Well, they haven't been exactly legal."

"Right."

"If some of those deleted calls involve drugs or . . . illegal firearms or . . ."

"Stalking. He stalked Teresa Leone. She filed a restraining order against him."

"Yes," she said. "I know. He was going through a really rough time, personally."

"Yeah, well. So was Teresa."

"He was in bad shape. Off the wagon. Even Lydia didn't know the full extent of it because it would have broken her heart. It was like a . . . a terminal illness."

I stared at her for a full ten seconds. *The things some women are willing to overlook in men, or, worse yet, defend . . . And he's just a friend. He's not even her type. She said it herself.*

"Anyway," she said, "you understand the problem."

I nodded. I understood my problem, too. I'd taken the case. There were good people who desperately wanted to find this jerk. It wasn't my job to convince them otherwise.

I opened Dylan's texts, which didn't seem to have been deleted. The most recent outgoing texts from Dylan were to his father and Sky, making excuses for missing the family Thanksgiving brunch and not being able to come in to work. Apparently, he'd been back in his office at some point before the Monday after Thanksgiving in order to drop off the phone. Or maybe, after he stormed into his office the previous Wednesday, slamming the door behind him, he'd just stayed there. And outside of bathroom trips (if that) he didn't venture out of his office for the whole of Thanksgiving weekend. It made sense, now that I thought about it. At the very least, it explained the crushed cans, the half-eaten sandwich, and the giant Hershey bar, which was enough for someone with zero concerns about his own health to survive on for a long weekend.

But why? What could have spooked Dylan Welch so much that he'd hide in his office for an entire four-day holiday?

I went back to the phone. The most recent texts to Dylan were from Sky and his mother.

*Are you alive?* Sky had texted yesterday. *Type Y to confirm.*

I looked at Sky. "I was trying to be funny," she said. "Little did I know that I was texting his desk drawer."

Lydia was not trying to be funny. *I don't care what you've done, my beautiful son*, she had texted today. *No one will be angry if you just please come home.* She was in his contacts as MOMMY. Despite my firsthand knowledge of Dylan's anger issues, lack of self-control, and deeply misogynistic leanings, it broke my heart a little. Even the most unlikable human beings were such vulnerable creatures.

I exited the Mommy thread and went back to the list of texts. After Sky, Lydia, and Bill, there was a sender marked ANONYMOUS. I opened it up for the hell of it, expecting one spam message. That wasn't what I found.

Sky gasped audibly. I barely kept myself from doing the same. There were more than two dozen messages from this blocked number, and every single one of them said the same thing:

MURDERER

I turned to Sky again. Her face had gone completely white. It seemed as though she'd forgotten how to blink.

"Sky," I said. "Do you have any idea who might have sent these to Dylan?"

She didn't look at me. Her gaze stayed riveted to the phone. "Yes," she said. "Yes, I do."

# NINE

S he did it," Sky said. We were one floor down from the corporate offices, in Gonzo's security suite. The head of security was an older guy named Maurice Dupree. He was a former Boston cop, and when Sky had introduced us, he'd recognized me—not from the *Globe* article, but as "Phil Randall's little girl"—which made me like him instantly.

At Sky's request, Maurice had taken us to a room full of CCTV monitors and called up footage from three weeks ago. What we were looking at had been recorded at ten a.m. in the hallway between Sky's and Dylan's offices—a thin, short-haired woman in a hoodie and jeans, raging.

"She's the one who texted Dylan," Sky said. "I know it."

The footage was recorded without audio, but as she kicked the walls, pushed over a large abstract sculpture, and fell to her knees, I felt as though I could hear her shrieking. She was facing a terrified-looking Sky, who stood in the doorway of her office, her hands raised, her fingers spread. *Calm, calm . . .* Sky moved toward the woman. She seemed as though she wanted to put her arms around her, but she barely made it two steps when the woman sprung to her feet and lunged at her, yelling something, her teeth bared. Sky jumped back quickly, the way you would from a biting dog. The woman collapsed again, face buried in her hands. The whole time, Dylan's door stayed shut.

"Who is she?" I asked.

"Rhonda Lewis," Maurice said, his gaze pinned to the screen as he and another guard moved into the frame, lifting Rhonda to her feet. He pushed a button on the console. The screen froze. I looked at the image. That frail woman, flanked by two big guards, her mouth wrenched open in a silent scream. "She's been in the corporate offices a few times, yelling at people. Defacing property," he said. "Sky didn't want to do much about it because she felt sorry for her."

"I still do," Sky said.

"I feel for her, too," Maurice said, "but I gotta confess I'd have called the cops after that particular incident."

"We did increase security," Sky said. "That metal detector is new."

Maurice let out an exasperated sigh. For a moment, they both seemed to forget I was in the room.

"What happened today was not good," Sky said. "But Rhonda did leave peacefully."

"After breaking a neon sign," Maurice said.

"I know, I know."

"And scaring Elspeth half to death. I understand how you feel, Sky. Really I do. But what the hell does Elspeth have to do with what happened to Rhonda's daughter?"

"Nothing, but—"

"Come on, man. Elspeth's just a kid. And that sign was freakin' expens—"

I cleared my throat very loudly. They both turned to me.

"What are you guys talking about?" I said.

Maurice looked at Sky. "You want to take this?"

Sky's back straightened. "Rhonda Lewis experienced a tragic event and, as a result, has exhibited behavior that's made us concerned for the safety of our employees," she said.

I looked at Maurice, then at Sky. "Excuse me?" Neither one of them said a word.

"If you want me to help you find your friend, Sky," I said, "you're going to need to be a little clearer."

Sky winced. "Sorry. I don't like phrasing things that way, either. But I have to."

I wanted to ask Sky why working at a company that observed Bottle Poppin' Fridays would necessitate talking like a member of the State Department. But I decided to save that for later. "What was the tragic event?" I said.

"Rhonda's daughter passed," Maurice said.

"How old was she?"

"Seventeen," Sky said.

"That's terrible," I said. "When did it happen?"

"About a year ago," Maurice said. "But Rhonda's only been coming around here since she lost the lawsuit."

I kept my voice calm. "Her daughter died from drinking Gonzo?"

A silence followed—so thick it made it hard to breathe.

"She died of cardiac arrest," Sky said finally.

"She was seventeen," I said.

"She had a heart condition," Sky said. "She drank three Gonzos in a row, mixed with alcohol."

I didn't say anything.

"We have very clear warning labels on our product," Sky said. "It's even part of our advertising—more caffeine than any energy drink on the market."

"I've got A-fib, and I wouldn't touch the stuff if you paid me a million bucks," Maurice said.

"It's why we weren't found liable," Sky said. "But I understand how Rhonda feels. Something like that happens to your child, you have to blame somebody."

I looked at Sky. It was hard to get past the change in her tone—as though she had a team of lawyers whispering in her ear. "She's done, then?" I said. "I mean, as far as the courts go?"

"No," Sky said. "She's filed an appeal."

I turned back to the screen, the frozen blurred image—Rhonda Lewis's face, her features twisted in agony, like a figure from a Goya painting.

"Does she have a husband?" I asked. "Any other family you know of?"

"She's a single mother," Sky said. "Daisy was an only child."

"Like I said, I feel for her," Maurice said.

Another silence crept into the room. I glanced at Maurice, twisting his wedding band.

"Sky?" I said.

"Yes?"

"Rhonda was yelling at you in this video. What was she saying?"

"Same thing she always says when she comes in here. She told me I have blood on my hands. And she called me a murderer."

"Like the texts that were sent to Dylan."

"Yeah," she said. "Exactly."

"Has Rhonda gotten into it with Dylan?" I said to Maurice. "He's the face of the company, after all. The CEO. I'd think she'd go after him harder than Sky."

"Nothing's happened between them in person."

"Why not?"

"Because he always hides from her."

"Wow," I said.

"Yep," Maurice said.

"That would really, really piss me off," I said.

"Me too," Sky said. "I'm sure that's why she sent Dylan those texts."

"Are you sure she stopped with texts?"

"What are you saying?"

I just looked at her.

Sky shook her head vigorously, like a kid who's just been

told that Santa Claus isn't real. "Rhonda isn't a violent person," she said. "She's hurting, but she would never physically harm anyone."

"I understand what you're saying," I said. And I did. But like I mentioned earlier, we humans are complicated creatures. And even if we weren't, this woman had plenty of uncomplicated reasons to break her peaceable streak with Dylan Welch. "I think I'll talk to Rhonda all the same."

# TEN

The only contact information Sky had for Rhonda Lewis was her lawyer's phone number. She called him. Surprising no one, he wasn't willing to offer up his client to aid in our search for the missing CEO of the company she was suing for the second time. "I'm not sure why I even tried that," Sky said after ending the call.

"You want to find your friend," I said. "You're willing to try anything."

Sky nodded. She shut her eyes for a moment, too choked up to speak. Could Dylan be that awful if he inspired such heartfelt emotion from an obviously intelligent woman? Well . . . yes, he could. It happened all the time, and with men even worse than him.

"I believe Rhonda sent Dylan those texts," Sky said. "I think they probably scared him. But I know that she didn't have any-thing to do with his going missing."

"What makes you so sure?"

"This is going to sound weird."

"Try me."

"During litigation, I saw Rhonda in a resting state," Sky said. "She wasn't raging. She wasn't screaming, so I was able to really *see* her. I was able to look into her eyes. I can read people, Sunny. And after being that close to her, I know that Rhonda Lewis isn't capable of that type of violence."

"You're right," I said. "That did sound weird."

"Okay, fine. But from a practical standpoint, she's suing us. Again. Why would she want to jeopardize that by . . . by doing something to Dylan?"

"That actually makes some sense."

"I just want to find my friend," she said. "And I don't want to waste time by focusing on the wrong person."

"How about this?" I said. "I'm going to *consider* Rhonda Lewis—meaning I am going to pursue the idea that she might possibly know where Dylan is and what happened to him. But I will continue to follow any leads I come across. And I will keep you and Lydia informed of everything."

Sky sighed. "Fair enough."

"Good."

The one thing that Rhonda's lawyer did mention during the call was that she was on leave from her job. And when I asked Sky where Rhonda had worked, she told me she'd been a nurse practitioner at an urgent care in Watertown. I looked up the address on my phone. It was just five minutes away from my shrink's office in Cambridge.

"I still think you're wasting your time," Sky told me as we said goodbye. "She's a nurse, Sunny. A *nurse*." Sky Farley, who had clearly never watched a true crime documentary in her life.

I stopped by security again on my way out and asked Maurice if there was anything else he wanted to tell me, now that the COO wasn't around. "Anything at all," I said, "that might help my investigation."

He told me the same thing that Elspeth had. "Sky likes everybody."

"Meaning . . ."

"Meaning, she sees the best in people all the fuckin' time, and while it's admirable, it's also annoying as shit," he said. "Oops. Pardon my French."

I had to laugh at that.

He grinned. "Yeah, Phil could cuss a blue streak, too, under the right circumstances."

"And I'm a chip off the old block."

"I can see that."

"So you're telling me that I shouldn't take Sky's opinion of people as the objective truth."

"That's right," he said. "Sky's been known to give employees second, third, and fourth chances when she shouldn't have even given them one. The head of Quality Management went to federal prison for insider trading last year. She wants to hire him right back as soon as he's served his term."

"She also thinks there's no way that Rhonda could have hurt Dylan," I said.

"And I couldn't disagree with her more on that."

"Really?"

"I don't mean any offense against Rhonda Lewis, and I feel awful for what she's been through and I'm sure she's a good person," he said. "But tragedies like hers do things to your soul. They make you capable of rage and violence you never thought possible. It's like my youngest says: 'Hurt people hurt people.'"

I gave him a look. "I hope she doesn't say it often."

"She's only eighteen," he said. "She'll grow out of it."

I smiled. He smiled back.

"So I'm going to try and find Rhonda and talk to her," I said. "But let's say she doesn't pan out. Is there anybody else you might know of who could make Dylan disappear, or make him want to?"

He rolled his eyes. "You ever meet Dylan Welch?"

"Yes."

"So you probably could imagine him making an enemy or two. Or ten."

"Hell, for a hot minute there, I was one of them."

"I'm not at all surprised," he said.

"Nobody specific, though? Nobody he spoke to security about around the time he went missing?"

Maurice shook his head. "Only Rhonda."

"What did he say?"

"After that one incident—the one you saw on video—he wanted my team and me to help him scare her away."

"He actually used those words? He said he wanted you guys to 'scare her'?"

"No. What he said was he wanted us to track her down so he could send her a message. He never came out and said it, but I think he wanted her roughed up."

"Jesus," I said. "She's a grieving mother."

"And he's Dylan Welch."

"Good point."

Maurice crossed his hands over his chest. "For Sky's sake, I hope he's okay and that you're able to find him," he said. "But I can't say I've missed him all that much."

# ELEVEN

After I left Gonzo's offices, I pulled Dylan Welch's phone out of my pocket. I'd never told Maurice or Sky that I was taking it. But the way I saw it, I didn't owe that information to them. It wasn't their phone any more than it was mine.

Dylan's battery was at only 5 percent, so when I got into the car, I plugged it into my charger. I set my own phone in the holder on the dashboard, told Siri the address of Rhonda Lewis's workplace, and maneuvered my way onto I-90 West, which I took toward Watertown. Driving was beyond slow-going, but that was no surprise. It was rush hour, and rush hour during holiday season in Boston was otherwise known as the Ninth Circle of Hell. I was used to it.

*Well, I used to be used to it.*

As I sat behind the wheel of my car in standstill traffic,

ignoring a podcast while surrounded by the incessant and pointless blare of horns, I couldn't help but think of the Jersey Shore right now, the empty beach roads as twilight approached, the only sound the soothing roar of Atlantic.

And the sunsets . . .

I hadn't planned on calling Richie. I'd texted him this morning to let him know that Rosie and I had arrived safely home, but beyond that, I'd been determined to let this day come and go without communicating with him. I'd even told him as much. *I love you,* I'd said as I was getting into my car, *but if I'm going to survive until the next time we see each other, I'll need a day or two to myself.*

But it was more than that. I needed distance from Richie in order to gain some perspective. Was a move to Asbury Park truly a good idea, or was I letting my heart (and other parts of my body) lead me into making the wrong decision? Obviously, I couldn't figure out the answer to that question unless I was on my own for a solid block of time.

But you know what they say about the best-laid plans.

Richie's phone started ringing before I realized I'd called him. He answered before I could hang up. "Well, this is a pleasant surprise," he said.

"For me as well as you."

"Huh?"

"This call," I said. "I wasn't even aware I was making it. It was basically an involuntary physical response."

"You mean like the type of thing that keeps you alive?"

"That's a little dramatic." In the background, I could hear

the thump of a mic, a guy saying "testing," then counting to ten. "It is good to hear your voice, though."

"Thanks."

Someone launched into a very loud guitar solo.

"Kind of," I said.

"Huh?"

"It's good to *kind of* hear your voice."

"Sorry, that's The Wild and the Innocent," Richie said.

"Who?"

"Tonight's Springsteen tribute band. They're doing a sound check."

"I'd say it's a little heavy on the sound."

"Let me take you outside, where we can be alone."

I grinned. "It sort of turned me on when you said that."

"That was my intention."

I heard Richie telling somebody he'd be back in a few as the drummer started in. "We're almost there," Richie said. I heard a drumroll, the crash of cymbals, a door closing. Muffled music, footsteps, and then quiet. A gust of wind. "Better?" Richie said.

"Much." I felt like I could almost smell the ocean.

Back in Boston, someone behind me leaned on their horn. "What the fuck?" I shouted.

"Are you okay?" Richie said.

I let out a sigh. Traffic had apparently moved two inches forward and I hadn't followed suit. I took my foot off the brake, and the asshat finally eased up on the horn. "I'm fine," I said. "I'm just . . . driving."

"Say no more," Richie said.

"Yet another aspect of Boston that you don't miss at all."

"All of that is canceled out by what I do miss."

I felt myself blushing. I wished I could travel through the phone. "Jeez," I said, "you do know how to lay it on thick."

"How are you, Sunny?" he said. "How has your day been?"

"Well, for starters, I took that Dylan Welch job."

"Really?"

"Really."

"What changed your mind?"

"His mother," I said. "She showed up at my office this morning, offered me more than triple what Bill did."

"Holy crap."

"I know."

"I realize that a mother's love is boundless," he said, "but that's a hell of a lot to pay to find somebody who's probably in a hotel room somewhere, eyeball-deep in cocaine and hookers."

"We call them sex workers, Richie."

"Sorry."

"Anyway, I'm not so sure it's that simple," I said. "Most people don't love Dylan Welch as much as his mother does. It's very possible he's hiding from one of them. Or . . ."

"One of them found him."

"Yep."

Richie was quiet for several moments. Anybody else, I would have asked if he was still there. But not Richie. That was just how he was—he never spoke before organizing his thoughts. Traffic moved a few more inches. I gazed at the car in front of me—a minivan with a bumper sticker that said MY OTHER CAR IS A BROOM. Good thing she decided to take the van.

Richie said, "Maybe you shouldn't be involved in this case."

I stared at my phone. That wasn't what I'd expected him to say. "What?" I said. "I've been involved in cases like this since you've known me."

"I know."

"It's me, Richie. It's what I love."

"And you're great at it," Richie said. "But there's a reason why cops retire early."

"I'm not a cop."

"True. Your job is more dangerous."

It was my turn to go quiet.

"I worry about you, Sunny."

I forced a laugh. "I haven't managed to get myself killed yet."

"You almost did," he said. "Back in July."

"That's an exaggeration."

"You were in a coma for three days."

I winced. The guy behind me honked again. I flipped him the bird and he leaned on his horn harder and yelled something out of his window that I couldn't hear. "You should worry more about me driving on I-90 with these lunatics."

Richie was quiet again. I waited for him to collect his thoughts, but it was taking too long.

"Where did all of this come from, Richie?"

"This weekend."

"What about it?"

"It was great," he said.

"Of course it was," I said.

"And it made me think."

"About what?"

Richie took a breath. Let it out. "I want to grow old with you."

I'd never thought it possible to be annoyed and deeply moved at the same time—and yet here we were. "Me too," I said.

"Really?"

"Look, one reason why I took this Welch case is because I've been thinking about getting a second place near you," I said. "With this kind of money, I could spend part of the year in Asbury Park at first, then stay longer. And then, if that works out, we could maybe think about giving living together another shot."

"What about your job?"

"I could move my business to Jersey."

More silence.

"Richie?"

"I want you to think about us," he said.

"I am thinking about us," I said.

"I want you to think about our future. I want you to think about being alive for it."

I gripped the wheel. I nearly said, *Since when do you get to tell me what to think about?* But I didn't.

"I'm not suggesting you retire," Richie said. "But maybe you should take on cases that are less . . . dramatic."

I inhaled sharply. "Pushing paper around a desk."

"They have computers now," Richie said.

"No kidding?" I heard the ding of a phone—not mine. Dylan's. "I'll think about it," I said.

"I love you," Richie said.

"I love you, too," I said.

We hung up, which was a lot better than arguing. I knew Richie's intentions were good, but still the conversation bothered me, and if I'd stayed on much longer, I would have told him so. My mother had said something similar to my father when she was convincing him to retire. And while he'd acquiesced, for her sake, it was hard not to think that in urging him to stay out of harm's way, she was missing a crucial part of who he was. That may have been okay for my dad—being in love with someone who didn't fully comprehend his soul. But was it okay for me?

Richie had come from a dangerous and powerful crime family. And even though he'd steered clear of the Burke business, he'd nearly been killed himself, more than once. I'd thought that made us simpatico—different sides of the same coin. Yet after this conversation, I wasn't so sure.

If I'd explained to the man I loved that the main reason I needed to hang up was to check a missing douchebag's text messages on a phone I'd stolen from his office, would he understand?

I doubted he would—and that made me sad. But at the moment, I was more interested in reading the douchebag's latest text.

# TWELVE

The text was from someone Dylan had named Trevor the Chemist. And it read simply: *WHERE R U?*

Trevor the Chemist. Sounded like a drug dealer—albeit a pretentious one. Maybe he went to Harvard, too.

While I'm not normally one to text and drive, I'd used the voice option to reply while I was still stuck in traffic. *I am not Dylan, but I have his phone. I am trying to help his parents find him. Where are you? Can we meet?*

There had been no reply. I'd waited for another ding all the way to Optima Urgent Care, where Rhonda Lewis was employed—an unassuming-looking building with a very crowded parking lot on what was otherwise a mostly residential street.

While waiting at the end of a rather lengthy check-in line, I looked at Dylan's texts once again to see if Trevor the Chemist had responded back when I'd been distracted by road rage. He hadn't. I tried calling his number. It went straight to voicemail. The mailbox was full, which felt kind of irresponsible for a drug dealer.

I scrolled through the rest of Dylan's texts as I moved closer to the front of the line. None were very interesting—mostly spam and old appointment reminders for Lamborghini tune-ups and body waxing. As far as his personal life went, I imagined Dylan was more of a Snapchat kind of guy, disappearing texts and all. I started to move on to his stored images. The most recent was a dick pic. Of course it was. I closed it quickly. *Why can't somebody invent an app that makes you unsee things?*

I was next in line now—just behind a young couple with a shrieking baby that they were both trying unsuccessfully to soothe. I turned my attention to the medical receptionist—a pale, wan guy about my age, with a tattoo of a phone booth on his forearm. TARDIS, from *Doctor Who*. I wouldn't have known what TARDIS was until a year ago. Tom Gorman was a huge fan of the British TV show—a Whovian, if you will, with a DVD library that dated back to early episodes from the seventies and included every single one of the fourteen doctors. Back when we were dating, he'd made me dinner and treated me to a *Doctor Who* marathon. And though I must confess that Tom had treated me to other marathons I'd enjoyed a good deal more, I did like the show. While the receptionist was checking the young family in, I went to the *Doctor Who* Wiki Fandom and refreshed my memory.

After the woman in front of me finished signing in, I stepped up to the desk. Mr. TARDIS glanced up at me with tired, watery eyes. He was wearing blue scrubs that matched his tattoo. His nametag said STEVE. "How can I help you?" Steve said in an exhausted monotone.

"First things first," I said. "Who's your favorite doctor?"

He frowned. "Here?"

I shook my head and pointed to the phone booth on his forearm. "You know what I'm talking about."

His face lit up. "Wait, seriously?"

"Come on. Everybody has a favorite."

"Ten," he said.

"Ah, David Tennant. A class act," I said. "I like thirteen, of course."

"Of course. Everybody loves her."

"Yeah, but if we're talking favorite doctor of all time . . . I'm going with the War Doctor. No contest."

"The War Doctor," he said. "That is a deep cut."

"I'm a deep individual."

"What's your name?" he said.

"Sunny," I said. "Like Jaz Samuels's toy rabbit."

"No way."

"Yes way," I said. "And believe me, you're the only person I'll talk to today who gets that reference."

His smile broadened until he positively glowed. "I'm Steve," he said. "Like Steven Taylor."

I pretended to know who that was. "Ah! Well, it's very nice to meet you, Steve," I said.

"Likewise."

"I'm wondering if you could help me out with something."

"Of course," he said. Still beaming. I imagined this guy didn't get a lot of attention from women—especially ones who shared his *Doctor Who* obsession. "By the way, you ever go to the Who-cons?"

"No, but I've always wanted to." I was improvising now. "I heard there was a good one in Worcester."

"You haven't lived," he said, "till you've been to the London one."

"I bet."

He sat there, gazing into my eyes, a look on his face like he was about to book us two plane tickets for Heathrow. This was starting to get uncomfortable.

"So what can I help you with?" he said.

I exhaled. "Do you happen to know Rhonda Lewis?"

"Oh. Sure," he said, the glow fading. "She works here. Well, I mean, she's on temporary leave right now. But . . . yeah. I know her."

"What's your opinion of her?"

He shrugged. "Nice lady. Good at her job. Why?"

"She ever mention the name Dylan Welch to you?"

"Um . . . I don't think so, but the name sounds familiar. Was he ever a patient?"

I shook my head. "Doubt it," I said. "He runs an energy drink company."

"You mean the one that killed Rhonda's kid?"

"Well . . ."

"That stuff is so unhealthy."

I cleared my throat. "There's warning labels."

"Kids don't read warning labels."

I looked at him. "That's true," I said. It was.

"I'm a private investigator," I said. "Dylan Welch has gone missing and I've been hired to find him. We found some texts from Rhonda on his phone, and I wanted to ask her a few questions about him, but I don't have any of her info."

He started typing into his computer. A nurse appeared and called out a name, and a woman stood up, her bloody hand wrapped in a towel.

"Just what I thought," Steve said.

"What?"

He cleared his throat. "If you want to give me your contact info, I can pass it on to Rhonda," he said, all business now. "And I promise not to exploit your friendliness and spur-of-the-moment *Doctor Who* research."

My face burned. "That isn't fair. I really do like the show."

He smirked. "Sure, Sunny," he said. "Regardless, thanks for looking me in the eye and talking to me like a fellow human. It's not often that happens in here, so I don't much care about the motivation behind it."

I took out my card, embarrassment coursing through me. I made an early New Year's resolution: Stop underestimating people.

I wrote my mobile number on the back of the card. "That's the best way to reach me," I said. "A lot of times—now, for instance—I'm not in the office."

I handed it to Steve. He looked at it.

"See?" I said. "My name really is Sunny."

He put the card in his wallet. I was about to say goodbye, but he stood up. "I can walk you out to your car, Sunny."

"That isn't necessary," I said.

Steve pulled on a coat. "I'm due a break anyway."

"Okay," I said, but I felt a little uneasy. I pulled my coat tight around me, my purse held close to my side, so that I could feel the compact weight of my .38. I grabbed my car keys out of my purse and clutched them in my hand, sharp edges out like claws. *What if he's genuinely angry about the way I faked being a fan? What if he's angry enough to hurt me?* An overreaction, to be sure—no doubt due in part to my conversation with Richie. Still, I did need to stop underestimating people, for the worse but also for the better. "Really, you don't have to," I said.

"I know." Steve pressed a buzzer on his desk. A nurse came out, and he told her he was taking a quick break. She took his place at the desk just as more people came in. It was an elderly couple, the woman leaning against the man, limping miserably, the man so frail he could barely hold her up. Never had I seen two people so completely focused on getting from point A to point B. They were sure not to notice a large man in scrubs and a puffer coat, leaving the building a little too quickly, a nervous-looking woman in tow.

# THIRTEEN

Steve held the door open for me. We walked outside into the cold air. It was early but past twilight already, the sky a deep amethyst.

My heart pounded, my head full of doubts. *Calm, calm . . .*

He slipped a hand into his coat pocket. Immediately, I went for my purse. He pulled out a pack of cigarettes. I breathed a sigh of relief.

"I'm assuming you don't smoke," Steve said after he lit a cigarette.

I shook my head.

"Good for you. It's a crappy habit," he said, taking a long drag.

"Like energy drinks."

"Not as bad as that."

I smiled and started toward my car. He walked with me.

"Okay, listen." He spoke very quietly, his lips barely moving. "I wanted to talk to you in private for a reason."

I looked at him.

"I have met Dylan Welch. Kind of."

"What do you mean, 'kind of'?"

"He was here once. As a patient."

I stared at him. "What?"

"He OD'd."

"How long ago?"

"Not very. Last month."

"You sure it was him?"

"When I was at the desk, I looked it up on the computer, so yeah. I'm sure." We were at my car now. I didn't unlock the door. I just stood there, waiting for Steve to say more. He didn't. He took another drag and blew out a thick white cloud. He was taller than I'd assumed he'd be. He looked bigger standing up, more serious in the dimly lit lot, his face shadowed like an informant from an old conspiracy movie.

"Did Welch come in alone?" I asked.

"Some woman brought him in," Steve said.

"What did she look like?"

"Hot—like a model/influencer. White teeth, big hair, tight dress, expensive-looking surgical enhancements."

"Sounds like his type."

"She was most guys' type," he said. "But as I recall that night, she wasn't in much better shape than him. Barely able to stand up herself. She kept saying it was a reaction to mango.

Guava. Something ridiculous like that. It's funny, the lies people tell when they come in here. Anyway, she was very opposed to taking him to the hospital. Said he wouldn't want it. So we worked on him here."

"What was done for Dylan?"

"We gave him Naloxone. Dr. Conrad—he was the physician on call that night—suggested he rest at least, but he wasn't having it. As soon as he came to, more or less, Welch cussed us all out and left with the guava girl."

"Was there a reason he cussed you out," I asked, adding, "beyond the usual?"

"Someone ripped his fancy-ass shirt while administering CPR," he said. "So maybe the usual."

"Jesus."

"Right? Asshole."

"Well, at least now I know that it was the same Dylan Welch," I said.

"Why are you looking for him?"

"I'm getting paid," I said. "A lot."

"Wow. Well, I guess it's nice that somebody cares."

"He's from a powerful family."

Steve puffed on his cigarette. "Hey . . . Sunny?"

"Yeah?"

"Please don't tell anyone I told you this, okay? I could really get in trouble."

"Never," I said. "I promise."

"For some weird reason, I trust you," he said. "Even though I probably shouldn't."

"No, you should," I said. I gave him a smile. "Really."

We stood there for a few moments, our shadows looming on the pavement like ghosts. In a way, I wished I did smoke, just to make things less awkward and give me something to do with my hands while I figured out how to bring up his coworker again. I decided that with Steve, the best approach was straightforward. "Was Rhonda there the night Dylan came in?"

He puffed on his cigarette and nodded. "She helped resuscitate him."

"She did?"

"Yep. It's her job."

"She never mentioned anything to you about knowing him, or . . ."

"No. She was totally professional. I assumed he was a stranger. When the two of them left, Rhonda said something like 'good riddance,' but I assumed it was because he was rude to the staff. I didn't think it was because he was basically her daughter's killer."

I didn't bother mentioning anything about the warning labels this time. I just thought of Rhonda, trying to lose herself in her job, only to come face-to-face with the man who destroyed her entire world. And what had she done? Saved his life. *Stop underestimating people.*

"This city can be insanely small," Steve said.

I looked at him. "It really can," I said. "It's nice in a way, but sometimes it makes me feel like I know too many people."

"It's why I like England," he said.

"You don't know anybody there."

"Not a soul."

"That sounds nice."

"It is."

"I've been kind of . . . craving space lately," I said. "Peace and quiet. A break from this town."

"Me too," he said.

I pictured Richie, Richard Jr., Rosie, and myself at this time next year, in Richie's apartment, decorating a Christmas tree. I'd be calm there. Relaxed. A small, safe client list, my days spent checking the online activity of workers' comp claimants or going over nannycam footage. Very little physical interaction with anyone other than the people I loved. My stomach seized up. I felt slightly nauseated. I heard myself say, "The thing is, my life here is tough to quit."

"I get that."

"Really?"

He nodded. "I'd never leave Boston for longer than a two-week vacation," he said. "It's a pain in the ass here, but it's *my* pain in the ass. You know? Plus, I love my job."

"I love my job, too."

"Even though both of our jobs apparently involve helping out the same dickhead."

I smiled. "We have something in common. For real."

"You have a boyfriend?"

"Yes."

"I figured," he said. "But it was worth a shot."

I laughed a little. He laughed, too. "Steve?"

"Yeah?"

"Thank you."

He took one last drag, then dropped the butt to the pavement and stepped on it. "I talk to Rhonda pretty often," he said. "I'll put in a good word."

"You think she'll ever come back to work?"

Steve shrugged. "I could see her moving away."

"Scary."

"Tell me about it." He gave me a meaningful look. "Of course, everything's got to end sometime. Otherwise nothing would ever get started."

"Huh?"

"It's a quote."

"Um . . ."

"The eleventh doctor?"

"Oh, right," I said. "Of course."

I thought I caught him roll his eyes.

We said goodbye and shook hands. I walked back to my car. As I was about to get in, I caught sight of a black RAV4 parked in a space behind me. Its engine was running. And there was a man behind the wheel with his head tilted back, a baseball cap covering his face. I watched a few seconds longer. The man didn't move.

I opened my door and slipped into the front seat. I started up the car. After I backed out of my space and pulled into the lot, I glanced once more at the RAV4. The car looked familiar. So did the baseball cap. I saw headlights flash on in my rearview, and so I left the lot quickly, making a series of turns that landed me on a dead-end residential street. I waited for several moments until I was sure I was alone. Then I called Richie's father.

Steve was right. This town could be insanely small.

# FOURTEEN

You're on the verge of making a big change in your life,"
Susan Silverman said.

"How do you know that?" I said. I'd just arrived at her office.
I was ten minutes late. We'd barely exchanged hellos.

"Just making a guess," she said, "because you look very
tense. And change tends to stress you out, no?"

"I'm tense because I nearly committed murder at least three
times on Route 16. I hate holiday traffic. Plus, I don't like being
late."

"Ah," she said. "My mistake." She looked as though she didn't
believe me. And the truth was, she was right not to. There was
a reason for doctor/patient confidentiality—it provided the
freedom to be honest. And from my own experience, therapy
worked only if you told the truth.

"Okay, you win," I said. I took off my coat and hung it on the hook. "I'm late because I took a whole bunch of turns to lose a RAV4 that I think was following me."

"Pardon?"

"I drove here from an urgent care in Watertown." I glanced at Susan Silverman, alarm clouding her serene features. "Oh, no, I'm fine. It was for a case I'm working on."

"Whew." I followed Susan from the waiting room into her office. She took a seat behind her desk. As always, I admired her outfit—a pale gray cashmere sweater and an immaculately tailored charcoal pencil skirt, paired with an elegant string of pearls and matching earrings. I'd never seen Susan wear the same thing twice, yet, sartorially speaking, she always managed to knock it out of the park.

I took the chair across from Susan. She also had a couch, and the first few times I'd seen her, I'd felt obligated to use it, with Susan sitting in a chair beside me. But once she sensed my awkwardness and told me I could sit anywhere I liked, this chair became my chosen perch, with Dr. Silverman sitting behind her desk, as though we were having a business meeting.

I loved this chair, truly. After years of therapy, the soft leather felt like the embrace of an old friend—one I could say anything to without fear of being judged. "So anyway, when I was leaving the urgent care," I told Susan, "I noticed a suspicious character in the parking lot."

"What do you mean by 'suspicious'?" Susan said.

"Well, he was sitting in his car, for one thing," I said. "But also, he was wearing a baseball cap. Who wears a baseball cap at this time of year?"

Susan shrugged. "I never thought about it."

"I mean, what's next? Flip-flops? A Speedo?"

"I . . . suppose it's unusual." She sounded as though she was trying her hardest to be charitable.

"Anyway, the cap was covering his face. Like he was pretending to be asleep."

She nodded. "It was an urgent care, yes? Couldn't he have actually been asleep? Couldn't he have just been someone's ride?"

"Yeah, but I never forget a face—or even a baseball cap—when it belongs to a guy who was holding a gun on me."

"Wait, what, now?"

"That job I was on back in July," I said. "Early on, I talked to this disgusting criminal named Moon Monaghan. He has ties to Desmond Burke."

"Your former father-in-law."

"Yes," I said. "And during that entire conversation, Moon had one of his lackeys sitting in a car about twenty feet away, aiming a gun at me in case I did or said anything he didn't like."

"Yikes."

"Like I said, Moon's the worst."

"Clearly."

"Anyway, I could have sworn this was the same car, the same lackey."

"Was the car unusual?"

"No. A black RAV4."

"And you said the man's face was covered."

"The baseball cap, though."

"Okay."

"Also his size. And his attitude. Exact same."

"Okay."

"You don't sound like you believe me."

"My job isn't to believe or disbelieve," Susan said. "I'm just here to listen." If she hadn't gone into psychiatry, Susan would have made a great politician.

I sighed. "Anyway, I called Desmond, and I asked him why Moon was having me tailed."

"What did he say?"

"He said he would talk to Moon, but he didn't know of any reason why he would do that. In fact, he said Moon wants little to do with me because he finds me confusing."

"Interesting."

"And then Desmond started asking me about my weekend with Richie. He asked if his son had popped the question yet, and when I said no, he told me to forget he ever said it."

"Aha."

"Aha?"

"I feel like I have a better idea as to why you're so tense."

"I told you why I'm tense."

"Because you believe you were being followed by a man in a baseball cap."

"I *was* being followed by him."

"Are you sure that's the only reason?"

"Isn't that enough of a reason?"

"How did you feel when Desmond Burke mentioned that Richie planned to propose to you?"

I exhaled. "Tense," I said. "Very, very tense."

I expected her to say "Aha" again, but thankfully she didn't.

As usual, Susan had successfully opened the floodgates. The words banged around in my heart until I had to say them out loud. "Richie wants me to retire."

"He does?"

"Well, not retire per se," I said. "But he wants me to stop taking dangerous jobs, which is pretty much the same thing."

"How do you feel about that?"

I folded my hands in my lap, lacing my fingers together tight, as though to keep them from escaping my hands. "Richie worries about me," I said. "It's understandable. He loves me. He wants me to stay alive."

"I am wondering how *you* feel about it," she said. "Not Richie."

My throat caught. I felt an awful pressure against the backs of my eyes. I wasn't going to cry—I knew that. But I wanted to very badly, which was, in a way, worse. "I feel . . . like I'm being forced to choose between the two things I love most."

Susan nodded slowly.

"And . . . and I'm mad at Richie for making me choose."

"Is he making you choose?"

"Well, it's not like he's issued an ultimatum. But . . ."

"But what?"

"I don't want him to worry about me."

She nodded again.

"What do you think?" I said.

"Do you care what I think?"

"Of course I do."

"Why?"

"Because . . ."

Susan steepled her fingers under her chin and watched me for a long while. "I think," she said finally, "that you should probably stop caring so much about what other people think. Including me. Including Richie. We might get worried for you. We might disagree with your choices. But trust me, they are *your* choices. You're the only one who has to live with them. And no matter how worried or upset we may be about what you choose to do with your life, we will survive."

Susan's cheeks flushed. In all the time I'd known her, I hadn't ever heard her say so many words at one time, or show this type of emotion. It made me think about her own relationship, about which I knew very little—though enough to understand that she might have had firsthand experience with fears like Richie's.

I felt a tingling in my chest. *Nerves,* I thought. Because I was, in fact, very, very tense.

It wasn't until the session was nearly over and I felt the same sensation, this time at my side, that I realized it wasn't nerves, but my purse. More precisely, it was Dylan's phone, zipped inside and set to vibrate. Someone was calling him.

# FIFTEEN

The incoming call was from Trevor the Chemist. "I have to take this," I said, looking back up at Susan.

She nodded, her features settling into their usual placidity.

I ducked into the waiting room. There was another patient in there—a Harvard professor type, his face buried in a library edition of *Of Human Bondage*.

I figured I should answer Dylan's phone where no one could overhear me, and so I pushed open the front door, hurried down the short flight of stairs, and stepped outside. A cold wind bit through my sweater. My teeth chattered. I wished I'd thought to grab my coat. "Trevor?"

"Who is this?" The voice was deep and strangely familiar.

"My name is Sunny Randall," I said. "I'm a private investigator."

There was a long pause. Then, finally, laughter. "No way."

I frowned. "Trevor? Do I know you?"

Another pause. I could hear voices in the background. The crackle of a radio. "This is Lee Farrell, Sunny," he said.

"Oh, God," I said. "Really?"

Lee Farrell. One of the best cops I knew. The best-dressed by far, even if that wasn't saying much. Happy as I usually was to talk to Lee, though, I wasn't thrilled at the moment. "You're calling me from Trevor's phone because you found it," I said, the situation dawning on me.

"Yes."

"Where?" I asked. Though from the tone of his voice, combined with the background noises, I already knew what he was going to say.

"Trevor's dead," he said. "We found the phone on his body. This was the last number he texted."

"Great," I said. "Just great."

"Did you know him?"

"Trevor? No," I said. "But I really wanted to talk to him. He was my strongest lead."

"Who are you looking for?"

"Dylan Welch," I said.

"CEO of Gonzo?"

I was surprised Lee knew who he was. "One and the same," I said. "His mother hired me today. He's been incommunicado for two weeks and she's worried."

"He obviously didn't take his phone with him."

"Nope," I said. "Strange, right?"

"Not if he didn't want to be tracked."

"True."

"Why do you have the phone?"

"He left it in his desk before he went missing," I said. "I took it into my possession. To aid in the investigation."

"You stole it?"

"You obviously aren't familiar with the principle of finders keepers."

He laughed. Typically Lee was a serious, by-the-books, Eliot Ness kind of guy—as though being a gay male cop precluded him from cracking a smile. But I'd always prided myself on my ability to make Lee Farrell break character. "I don't know, though," I said. "I don't think I'm getting paid enough to look at some of these *saved photos*, if you know what I mean . . . I should have probably disinfected this thing before I borrowed it."

Lee laughed again.

"Straight men, am I right?" I said. And he laughed more. As ever, it felt like a triumph.

"Can you meet me here at the crime scene?" he said.

"Yeah of course," I said. "I just have to grab my coat."

He gave me an address that he explained was in Southie's industrial area, on the waterfront. Then we hung up. I pushed the town house door open again, found my coat, and apologized to Susan. "It's the police," I said. "I need to go. It has to do with my job."

"I understand," she said. "And I'm willing to wager that if Richie were here, he'd understand, too."

I wasn't sure about that. In fact, if I'd been low on cash, I'd have taken her up on that wager and doubled it. But Susan meant well. And I had a crime scene to get to. So I just thanked her and left.

# SIXTEEN

Before getting into my car, I surveilled the area around it. No sign of the RAV4. I got behind the wheel and took a quick, aimless drive through Cambridge just to make sure no one was following me before giving Siri the address of the crime scene.

Once I was officially on my way, I called Blake. "Go ahead and lock up," I told him. "I won't be back in the office until tomorrow morning."

"Okay, awesome," Blake said. "Did you find Dylan yet?"

"Not yet."

"All right," he said. "So, like, when you do find him, tell him, like . . . my compliments to the chef."

"Huh?"

"Gonzo," he said. "It's actually delicious."

"I thought you hated Gonzo."

"I don't think I gave it a fair chance," he said. "I saw one of my favorite skaters on YouTube drinking it, and, you know, with you taking the case and all . . . I thought I'd give Gonzo another try."

"That's charitable of you."

"It's super-good, Sunny. I really feel energized."

"Well, I guess that's what it's supposed to do," I said.

"You should try one. I bought a twelve-pack for the break-room fridge. Maybe when you come in tomorrow morning . . ."

"I'll take your word for it."

"Your loss, dude," he said.

"Yeah. I think I'm just too old for that stuff."

"Okay, so after I lock up I guess I'll head out to the gym. Take advantage of the energy. Pardon the pun."

It wasn't really a pun, but I didn't point it out. "Great," I said.

"Where are you right now?"

"On my way to a crime scene on the waterfront," I said.

"Wait, what?"

"Lee Farrell called me. There's been a murder."

"Not Dylan."

"No," I said. "I believe it's a drug dealer, actually. But from the looks of things, Dylan may be a suspect."

"Seriously?"

I told Blake I'd let him know what happened, but that cases like this one were often full of surprises, and that if things turned out the way I feared they might, it wouldn't be the first time I dealt with a missing person who morphed into a person of interest.

Blake was quiet for a long time. "*Morphed* is a sick word," he said finally. "I've gotta start using it more."

"Have a good workout," I said. "See you tomorrow."

"Bye, Sunny."

We hung up. I saw a gas station and pulled into it, parking the car momentarily. I grabbed my steno pad out of my purse and scrolled through Dylan's contacts, copying down names and information. I was 99 percent sure that Lee would ask me to turn over the phone, so now was the time to take everything from it that I could. It was interesting to me that very few of the contacts on this phone matched up with the names on Lydia's list. I did recognize one of them, though. Anna Horton. Under "relation," Lydia had referred to her as *Prom Date—Junior High*. When I'd called her from my office, I didn't think she'd know or care about what Dylan had been doing for the past fourteen years—let alone the past two weeks. And sure enough, the call had gone straight to voicemail, so I'd put her on Blake's list of people to email. Yet here she was among his iPhone contacts. *Interesting* . . . On impulse, I hit speed dial again. Again it went to voicemail, and again I left a quick message. Couldn't hurt, I reasoned.

I looked at Dylan's photos next. More dick pics. A few shots of fancy cocktails. An artful photograph of massive amounts of white powder on a glass-topped coffee table, Dylan's face shown in the reflection.

*Lee's going to love this,* I thought.

I came across some screenshots taken from Instagram, all of scantily clad influencers in suggestive poses. I didn't want to think about why he'd saved these.

Amid all this brain bleach–worthy material, though, was a shot of Sky and Dylan and a few of their coworkers holding up Gonzo cans in the middle of the Common. The picture stood out for its wholesomeness, everyone in it happy and healthy and wearing plenty of clothes. I took out my own phone and snapped a picture of it. The influencer shots, too. Maybe he actually knew some of them. The other images I had no need for. (And I was willing to wager that the women he sent them to felt the same.)

Once I was done, I filled up my tank, charged my phone, and got back on the road.

Instead of thinking about anything complicated, I focused on Siri's directions.

It was quite soothing—just stopping at red lights and making all the necessary turns to get to Soldiers Field Road, without letting my mind wander into more complicated places, such as my future, whether or not I was willing to give up the work I loved for the man I loved, or even how Trevor the Chemist had wound up dead when he had plans to meet Dylan Welch.

Traffic eased up once I got closer to the waterfront. After about ten more minutes, I reached a desolate stretch of industrial buildings—warehouses and manufacturing plants. In five years or less, they'd all be gutted and renovated into high-end condos. But for now, it was exactly the type of area where you'd expect to find a dead drug dealer.

I stared at the bleak road, my hands on the wheel with nothing on my mind, as though the car and I had morphed into one. I heard Blake's voice in my head. *Morphed is a sick word* . . . And I realized that I should have told Blake to get a Christmas tree for the office. He'd been bugging me about that for weeks—Blake loved Christmas almost as much as he loved Rosie. But I'd been putting him off, refusing to believe that Christmas would be here soon, and then New Year's, another year behind me, and what would the coming year bring? Changes? Mistakes? Missed chances? Wrong turns?

*There I go again . . .*

"You've reached your destination," Siri said, bringing me back to reality.

I looked at where I was—the cop cars teeming outside, lights flashing. I'd expected a vacant lot, a dark alley, a secluded garage—the type of place where Trevor the Chemist would secretly meet up with a wealthy scumbag like Dylan Welch.

But that wasn't the case at all. The address Lee had given me was a working factory. Save for the cop cars, the parking lot was mostly empty—but that was because, as Sky had told me, it was closed for the month. I noticed the lit-up logo. The familiar red letters: GONZO MANUFACTURING. Weird place to meet a drug dealer.

# SEVENTEEN

Trevor "The Chemist" Weiss was not a drug dealer. He was an actual chemist, who, until this afternoon, had worked in product development—i.e., the lab—at Gonzo's manufacturing plant. According to Lee Farrell, who, at this point, had only Trevor's phone, a lanyard taken from his desk drawer, and the driver's license found in his pocket to go on, Trevor Weiss was even younger than Dylan and Sky. A kid, really. And so, as I stood next to Lee in the basement level of the Gonzo factory, gazing down at Trevor's lifeless body, which lay between two enormous mixing tanks, blood pooling beneath, I was moved by the cruelty of it all, the waste of a life that had barely begun. He'd been shot through the heart at close range. According to one of the techs from the medical examiner's office—a woman named Giselle who was now bagging Trevor's hands—he'd probably died instantly. No pain. Most likely, he hadn't even been afforded enough time to be surprised.

This was not a place where anyone would expect to find Trevor Weiss, dead or alive. He worked in the testing labs, which were three floors up from where we were now. And besides that, as Sky had told me earlier today, the factory was closed for the month of December. Had Trevor Weiss really come down here to meet Dylan—and if so, why? I said all that to Lee, but it was more intended for myself. Thinking out loud, as it were.

"I'm not sure on the why," Lee said. "But an empty factory is as good a place to meet as any if you need privacy. Plus, Dylan Welch and Trevor Weiss presumably had access to the key codes, so they could get in without setting off alarms."

"True . . ."

I thought about my own run-in with Dylan six months earlier—how wasted he'd been at the time, sweating, shaking. Off-the-rails paranoid to the point of delusion. I remembered how he'd held a gun on me. And how, though I'd been relatively certain he didn't know how to shoot it, I'd been equally sure that he was willing to try.

"It's a good, quiet place to kill somebody, if that's what you're looking to do," Lee said.

"Yes," I said noncommittally.

Lee was looking at me in a way I didn't like—as though there was something important I wasn't telling him, which was, in fact, true. But Lydia Welch had specifically said she didn't want the police involved. And though it appeared that she'd soon have no choice in the matter, I owed it to my employer to let her know about Trevor Weiss's death before Lee learned (which he would, with or without my firsthand information) that Dylan Welch definitely had access to a gun.

"Dylan has been missing for two weeks," I tried. "Wherever he is, he doesn't have his phone on him. I find it hard to believe he'd rematerialize just to meet some random lab tech from his own company . . ."

"And kill him," Lee said.

"Yes," I said.

"Unless that lab tech had something on him," Lee said. "Something that might have scared him into disappearing for two weeks."

I swallowed hard. Lee was making a little too much sense. "Who found the body?"

Lee gestured at a middle-aged man standing about twenty feet away from us, talking to two uniforms. "He didn't know either one of them," Lee said.

"Who is he?"

"Ted Blankenship. Works on the assembly line," Lee said. "Apparently, he'd been down with the flu since December first, and so he wasn't able to clear out his locker for the month. He felt better today, and showed up at around six to get his stuff. He saw the blood first. Thought it was leakage from one of the tanks, so he went to investigate. That's when he came across the body."

"Allegedly," I said.

"Allegedly," he said.

"He could be a suspect."

"Yes. But Ted Blankenship has never met Trevor Weiss."

"Allegedly."

Lee gave me flat eyes. "He seems legitimately shocked," he said. "I don't make him as our killer."

I took a closer look at Ted Blankenship. He held a white handkerchief to his forehead that was roughly the same color as his skin. One of the uniforms was handing him a tarp to put around his shoulders because he was shivering, visibly—even from this distance. And from what I could see of his face, *You look like you've just seen a ghost* would have been the obvious conversation starter. "I get what you mean."

"Shitty way to start a vacation," Lee said. "Of course, if it wasn't for Ted Blankenship, he and all his coworkers would have been greeted with an even worse sight the day after New Year's."

I nodded.

"You ever meet Dylan Welch?" Lee asked.

"Once."

"What did you think of him?"

"Not much."

"But now you're working for his parents, trying to find him."

"His mother," I said. "Yes."

"Why?"

"She's paying me a small fortune," I said. "And it just so happens that at this point in my life, I could really use a small fortune."

"Any reason why his mother hasn't called the police?"

I cleared my throat. "Come on, Lee. Dylan Welch is a grown man and not what you'd call reliable. He disappears all the time—goes on benders, winds up in rehab . . . You guys wouldn't want to pour your limited resources into finding somebody like that."

He nodded. "You've got a point," he said. "You have his phone?"

I started to hand it to him, then stopped. "Can you keep in touch?" I said. "Tell me anything you find out about Trevor Weiss?"

"Such as . . ."

"Well, he's young. Smart. Works at Gonzo, but in the lab. And in an entry-level job—not management."

"Yes."

"I just can't imagine him being somebody Dylan Welch would know, let alone arrange to meet in private with." *Unless he was dealing drugs on the down-low. Or dating a girl that Dylan was stalking.*

"I called his supervisor, who's on his way. We have his laptop. His phone. We'll find out who Trevor Weiss really was. Who he was associating with and why. And we'll find out why his last text was to someone whose family regards him as a missing person."

"So that's what I'd like to know."

"I'll tell you what I can."

"Speaking of his phone," I said. "I'm assuming there aren't any messages from Dylan on it."

"Just the one you sent."

"Don't you find that weird?"

"I find everything about this weird."

"Yeah, but this especially," I said. "Dylan and Trevor obviously had a plan to meet. Trevor showed up and texted Dylan, asking where he was."

"Yep."

"But where are the texts or phone calls where they made the plan in the first place?" I said. "What did they do, pass notes?"

"Good question," Lee said. "Of course, we'll contact his phone company. Recover any deleted texts, voicemails, records of calls."

"And . . ."

"I'll let you know if we find out anything."

"Thank you," I said.

"Within reason," he said.

"Of course."

He locked his gaze with mine. "I presume you'll do the same."

I picked at a fingernail. "Don't I always?"

"You tell me, Sunny," he said.

"I do," I said. "Within reason."

I handed him the phone and he dropped it into a bag. "For what it's worth," I said, "I don't think Dylan would have shot Trevor Weiss. Not like this."

"Like what?"

"Skillfully. At close range. Without hesitation."

"Any reason why you believe that?"

I shook my head, forcing the image out of my mind: strung-out Dylan Welch, his face gleaming with sweat, the gun held in his trembling hand. "Just a feeling," I said.

"We don't put a lot of stock in feelings," Lee said.

"I know," I said. "But my feelings are more reliable than most."

He smiled. "Good luck with this job, Sunny," he said.

"Thanks," I said. "I'll need it."

We said our goodbyes, and I left the factory feeling more in the dark than ever. Did Dylan really shoot Trevor? Or did someone shoot both of them, and his lifeless body simply hadn't been found? For Dylan's mother's sake, I hoped neither possibility panned out. Dylan's mother, whom I definitely needed to call.

On my way out, I nearly bumped into a worried-looking middle-aged man. He wore baggy gray sweats and a misbuttoned wool overcoat, clearly thrown on in a hurry. He was my height and bald, with embryological features and huge, pale eyes like a baby's. He stuck out his hand. It was trembling. "Rand Carlson," he said. "I was asked to answer questions about Trevor Weiss?"

"Are you his supervisor?"

"I run the lab here," he said. "Trevor required very little supervision." He gave me a nervous smile. I nodded politely but didn't smile back. It was clear he thought I was a cop, and I saw no reason to relieve him of that notion.

"Did you ever see Trevor with Dylan Welch?" I asked.

"The CEO?"

"Yes."

"No," he said. "But that doesn't mean much."

"Why not?"

"I only saw Trevor within the confines of this factory," he said. "We're not social here like they are in corporate."

"Sure."

"And as you might guess if you've met him, Dylan Welch has never visited our lab."

"Not even once?"

"Well, he was here when we cut the ribbon on the factory," Rand Carlson said. "But by and large, Mr. Welch isn't the kind of person who likes seeing how the sausage gets made, so to speak."

"He's not a scientist," I said.

"Correct," he said.

"Not much of a CEO, either?"

"That's a matter of opinion," he said. "I think he's more of a . . . delegator." He seemed pleased with himself for finding the right word.

"How about Trevor?" I said. "Anything unusual about his behavior lately?"

"Unusual?"

"Did he seem tense or agitated during those weeks before vacation? Was he on his phone more than is typical? Eating less? Performing at a lower level? Or maybe it was the opposite and he was spending more hours at the office than usual?"

Carlson bit his lip, those eyes widening more than I'd thought possible. His mouth grew tiny and his skin flushed—his infantile face conquered by a dawning idea.

"What is it?"

"Just what you said about spending time at the office," he said.

"Yes?"

"Four or five months ago, corporate wanted to brainstorm new ways to change the formula," he said. "The COO asked for my best and brightest, and Trevor is young and brilliant—graduated MIT at just nineteen. I sent him over. God, I mean to say he *was* young and brilliant. I can't believe he's . . ."

"How did he seem to feel about that? Being sent over to corporate?"

"Happy. Excited," he said. "At least at first he was."

"And then?"

"Then, maybe . . . I don't know. Tired, I suppose. A little on edge. Those business and marketing people can be very draining. We're pretty much all introverts. They're the opposite. I think he was glad to come back to the lab."

"So you're telling me that, even though you've never seen Dylan Welch within the confines of your office, Trevor potentially had ample time to meet Dylan and get to know him."

"Yes, yes!" He grinned, his face brightening as though he'd just discovered we spoke the same language. "That's exactly what I'm telling you."

I nodded. "Trevor never mentioned Dylan, though."

"No."

"You never knew about Trevor making plans with Dylan Welch, attending a party he threw, et cetera."

"No, but also, now that you mention it, I did see him on his own phone a lot. He was leaving the lab to take calls. He'd go to the stairwell. It got to a point where I reprimanded him for it once. Which is something, for Trevor. Like I said . . ."

"He was your best and brightest."

"Yes," he said. "My God . . ." He swallowed hard, his thin neck moving visibly. "Trevor's gone. He's . . . I'm sorry. I just can't believe this happened."

"That's okay," I said. "Take a deep breath."

He did. Then he took another. "Thank you," he said. "That helps." He swatted at his dry eyes, as though he was preemptively wiping tears away.

I waited for him to either stop doing that or actually cry. He did neither. It didn't faze me. Everyone experienced shock in different ways, and some people weren't criers. Especially men in clinical professions. He covered his face with both hands and took several more deep breaths until finally he was able to compose himself.

"Who did you think the calls were from?" I asked.

"At the time, I assumed it was the receptionist. Elspeth," he said. "She picked Trevor up a few times after work. I . . . I think he was sweet on her. Do you know who she is?"

"I do," I said.

"Nice girl," he said.

"What about now?"

"Pardon?"

"You said 'at the time' you thought it was Elspeth calling. Have you changed your mind now?"

"Well, you know what they say about hindsight," he said.

"I do," I said again.

Carlson rubbed his chin, his big babyish eyes staring off into the distance. "Looking back on his demeanor during those calls," he said, "he didn't seem like he was talking to a young lady."

"How so?"

"He seemed intense," he said, "you know . . . serious . . . like what he'd just been discussing was important."

"You don't think a call with a young lady could be important?"

He sighed heavily. "Come on," he said. "You know what I mean."

"I do."

His cheeks flushed.

I crossed my hands over my chest. "Thank you, Mr. Carlson," I said. "You've been very helpful."

"Is there anything else you need," he said, "or can I leave?"

"Well, I'm sure the police will want to talk to you. They're all inside the factory. Lee Farrell is the detective in charge."

His face fell. "Wait, you aren't the police?"

"Nope."

"Shouldn't you have told me that?"

I'd already started toward my car, but I turned around and smiled warmly. "Shouldn't you have asked?"

# EIGHTEEN

I made two calls from my car. The first was to Gonzo's corporate offices, which were closed for the day. I used voice prompts to get to the staff directory, then left a message for Elspeth, whose last name, I learned, was Wasserman. "I'm hoping we can talk," I told her. "It's important." I gave her my name and phone number and reminded her that we'd met earlier that day. I didn't say anything about Trevor's murder for a number of reasons—one being that it was never a good idea to be recorded asking someone to call you about an ongoing police investigation; another being that if the police hadn't gotten to her yet, I couldn't imagine a worse way to find out about a friend's death than from office voicemail.

Next, I called Lydia Welch. She picked up immediately. "Did you find him?" she said.

"Not yet," I said.

"Well, I'm still glad you called," she said. "Bill wants to meet with you and we both want a full update. Can you come to our place tomorrow, please? I can have our chef prepare a marvelous luncheon."

"Of course," I said. Not that I had any desire to spend more time with Bill Welch than I already had—marvelous luncheon or otherwise. But with Lydia paying what she was, saying no wasn't really an option.

"I'm going to invite Sky Farley as well. You met her today. Isn't she lovely?"

"Yes, I did, and yes, she is."

"Splendid."

"I do have some news," I said.

"Oh, why on earth am I taking up the conversation?"

"Unfortunately, it isn't what you'd call great news."

"Tell me."

"I think you should expect a call from the police."

"Why?"

"A young chemist from the Gonzo lab was shot to death today," I said. "His last text was to Dylan. Apparently, they were supposed to meet?"

"Today?"

"Yes."

"But . . . But Dylan's been missing for weeks."

"Missing to you," I said. "Missing to his friends. But presumably, hopefully . . . he's out there somewhere."

"Yes, of course," Lydia said. "I know in my heart that he is. But are you telling me . . . Do you think . . ."

"I don't think anything."

"Do the *police* think my son murdered this person?"

"It's very early stages," I said, staring at my phone. *Could be tapped. It's been tapped before.* "I can explain more to you in person."

"Oh, God. Dylan is being accused of shooting a man to death. And he's not even around to defend himself."

"He isn't being accused of anything," I said. "The police have an interest in questioning Dylan—and, in his absence, they'll want to speak to you and your husband." The car behind me was driving too close, its halogen lights burning into my rearview. I switched lanes.

"Should I call our lawyer?"

"I don't think it's necessary at this point," I said. "But go ahead and do what makes you feel comfortable."

There was a short stretch of silence. Then Lydia spoke. "It's like that high school party all over again." She said it very quietly—more to herself than to me. She didn't think I knew what she was talking about, but unfortunately I did. I could practically see Dylan writhing on the sidewalk, just as he was six months ago, strung out and bleeding and delirious. Dylan, confessing to me about something that had happened when he was a drunk and horrible teenager. *The girl was into it,* he had said. *She wanted me. She only got weird afterward.* I hadn't asked follow-up questions back then and I didn't want to now. My stomach felt sour. I needed to change the subject.

I said, "I gave Dylan's phone to the cops."

"You had Dylan's phone?"

"Yes," I said. "It was in his office. I found it."

"How could that be? He never goes anywhere without that phone."

"Well, he might have had to leave in a hurry—for whatever reason—and forgotten it," I said. "He could have purposely not taken the phone so he wouldn't be traced. Or he could have simply decided to buy a new phone."

"'For whatever reason,'" Lydia said.

"Excuse me?"

"You said he could have left in a hurry for whatever reason. As though . . . he was being chased. Or someone abducted him. Or . . . Or . . . he was off . . . planning the murder."

"Or he took a spur-of-the-moment vacation or he fell in love and wound up running off with her," I said. "Please, Mrs. Welch. You'll do yourself a huge favor—and me, too—if you don't jump to conclusions."

"Lydia."

"What?"

"Call me Lydia."

*God, she's all over the place.* "Please, Lydia."

"Thank you."

"Just try and stay with me here, Lydia," I said.

"I'm with you," she said.

"All Dylan did was receive a text. That's it," I said. "That is the only thing that makes him a person of interest."

"I'm calling the lawyer."

"The term *person of interest* only means that Dylan may have information that could help the investigation."

"That's it?" she said.

"That's it," I said. "It's very different than being named a suspect. There's no proof that Dylan and Trevor ever saw each other."

"What did the text say?"

"It said, 'Where are you?'"

"That's damning."

"Not really."

"Did you reply?"

"Yes," I said. "I texted that I had Dylan's phone and that we are looking for him. But I never got a response."

"What time was this?"

"Two-thirty," I said. "The police called around six, telling me the body had been found. I just got through meeting with them."

"What was his name? The chemist?"

"Trevor Weiss," I said.

I could hear Lydia's shaky breathing through my Bluetooth. The halogen lights swung in behind me again. *Jesus.* Any closer and they would have been inside my car. I opened my window and shouted, "Hey! Anybody ever teach you about boundaries?"

"What?" Lydia said.

"Sorry. I was just talking to another driver."

"Ah." She said it as though she completely understood. I appreciated that.

"Do you know the name at all?" I said. "Trevor Weiss?"

"I . . . I don't think so," she said.

I reached a traffic light and made a right turn. It wasn't the fastest way home, but it was worth it if I could lose the tailgater.

"I know Dylan didn't spend a lot of time at work," I said. "No reason why he'd know a low-level scientist from Product Development."

"Yes, that's exactly right . . ." She sounded strange and sort of dreamy. "He didn't spend a lot of time at work."

"Is something wrong?" I said, just as those needlessly bright headlights returned. I sped up, suddenly. The traffic light in the distance felt like a finish line.

"I don't know if this means anything at all," Lydia was saying. "But I just had a memory. Dylan was at our home. He kept taking phone calls, speaking very quietly or moving into another room. It happened several times."

"Uh-huh?" I peered into my rearview, then turned around. *Lost him*, I thought. *Finally*.

"I told him he was being rude," she said. "That he shouldn't take phone calls during visits home. But Dylan swore to me he was talking to someone from Gonzo. A research scientist. He said it was an important business matter. I just said, 'Honestly. How stupid do you think I am?' I love my son, but he wouldn't know an important business matter if it punched him in the nose."

"He never said the research scientist's name?"

"If he did, I don't remember," she said. "I would have bet all my savings at the time that he was lying and it was one of his sleazy drug friends. Whispering the way he was. I actually heard him say . . . and I quote, 'What's the point if there's no buzz?' Who says that to a research scientist?"

"How long ago was this?"

"Around a month ago."

*The same time he went to urgent care.* I saw the headlights again, the car catching up with me. Quickly, I turned around to see its logo glinting in a streetlight. It was a RAV4. A black one. I swore under my breath.

"Pardon?"

"I have to go."

"But . . . But I have more questions."

"I'll see you and Bill tomorrow for the luncheon. Name the time and give me your address, I'm there."

"All right, then."

I turned around again. The driver clicked on his dome light, for just a few seconds. Long enough for me to see the baseball cap. Then he waved.

Lydia was saying something about whether she should text or email me her address. "Either way," I said. "I'm flexible."

Then I pushed the pedal to the metal.

# NINETEEN

*Maybe Richie has a point about my job,* I thought as I swung into a sharp right turn that nearly made my car flip over. My next thoughts were, in quick succession, *I wish I could drive like Spike*—because Spike was the fastest and most skillfully reckless driver I knew. *Where are the police when you need them?* And finally, *Rosie hasn't had dinner.*

My solution to the first two of the latter thoughts was to floor it until the next light, then make an unexpected and extremely illegal left turn—the light was red—and pray that I'd get pulled over.

I didn't get pulled over.

As I tore down another deserted street full of abandoned-looking warehouses, those halogen headlights burning through my windows, I kept thinking about Rosie, and how, if this asshole were to succeed in getting me into a fatal accident, no one would know enough to check up on her for close to twenty-four hours. She'd be stuck in my apartment—hungry, frightened, and alone—until tomorrow afternoon at three p.m., when my fourteen-year-old neighbor, Cara, would innocently show up at my front door and use her spare key, expecting to take Rosie on her daily walk. (I paid her once a week for this.) Would Rosie be able to get by until three p.m. tomorrow with no food, no walks, no *me*? And after that, who would take her? Spike? Richie? Would she be able to survive without me? What if she couldn't?

*What a terrible thought.*

I blazed through another red light. The RAV4 didn't slow down by even a fraction. It was as though Baseball Cap and I were the only two people left on earth, free to break any driving law we wanted to, with no repercussions. "Where are all the cops?" I said it to the windshield. And then the answer came to me.

The entire Boston Police Department was at the Gonzo manufacturing plant. An exaggeration, sure. But I happened to know that there were at least a dozen cop cars in the Gonzo factory parking lot. And I now had a plan. I'd lead him there.

My phone was mounted on my dashboard. I pressed the button and asked Siri for directions back to the crime scene. Cheerful as ever, my AI complied.

Siri told me to take a right at the next light. I did. So did the RAV4. She told me to go straight for three blocks, and I did. He did the same. She said to make a left at the next stop sign and I accidentally took a right and wound up on a dead-end street. He followed me. Siri politely told me to "safely make a U-turn," which almost made me laugh. I wasn't doing anything safely tonight. I threw my car into a U-turn and the RAV4 stayed where it was, then sharply pulled forward, its grill careening toward me. I jammed my foot on the brake. So did he. My heart pounded up into my throat, my ears, my hair. "Jesus Christ." I whispered.

We'd stopped short of a head-on collision. By inches. Millimeters. I was relieved, then terrified, then very, very angry. Adrenaline coursed through me.

He got out of the RAV4 and walked toward me. I thought about putting the car in reverse, but there was a telephone pole right behind me. So instead I reached into my purse. Got my hand on my .38 and slipped it out.

He moved closer. He was a big man with square shoulders. He wore a bulky black leather jacket with fur at the collar that looked real. This wrap of his managed to be tacky and expensive-looking at the same time—the worst of both worlds. Plus, it didn't work with the baseball cap. It was as though this guy couldn't decide what season it was and wanted to make sure he was covered.

He moved closer. Close enough so I could get a good look at his face. I recognized him. That cap. That smile, the meaty jaw half hidden by the scope of a gun the last time I saw him. He was Moon Monaghan's guy. No question.

*Thanks a lot for taking me seriously, Desmond.*

Moon's guy knocked on my window. I opened my door and

stepped out slowly. The air felt about ten degrees colder than it had outside the factory, the temperature dropping quickly, the way it always did at this time of year.

He was a tall guy. So tall that when I raised the gun straight out in front of me, it was aimed at his stomach. I raised it higher. "Stay back, asshole," I said.

He stared at me for a few moments, his hands in the pockets of that bulky, cheesy fur-trimmed jacket. It looked worse up close. The fur was either fox or dyed rabbit. Or dog. It could have been dog.

"Where is he?" he said.

"Where is who?"

"Dylan Welch. Say where he is, you won't get hurt."

"First, I feel like if one of us is going to do the threatening, it should be me." I released the safety.

"You kidding me?"

"Get your hands out of your pockets."

He took his hands out of his pockets. He was holding a gun in one of them. "Oh, now, come on," I said.

"What?"

"Drop it."

"No."

I switched positions and fired. The bullet hit the concrete half an inch from his foot. Close enough so he knew that I'd missed intentionally and that next time, he might not be so lucky. His eyes went big. "Jesus Christ, lady," he said. "What the fuck is wrong with you?"

He looked rattled. I was glad. When you're a woman and

you're dealing with guys like this, it's best if they think you aren't playing with a full deck.

He said it again. "The fuck is wrong with you?"

"I said *drop it*, you piece of shit."

He dropped the gun, proving my point.

"Shooting me would be a mistake," he said. "There's lots more where I come from."

"Yeah, right. Like cockroaches," I said.

My headlights were still on and illuminated his face. He was sweating. A lot. His skin shimmered. Droplets fell from his forehead, his nose.

"What do you want with Dylan Welch?" I said.

"None of your business."

I aimed right between his feet and fired again. Bits of pavement went flying. He yelped. That's right. Mr. Cool-as-a-Cucumber Professional Sniper made the same sound Rosie did if you accidentally stepped on her tail. I found it tremendously satisfying. "Next time," I said, "I'm aiming two feet higher."

His jaw dropped open. I had no doubt he believed me.

I said it again. "What do you want with Dylan Welch?"

"He owes money to the firm."

"Moon and Desmond?"

"No, just Moon," he said.

"Desmond doesn't know about it."

"I have no idea what Mr. Burke knows and doesn't know."

"That's noncommittal of you."

"Huh?"

"Never mind," I said. "What does Dylan owe you money for? Drugs?"

"Medical supplies."

"Cut the crap. I'm not a cop."

"You wearing a wire?"

"You've been chasing *me*. This meeting wasn't by choice. Why the fuck would I be wearing a wire?"

He looked me up and down, computing the situation in his thick head. Then he actually grinned. "Can you prove you ain't wearing a wire?"

*Idiot.* I raised the gun two feet.

"Okay, okay! It's drugs."

"What kind?" I said.

"Designer stuff. From overseas. He owes us a lot. He said he was good for it and then he just . . . disappeared. Like Moon says, that's a dumbfuck thing to do."

"A real wordsmith, that Moon."

"Huh?"

I sighed. "What do you mean by 'designer stuff'?"

"I . . . I don't know. Powerful shit. Moon figured he was good for the money because he's bought from us before. We didn't expect him to run away."

"Why do you think I know where he is?"

"We've been tracking his phone. You have it. Or you had it."

"The police have it now."

"Wait, what?"

"Welch is missing," I said. "I'm trying to find him, just like you are."

"Why are you trying to find him?"

"I was hired to."

"By who?"

"None of your business."

"He doesn't have his phone?"

"No, genius. He doesn't have his phone. He hasn't had it for two weeks."

"You gotta tell us when you find him," he said.

"I do, huh?" I took a few steps closer, the gun still pointed at his crotch.

"Fuck." He started to tremble.

I walked up to him and plucked his gun from the pavement. I dropped it in my purse.

"That's . . . That's *mine*." He said it like a two-year-old on the cusp of a temper tantrum.

I stood up and resumed my stance. "Here's what I'm going to do," I said. "I'm going to get in my car and drive away. Here's what you're going to do. You're not going to follow me."

"What about my gun?" he said.

"I'll give it to Desmond. If he thinks you deserve it, I'm sure you can have it back." I offered up a cheery smile.

He said something I couldn't hear. I could tell it wasn't very nice. I turned and shot out one of his tires. "Watch the way you talk to a lady."

His face reddened. "What the . . ."

"You're lucky it's just a tire."

I held my gun on him as I eased into my car and closed the door. I kept it aimed at him when I started it up and drove away. It wasn't until I was back in traffic again on Soldiers Field Drive, and both guns were safely in my purse, that I was finally able to start breathing.

# TWENTY

I shouldn't have put off the judo lesson," Spike said.

"Hey, the gun worked out pretty well for me," I said.

"I know, but knowing a martial art is a good backup if your gun jams or you run out of ammo," he said. "Plus, it gives you confidence. Big-dick energy."

"I've already got that," I said.

"Yeah, you do," Spike said.

It was late, and we were at my place, finishing our second glasses of wine. Spike had been the first person I called once I got home and fed Rosie. Not Richie, because I knew how he'd react. And when I'd told Spike everything that had happened to me today, he'd done exactly what I'd expected him to do. He'd listened without judgment. Without saying anything really, except *Come to the restaurant. Bring Rosie. Dinner's on me.*

It was only then that I'd realized how exhausted I was, physically and emotionally. I'd told Spike I couldn't imagine anything worse than leaving my apartment again. And again, as ever, he understood. Since it had been a slow evening at the restaurant (Mondays always were), he'd stayed just one more hour and tasked his manager with handling the rest of the night and closing up. Then he'd headed over to my place, with three bottles of his best cabernet and a soup bone for Rosie.

I didn't deserve Spike. Lucky for me, he didn't seem to know that.

"So let me get this straight," Spike said. "You got a text today from this chemist guy . . ."

"Actually, it was Dylan Welch who got the text."

"Dylan Welch. Who has been missing for two weeks. Without his phone. He's somehow arranged to meet with this chemist today at the Gonzo factory, which is closed. And a couple hours after texting Welch, asking where he is, the chemist is found dead."

"Yes."

"Cops are involved."

"Very."

"Meanwhile, Welch has managed to get the Mob after him."

"Uh-huh," I said. "And don't forget the grieving mother."

"Right," Spike said. "Jesus."

"I know," I said. "We haven't even started on all the women he's pissed off." Which reminded me. I needed to call Teresa Leone.

Spike poured himself another glass of wine—a longer and more difficult process than it would have normally been. Rosie was now sleeping in his lap. He didn't want to disturb her, and so he had to disengage the top half of his large body from the lower half. Somehow he managed to do it without waking Rosie or spilling a drop. Spike liked to call himself "big but agile," and I had to agree. I was impressed.

"Please tell me again," he said after draining his glass, "why you decided that this asshole was worth finding?"

"The paycheck," I said.

"Oh, right."

"But that may be not as important as I thought."

"Wait, what? Why?"

I shrugged.

"You're not reconsidering the Jersey Shore, are you?"

I took a big swallow of wine and felt the warmth of it in my chest, my stomach. My cheeks and nose flushed. I absorbed it all.

Rosie was snoring softly. Spike scratched her ear. I patted her on the back, remembering her in bed with Richie and me this weekend, squeezed in between us, muttering in her sleep. How natural that had felt. *That was vacation, though.* To me, vacationing with a man had always felt like acting in a play— the lines rehearsed, the time limited, everything a little too perfect and heightened and unnatural.

"Richie wants me to stop taking dangerous jobs," I said.

"Well," Spike said, "you'd better not tell him about this one."

I finished the rest of my glass and set it down on the coffee table. "Hey, I got hired to find a missing rich douchebag . . . by his mommy," I said. "You have to admit that on paper, that doesn't seem very dangerous."

"That's true, I guess," Spike said.

"It is," I said. "By the same token, I've taken jobs that made me want to up my life insurance policy, and they wound up putting me to sleep. You know . . . there's no telling how dangerous a case is going to be when you accept it. Which is one reason why I love my job. I've never done well with predictability."

"Have you explained this to Richie?"

"Hell, no," I said. "I can't even explain it to you."

"No, no. I get it."

"You do?"

"Yes."

I poured myself more wine and took a lengthy sip.

"You are going to need to talk about this with him," Spike said. "No matter what either one of us happens to think."

"Do you talk things like this through with Flynn?"

"Things like this? With Flynn?" Spike said. "He's a foodstagrammer, Sunny. I've never been afraid he'd lose his life on the job."

"You know what I mean. Once a relationship reaches a certain point, you start thinking about the future."

"I don't know. Flynn and I aren't like you and Richie. We just started dating a few weeks ago."

I smiled. Spike and Flynn Tipton had been together for six months. At the start of their relationship, he'd described it as a much-needed fling or a breath of fresh air following his breakup with Sam, the morning-show anchor. *It's just a one-night stand,* he used to say back then. *Okay, maybe a three- or four-night stand. Five. Six, tops.*

Spike was like me. He could stay in a relationship forever—just so long as no one made him define it or make sacrifices for it, and he had to think of it only from day to day to day. "You understand how I feel," I said, "don't you?"

"Sure."

"Good."

"For what it's worth, I understand how Richie feels, too."

"Jesus, would it kill you to take sides?"

Spike laughed. I laughed, too. I drank more wine. He poured himself another glass. I was starting to get a little tipsy—that wonderful stage in drinking where the stress lifts and nothing really matters as much as you thought it did and so you may as well enjoy yourself.

Rosie stretched in her sleep and yawned. I was pretty sure she was at that exact same stage, no alcohol needed. "Maybe Rosie is my one true soulmate," I said. But Spike didn't seem to hear me.

"You are going to sit down with Richie and discuss this," he said. "You're going to hear each other out and come up with a compromise."

"Is that supposed to be a question?" I said. "Because it didn't sound like one."

"It wasn't," Spike said. And then my phone rang. "Speak of the devil," Spike said. Indeed, it had to be Richie. Who else would be calling me at eleven p.m.?

It wasn't Richie. On the screen, I saw an unfamiliar number with a Boston area code. I tapped the green dot and put the call on speaker. "Hello?"

"Sunny Randall?" The caller sounded young and female and breathless. I looked at Spike. He shrugged. "Is, uh . . . is this you?" she said.

"Yes, this is Sunny," I said. "Who is this?"

"Elspeth. From Gonzo?"

"Oh, Elspeth. Hi. Thank you so much for returning my—"

"I'm outside right now."

"Okay. Why are you outside?"

"I mean, I googled your address and I'm pretty sure I'm right outside your apartment. Is it all right if we talk, like . . . in person?"

Spike's eyebrows shot up.

I walked over to my street-facing window and pushed the curtains aside.

Elspeth Wasserman was standing directly below my apartment. She was the only person on the street. But even if she hadn't been, there would have been no mistaking her in that all-white outfit, that winter-white coat, silver baubles dangling from her wrists as she grasped the phone. Elspeth's hair was a mess and she was breathing hard, her slim body doubled over, as though she'd run all the way here from the Gonzo offices. Had she?

I wanted to ask Elspeth that. I also wanted to ask her if it had really been that easy to find out where I lived, but she seemed too emotional to answer either of those questions. So instead I just said, "Sure," and buzzed her up.

# TWENTY-ONE

I was glad Spike had brought three bottles of wine. I'd thought it a little excessive when he'd first shown up, but seeing as Elspeth had downed two glasses before she was even able to speak, it now seemed like good planning.

We were all sitting at my kitchen table, with Rosie beneath it, reacquainting herself with her soup bone. I'd introduced Elspeth to Spike, but she kept giving him scared sidelong glances—as if he was an undercover cop or a bodyguard I'd hired for the sole purpose of keeping her in line.

She poured herself another glass. I placed my hand on her arm. "You want to tell me what's going on?" I said.

Elspeth swallowed her wine, then set it down on the table. A tear spilled down her cheek. "Trevor," she said. "I . . . I knew him. I liked him."

"I know you did," I said. "I'm so sorry."

"We weren't, like . . . dating. But we were sort of . . . getting to know each other." She lifted the glass to her lips and drained the rest of it. This was her third glass of wine in less than ten minutes. And she was toothpick-thin. I was getting worried about her blood alcohol level. Spike and I glanced at each other. I wondered if she'd pass out before revealing whatever it was she'd run all the way here to tell us. She poured herself another glass and took a swallow. I saw Spike's hand moving toward the bottle and sliding it away from her. It seemed like an unconscious reflex. Bar owner's instinct. I shook my head at him. He slid the bottle back.

"If I tell you guys something," Elspeth said, "will you promise not to tell the police?"

I blinked at her.

"Why don't you want us to tell the police?" Spike asked.

"Because," she said, "it will get me killed."

Spike raised an eyebrow. I looked at Elspeth. "I promise you that we'll do everything we can to keep you safe," I said. "But that's the best I can do."

She swallowed more of her wine. "Okay, I understand." Her voice was clear, her speech un-slurred. I was impressed. For someone who weighed maybe a few pounds more than Rosie, this girl could definitely hold her alcohol.

"Dylan Welch isn't really missing," she said.

I stared at her. "How do you know that?"

"Because he's been talking to me," she said. "And because he killed Trevor."

Spike's jaw dropped open. So did mine, but unlike Spike, I managed to shift it back into a position where I was able to speak again. "Do you have proof of what you just said?"

Elspeth nodded. She was crying now, silently, her shoulders heaving, her face wet from tears. I excused myself, grabbed a box of Kleenex from my nightstand, and headed back to the kitchen.

When I returned, Elspeth was scrolling through her phone as Spike watched her, his big arms folded over his chest.

"What's going on?" I said.

Spike said, "She's finding the proof."

I placed the Kleenex in front of Elspeth. She took one and dabbed at her eyes while continuing to scroll. Finally, she tapped the screen. Dylan Welch's voice oozed out of it. *Hate to be the bearer of bad news, babe. But your boy got smoked. When the cops call, play dumb. I know you're good at that. Ha.*

I felt nauseated—a visceral response to that rich-boy lilt, the pseudo-gangster phrasing. The obvious sociopathy. It was Dylan Welch, no question. Missing or not, loved by his mother or not, he was truly a shithead. I looked at Elspeth. Asked the obvious questions. "When did you get this message? Who is he talking about?"

"Trevor." She looked at me like I was an idiot. "I got it this afternoon when I was leaving work. The police called, like . . . a couple hours later? I didn't pick up. I was too scared. But I knew. Dylan killed Trevor."

"Is that a voicemail?" Spike said.

"It's an audio text message," Elspeth said. "He's been sending them since he supposedly went missing. Telling me to do things."

"What kind of things?" I asked.

Elspeth took another swallow of wine and went back to her phone. "I'll find you the first one," she said as she scrolled. "Okay, here it is." She tapped the screen.

*Els. It's Dylan. I need you to go to my apartment. Take the gun that's under the bed in a box. Put it in your car. Drive to 67 North Washington and park it there. Doors unlocked. Then walk or take the T to work.*

"I texted back that I didn't want to do that, and then he sent me this." Elspeth tapped her screen again, and again we heard Dylan Welch. *You're in a good place now, Els. You're solidly on the ground floor of an up-and-coming company and the elevator is right there, babe. You're in line for a promotion. Marketing job with your name on it, plus shares in the biz. Don't fuck it up and ruin your rep. I can make it so you never work again.*

"What did you say then?"

"I told him no again. Then he sends this." She played the next audio message. We listened. It was still Dylan's voice, but deeper, more menacing. As though someone had swiped from him even the pretense of compassion. *Okay, bitch, you wanna play like this, fine. Here's what's REALLY happening: I'm watching you. My friends are, too. You know what we love to do? You'll never guess, so I'll tell you. No, no. I won't tell you. I'll just let you find out.*

She slid her phone to me. Attached to the audio message was a video—a sniper's-eye view of Elspeth taken through her apartment window. She was in her bathroom wearing a towel, blow-drying her hair. Completely oblivious. "I said yes after that," she said.

"Understandable," I said. I slid the phone back to her.

I looked at Spike. He was gaping at Elspeth. "What a shit holiday season you've been having," he said.

She actually laughed at that. "Right?" she said. "Merry Christmas to me." Then she started to tear up again.

"Hey," Spike said. "Hey, kid." He poured her more wine.

I thought back to my visit to Gonzo—how stressed Elspeth had seemed when I'd introduced myself. The twitching eyelid. The bizarre response (*Find who?*) when I'd told her I'd do my best to find Dylan. I'd assumed Rhonda Lewis's latest visit had freaked her out. But apparently she'd been hiding something far freakier, for weeks.

"What else has Dylan Welch asked you to do?" I said.

"He gave me a list of files on his work computer and told me to go into his office after-hours and permanently delete them," she said.

I thought of the scant number of documents I'd seen on his computer, how I'd attributed it to laziness. "Do you know what the files were?"

"I didn't open them," she said. "They had numbers in their titles. I didn't care. I just wanted to get out of there before I got caught."

I nodded.

"Now I think they must have been something really bad, right? And maybe Trevor found out about them. And

Dylan . . . or . . . or one of his friends . . . They wanted to shut Trevor up."

I nodded again. What could I possibly say to that? It made sense.

"Was Trevor acting different before he died?"

"Kind of."

"How?" Spike asked.

"He used to really love going to work," she said. "But over the past few days before the factory went on break it was like . . . he couldn't get out of there soon enough. It seemed like he hated his job. Hated the lab. He talked about burning it all down and then going to med school."

I looked at her. "He used that phrase? 'Burning it all down'?"

"Yeah."

"That seems a little dramatic if you're talking about quitting a job. Did Trevor often say things like that?"

"No," she said quietly. "No . . . he didn't. He wasn't dramatic at all." She poured herself more wine and drank it. Spike and I drank our wine. Outside the apartment, someone rode by on a motorcycle, the roar of it echoing down my street.

"Maybe it's my fault Trevor died," Elspeth said.

"Stop," Spike said.

"I got him his gun," she said. "I enabled him."

"Don't think that way," I said.

Elspeth drained the rest of her glass. Rosie chewed on her bone. For several moments, that was the only sound in the room.

Finally, I spoke. "Is there anything else that Dylan asked you to do?" I said. "I mean . . . besides erasing those files?"

"He left a burner phone in my car and gave me a number to call," Elspeth said. "When the person answered, I had to tell them 'Dylan Welch is dead' and hang up."

"And you did that?" I asked.

"Yes," she said. A tear slipped down her cheek. Then another. "He . . . He made me text him after each date I had with Trevor. Tell him everything we talked about. It was just boring stuff. But it made me feel sick. Like . . . Like I started making excuses not to see Trevor. Just so I wouldn't . . . I wouldn't have to . . . I didn't want to do any of those things, but I felt like I didn't have a choice."

Spike handed her a Kleenex.

"Of course that's the way you felt," I said.

"He has eyes on me," she said as she wiped her face. "He told me he has eyes on me. He called me. He left me those audio messages. Every single day he would remind me that I was being watched. The only reason why I felt safe coming here is because the cops are after him, and I figured maybe he's laying low."

Elspeth started to cry more. I put my hand on her shoulder. "You can stay here if you want," I said. "Call in sick tomorrow."

"I can't," she said. "I mean . . . thank you. But I have to act, like . . . normal. He's watching. He's got . . . friends." Her speech was starting to slur. She put her head down on the table. Rested it on her folded arms like a kid at naptime.

"If this makes you feel any better," I said, "Dylan definitely has more enemies than friends."

Elspeth said nothing. Her eyes were closed. I started to repeat myself, but Spike shook his head. "She's toast," he said.

Elspeth was snoring softly. She sounded like Rosie.

"Looks like she is staying here," Spike said. "Whether she wants to or not."

I nodded. "I'm going to turn down the bed in the guest room."

"Make sure there's a trash can next to it," Spike said.

"I will." I stood up. I was a little unsteady on my feet, but otherwise I felt okay. I poured three glasses of tap water—one for me, one for Spike, and one for next to Elspeth's bed, along with a bottle of Advil, should she need it.

Returning to the table, I found myself detouring to the living room window, pushing aside the draperies, and searching the streets for Dylan or his "friends." Anyone connected with him who might have noticed a young woman dressed completely in white and silver, talking on the phone in front of my apartment, seemingly on the verge of a panic attack. I didn't see anyone. The hairs on the back of my neck said otherwise.

"Hey, Sunny?" Spike said.

"Yeah?"

"You want me to stay, too? I can take the couch."

"Would you mind?"

"Of course not."

I smiled. There was no one in this world who understood me as well as Spike did.

# TWENTY-TWO

When I woke up at seven-thirty, Spike was still asleep on the couch. Elspeth was in the kitchen, wearing the yoga pants and T-shirt I'd lent her to sleep in during her tiny window of being awake. They were maybe a size or two too big, but she looked cute and comfortable in them—and shockingly fresh-faced for someone who'd polished off an entire bottle of wine before bedtime. That was twenty-two, I supposed.

The T-shirt was from Richie's old saloon. I hadn't really looked at the shirt when I'd given it to Elspeth, and now it felt like the universe was snapping its fingers in front of my face, telling me to pay attention. Richie's saloon was no more. He'd sold it to a big corporation, which had turned it into one of those soulless birthday-party places for kids, with overpriced food, rooms full of video games, and carefully measured drinks for the parents. Richie was in Jersey, waiting for me to decide if

I wanted to change my entire life, too. He wouldn't wait forever. Time was marching on. And as much as I wanted to step on the hem of its cloak and trip it, I was powerless.

Elspeth had already made a pot of coffee and she was drinking a cup. "I hope you don't mind that I helped myself," she said. Her eyes were wide and apologetic and slightly confused. I must have been looking at her funny.

"Of course not," I said. "Sorry. I'm just a little . . . um . . . distracted."

"I get it," she said. "Listen, thanks for letting me stay here last night. I'll be out of your hair soon."

"You can stay as long as you like."

"I have to get home to change for work."

"You can borrow some of my clothes."

She looked at me. "Do you have anything in white wool? I have to match the color scheme and they keep it so cold in there, even in the winter."

"I think I do," I said.

I went back into my bedroom and looked through my closet. I pulled out a white Armani suit I'd bought on a whim while visiting L.A. with Jesse Stone. It had been a business trip—we were both investigating the same case—but we'd managed to squeeze in quite a bit of pleasure. Coincidentally, we'd hooked up in a boutique dressing room at one point—something I'd never even considered doing before that trip (or, come to think of it, after). But that hadn't been when I'd bought the Armani. I shut my eyes and pushed the memories out of my mind. Jesse and I were no more—and we'd been no more for quite a while.

It was just like my brain to ambush me like this, broadcasting the most inappropriate images at the most inappropriate times.

I focused on the suit. It looked like it might fit Elspeth, if she buttoned the jacket and maybe wore a belt. I brought it out to her, along with a white satin Dolce & Gabbana blouse I'd purchased right here in Boston, no memories attached. I walked into the kitchen and held them up.

Her eyes lit up. "Are you sure I can wear these?"

"You bet."

She put her cup of coffee down. I handed her the clothes. "I'll get these back to you right away," she said. "I'll get them dry-cleaned."

"You don't have to do that."

"No, no. You're a life saver, actually. I just remembered it's my office Christmas party this morning."

"This morning?"

"Well, late morning. It's like a brunch thing. At the Loews."

"Fancy."

"Right? So now I'll feel like . . . appropriately dressed."

"Glad to be of help."

Spike walked into the kitchen, yawning and stretching. I'd seen him wake up many times over the course of our friendship. He'd always reminded me of a bear coming out of hibernation, and this morning was no different.

"Morning, Spike," Elspeth said.

"Morning, kid." Spike held up Elspeth's phone. "You left this in the kitchen last night, so I charged it for you."

Elspeth stared at it, the smile slipping from her face, the

previous night creeping up on her, overtaking her. "Did . . . Did you check the texts?" she asked.

Spike shook his head. "I didn't want to invade your privacy," he said. "But I heard it ding a couple times."

Elspeth took it from him with shaking hands. She tapped the screen and looked at it. Then she dropped it on the table.

I looked at her. "Are you okay?"

She shook her head.

I pointed to the phone. "You mind?"

She shook her head again. Spike moved closer to me. I picked up the phone. A series of texts striped the screen, all from that same number.

*BE SMART. PLAY DUMB.*

*IF U TALK, U R DEAD*

*Wanna join Trevor????*

*Bitch.*

*I'm always awake. I'm always watching.*

"Jesus," Spike whispered.

The last text contained an image of the front of my building at night, my face in the living room window, my hand holding back the curtain. The shot had been taken after Elspeth had fallen asleep, when I'd peered up and down the street and seen no one.

The hairs on the back of my neck had been right.

I looked at Elspeth. She'd put down my clothes and she was trembling, her arms pressed against her stomach, as though she was literally trying to hold herself together.

"I can't talk to the police," Elspeth whispered. "He'll know. He's watching."

My gaze returned to the screen, a thought sneaking up on me. "We can draw him out," I said. "I know something about him that he may not even know himself."

"What do you mean?" Elspeth asked.

"You mind if I text him?"

"What are you going to say?"

I took the phone from her and typed in a text: *Heads up: Moon Monaghan's guys are after u. They say u owe them a shit-ton of money and if you don't pay up, U R gonna be dead for real.*

It wasn't up to my usual standards eloquence-wise, but I figured I'd put it into language that a wannabe gangster like Dylan could understand and respect. I showed the text to Elspeth. "It's the truth," I said. "Before I got home last night, I got chased by this Mafia asshole because I had Dylan's phone and they were tracking it. He nearly got us into a car accident." I looked at Spike. "Shit, that reminds me. I still have his gun in my purse."

"Jeez, you're so absent-minded lately," Spike said. "Call Desmond. Do I have to write it on your hand?"

"No, you don't," I said. "I just happen to have a lot on my mind."

"Obviously."

Elspeth's gaze darted from me to Spike and back again, as though she was watching a tennis match. "You guys lost me," she said.

I put my back to Spike and spoke directly to her. "Okay, so as I was saying, Dylan really does owe money to Moon, and this text could scare him into doing something."

"Like what?" Elspeth said.

"Like . . . paying up. Maybe moving around some funds to do it. We could keep our eyes on his accounts. And I can keep my eye on Moon."

"How?"

"His boss is my ex-father-in-law."

Her eyes widened. "Wow. Small world."

"Small town," I said.

"Seriously."

"At the very least," I said, "this should give Dylan something else to focus on besides, well . . . you."

Elspeth nodded. "Send the text," she said.

I did. We watched the screen. We saw bubbles. Then stillness. Then bubbles again. We kept watching. We waited. But the reply never came.

"Looks like somebody's a little spooked," Spike said.

Elspeth smiled. She picked up the clothes I lent her. "I fucking hope so," she said.

# TWENTY-THREE

Rosie woke up. I fed her. Then Spike, Elspeth, and I all had breakfast at the kitchen table—coffee, orange juice, a fruit salad I'd thrown together quickly, and these really good bagels I'd picked up at Mamaleh's a week ago and frozen. Spike wolfed down two bagels in quick succession. Elspeth picked at some of the fruit, explaining she wanted to save room for her office holiday brunch. We talked about the weather, the holidays, our families, sports, politics even—anything and everything but Elspeth's murderous, missing boss. The whole time, though, we all kept stealing looks at her phone, which sat next to the plate of bagels like a bomb about to detonate.

Toward the end of breakfast, it dinged once.

"Can you look at it?" Elspeth said to me.

I read the text and exhaled, realizing only then that I'd been holding my breath. "It's from your mom," I said. "She's reminding you to wish your aunt Debbie a happy birthday."

Elspeth smiled. "Still nothing from Dylan."

"Nope."

We all went to various rooms to get ready for work. I kept a few of Spike's shirts and jeans in my guest room closet especially for his occasional overnight stays, and he availed himself of those and showered and changed in the guest bathroom.

It took me a little while to decide what to wear, since my no-doubt busy workday also included a luncheon with the Welches. Ultimately, I settled on a Burberry wool dress in a deep red plaid, paired with a black Tom Ford jacket and low-heeled, black Bottega Veneta boots—hopefully covering all bases in terms of comfort and understated chic.

Elspeth looked spectacular in my white Armani suit—like a young power broker. Spike said he'd drive her to work and make sure she got to the office safely. "Let me know when you're leaving," he added. "I'll escort you home, too."

"You don't have to do that," she said.

"I know," Spike said. "But if I don't, I'll worry."

She smiled. "Thanks."

As she was grabbing her coat, Elspeth's phone dinged again. We all looked at it. It was from Dylan this time. *How do u know about Moon?*

I took the phone and replied. *His guy came by the office.*

Bubbles again. A solid thirty seconds of them, at least. And then, finally, the reply arrived.

*Thx*

"Thanks? That's all?" Elspeth said.

"Apparently," I said.

"What does it mean?"

Spike took his coat from the couch and put it on. "I think it means you've got some time to yourself," he said. "But I wouldn't count on it being for too long."

He and Elspeth and I said goodbye. I closed the door. Two seconds later, there was a knock. I opened it. "Call Desmond," Spike said.

"Okay, okay."

I watched the two of them walk to the elevator and closed and locked my door. Then I called Desmond. It was still before nine, but knowing my former father-in-law, he'd already been up for at least three or four hours.

Sure enough, he answered quickly. "Sunny?" he said. "Again?"

"Hi, Desmond."

"Did my son—"

"No," I said. "No, he did not. I'm actually calling about a gun."

"What?"

I opened my purse, pulled out the thug's gun, and looked at it. I found it clumsier than my .38, but that could have just been a familiarity thing. "It's a Ruger MAX-9," I said. "I took it from that idiot I was telling you about. Moon's guy. Baseball cap. I told him I would give it to you and he could ask you for it."

"Let me clarify this," he said. "Moon Monaghan truly is having you followed?"

"Was," I said.

"Why?"

"Well, it's not me he's after. It's Dylan Welch, whose phone I had. Ever hear of him? He owes Moon money. Moon's people have been tracking him through his phone, but he's gone missing. I've been hired to find him, which is why I had the phone he left behind—the same one they were tracking. Make sense?"

There was a long pause on the other end of the line. "Yes. I've heard of Dylan Welch," Desmond said finally. His voice was as dry and heavy as dirt on a grave.

"So . . ." I cleared my throat. "How can I get this gun to you?"

"I don't give a fuck."

"Pardon?"

Desmond didn't say anything for a long while. I could sense his anger, but I wasn't sure about its source. It made me feel as though I had to forcibly drag it out of him—which made *me* angry, too. At times like this, he reminded me of his son, and not in a good way. *May as well accomplish something while I'm waiting for him to talk.* I put Desmond on speaker, unloaded the gun, and placed the ammo beside it on the kitchen table. The whole time, he remained quiet. Once I was certain the gun was safe, I took Desmond off speaker and picked up the phone. "Okay, I give up," I said. "What's wrong?"

"Dylan Welch is a prick," he said.

"No argument there," I said.

"He's owed us before. We've had him followed before. He's a waste of our time, money, and manpower. I've informed everyone within my organization not to work with him again."

I took a breath. "Oh," I said.

"Moon didn't listen to me."

"To be fair," I said, "Moon is a bigger prick than Dylan. And unlike Dylan, he's old enough to know better."

"Moon always listened to me in the past," Desmond said. "He always did as I asked."

"He probably forgot about Welch," I said. "Moon is an idiot."

"It isn't that," he said quietly. "He thinks I'm . . . slowing down."

I knew what he meant. My dad had said similar. You get older, people don't take you as seriously. *They know you're going to leave the party soon, so they stop bothering to serve you drinks,* Phil Randall would say. And while it did upset me when he made depressing observations like that, I could see it sometimes in the way strangers treated him—waiters or sales clerks looking to me for verification, as though what he'd just requested didn't matter. As though this decorated and revered police chief had somehow regressed back to toddlerhood, simply by virtue of his cane. "It isn't you," I told Desmond. Same as I would have told my dad. "It's him."

Desmond cleared his throat. "I'll send one of the boys to your office to pick up the gun," he said. "When is a good time for you?"

"Between ten and eleven works, or late afternoon," I said. "I have a luncheon at noon on Beacon Hill."

"You do, eh? That sounds lovely." This made me smile. It always did, hearing this hardened criminal describe something as "lovely." Yet it was a word he said often. It brought out his Irish lilt.

"I don't know how lovely it will be," I said. "The luncheon is with Dylan's parents."

"Well, then. You'll have some news for them, won't you?"

And for the first time, I thought about what that luncheon was going to be like. The good news/bad news speech I'd soon be forced to deliver about Bill and Lydia Welch's only son. *The good news is, he's alive . . .* I cringed. "You and Phil have it pretty lucky, you know that?" I said. "I mean, as far as your offspring goes, you've pretty much hit the jackpot."

It was a bit of an exaggeration. Richie and I had messed up plenty of times in our lives, and my sister, Elizabeth, was no walk in the park. But compared to Dylan Welch . . .

"Don't I know it," Desmond said.

I smiled. "And don't worry about Moon, okay? He's a waste of space. A moron. I meant it when I said that's no reflection on you."

He let out a long, mirthless chuckle. "He made a big mistake," he said. "But it doesn't matter. Life's too short. I'm already over it."

I didn't say anything, but I knew he wasn't.

# TWENTY-FOUR

When I showed up at the office, Blake was involved in an animated discussion with an enormous bald guy. I'd seen the bald guy before—with Desmond, in fact—but even if I hadn't, I'd have clocked him as Burke muscle. When it came to henchmen, Desmond had a type: enormous, scary-looking, silent, and very often hairless. (I'd always imagined that last requirement had to do with not leaving any DNA.)

This dude ticked off all the boxes—save for the silent part. "Three hundred," he was saying now. "I used to bench-press three-fifty, but then my shoulder started bugging me."

"Respect, man," Blake said. "My limit is two twenty-five."

"Ever do chin-ups?" the bald man said.

"Noooo. What a great idea, bro. So old school. You put in a bar?"

The bald guy launched into a lengthy response about chin-up bar installation. They were both drinking cans of Gonzo. Neither one of them seemed to notice I was in the room. I took off my coat. I hung it on the hook by the door and cleared my throat loudly, interrupting Blake's enthusiastic and detailed question about leg lifts.

"Oh, hi, Sunny," Blake said. "I didn't see you come in. Where's Rosie?"

"Sorry, I had to leave her home again," I said. "She had a late night, and she was sleepy."

"We should get a dog bed for the office. I could keep it right out here with me."

"Not a bad idea. I'll think about it." I looked at the visitor. "Who is this?"

Blake finished the rest of his can and stood up. "This is Charlie. He's an associate of Mr. Burke's."

"Yes, I was expecting you," I said.

Charlie rose to his feet, all business now. "Mr. Burke says you got something for me." He gulped from his Gonzo can and belched softly.

I'd wrapped Moon's thug's Ruger in a scarf I no longer wore and put the ammo in an empty box I'd found at home. I removed both from my purse and handed them to him. It felt good to get rid of the gun—like I'd accomplished something.

"Thank you," Charlie said.

"Great meeting you, man," Blake said.

Charlie put the gun and the ammo into a gym bag that I hadn't noticed he'd brought with him until now. He took another swallow of Gonzo. Then he looked at Blake. "Same, bro, same," he said. "And try the chin-ups. You won't be sorry."

"I will for sure."

He set his can down on Blake's desk. "You guys recycle?"

"Just leave it," Blake said. "I'll take care of it."

"I didn't finish the whole thing."

"No worries. I'll spill it out."

After Charlie left, Blake sat back down. "Awesome human being," he said.

"He seemed fine," I said.

Blake brought Charlie's Gonzo can to his lips and drained the rest of it.

I stared at him.

"What?"

"Well, first, there are a lot of winter bugs going around, so it's probably not a great idea to polish off cans left by strangers."

Blake's cheeks flushed. He let out a nervous laugh. "I thought that was mine," he said. "Guess I wasn't thinking."

"Second, how many of those have you had?"

"Just two. Maybe two and a half."

"It's ten in the morning," I said. "Not trying to act like your mom, but I'd suggest you at least move on to coffee."

Blake sighed. "You're right," he said. "I'm just going to throw these into recycling."

I followed him into our breakroom, which was really just a converted closet. Blake had been the one to suggest we create one, and I'd accommodated him by installing overhead lights, a sink, a small refrigerator, and cupboards. Then I'd thrown in a couple folding chairs and the coffee maker and called it a day. There could have been more forethought put into the design. The walls were plain white, the floors white linoleum, and, of course, considering the room's previous life as a walk-in closet, there were no windows. I couldn't imagine anyone taking an actual break in here, but functionally speaking, it worked. Blake could make coffee for clients, and he could also offer them juice, bottled water, even snacks. Plus, the fridge enabled us to bring lunch to work if we wanted to, decreasing our need for expensive takeout. It had been a good idea, and it had been Blake's idea. And it made me think about how important it was to take young people like him seriously. Which, of course, brought my thoughts back to Elspeth—the calls, texts, and audio messages she'd been forced to contend with. The guy she'd just started to like, shot dead. Her every waking moment filled with anxiety, terror. It was no way to live for anyone—but Elspeth was barely out of her teens. That was the problem with people like Dylan. They never picked on anyone their own size.

Blake threw the Gonzo cans into the recycling bin. I glanced inside. There were five other empty cans in there. "Yeah, you really might want to try and ease up on this stuff."

"It's got vitamins, though. Niacin. $B_{12}$."

I gave him a look.

"Yeah, well, anyways, what's going on with Dylan? Do they really think he killed that drug dealer?"

"He wasn't a drug dealer." I walked over to the coffee maker and poured myself a cup. "He was a Gonzo employee. A chemist."

Blake's eyes widened. "So, like . . . he helped put together this formula?"

"Yeah, I assume so."

"Interesting." He moved to the refrigerator and started to take out one of the four remaining cans of Gonzo, but stopped when he caught me staring. "I mean, he kind of *was* a drug dealer, in a way. I can't get enough of this stuff."

"Yeah, but I suspect that's mostly marketing, endorsements. You saw that skater drinking it, you bought in. I'm sure a lot of people felt the same way when they saw you drinking it on Instagram—and you hated it back then."

"I'm telling you. It tastes different now."

"Okay, I believe you."

"I'm just saying . . . Maybe the guy got killed because of that formula. You know? I mean, like . . . maybe he was trying to sell it to some other company and Dylan found out and got pissed."

I took a swallow of my coffee and thought about it. "That idea would make a lot of sense," I said, "if Dylan Welch wasn't who he is."

"Meaning . . ."

"Meaning, according to his mom, he's got no interest in the business. He just thought up the name, went to a few meetings, and checked out, and now he's only in it for the parties and the influencers. He spends most of his time out of the office and leaves all the real work to his employees."

Blake shrugged. He poured himself a cup of coffee and gave me a look. "His mom said that."

"Yes. So?"

"I mean . . . how well does your mom know you?"

I drank my coffee. He drank his. "That's a really good point," I said.

"I know," Blake said.

"I think maybe those vitamins make you smart," I said.

"Nah," he said. "I've always been like this."

I took one of the chairs. He took the other. And there we were, Blake and me, actually using the breakroom.

# TWENTY-FIVE

In addition to their many other properties on the East Coast and around the world, Bill and Lydia Welch owned a renovated brownstone on Beacon Hill that dated back to the Colonial era. This was where they typically spent November and December. It was where they held the annual holiday party that had always made the society pages, back when there were society pages. And it was where our luncheon was to be held.

Lucky for me, the Welch brownstone had been photographed for *Architectural Digest* a little over a year ago, so I had been able to look it up online and gawk at the pictures before I was scheduled to arrive. As a result, when I did show up, I was suitably blasé about my surroundings. (Or, at the very least, I wasn't tempted to beg for a tour.) Their home was truly beautiful—a marvel of polished mahogany, creamy crown moldings, and immaculate, multi-paned windows of antique leaded glass that made the snow-dusted street below look like a Victorian Christmas card. The thing that impressed me most, though, was how much care and effort had gone into restoring the space to its original beauty. It was as though before embarking on the renovation, Bill and Lydia had looked at their failure of a son and decided that this time, they were going to get things right.

A tuxedoed butler greeted me at the door and took my coat. His close-cropped silver hair shimmered in the soft lighting. "You must be Ms. Randall," the butler said to me. He spoke in a refined British accent, and he carried a silver tray with a single tall glass of iced tea placed atop it. It was all so what-you-would-expect-from-old-Boston-money, it almost felt like cosplay. The butler introduced himself as Balthazar and handed me the iced tea. He was wearing white gloves. "Jasmine and mint," he said.

"That sounds delicious," I said. I took a sip. It was.

"May I take your phone?" he said.

"Pardon?"

"The Welches have a strict no-phone policy during their luncheons," he said. He slipped two iPhones out of his jacket pocket. "As you can see, I have theirs as well."

I thought it was an annoyingly presumptuous request—as though no one could be trusted to stay off their phone for an hour, and so they had to be treated like junior high school kids. But it wasn't a hill I was willing to die on. I removed my phone from my purse and handed it to him.

I followed Balthazar through the large foyer, past an enormous Christmas tree, and up to a grand mahogany staircase, which we climbed together. Perhaps it was because of all the wine I'd consumed the night before or simply the lack of a chance to get to a gym the past several mornings, but I found myself taking the stairs a little slower than usual. At one point, I stopped and sipped some iced tea to fortify myself and almost ran into a man in a suit who was hurrying down the stairs, his head lowered. All business. He looked familiar to me, and so I turned and watched him leave before I realized the butler was waiting. "I'm sorry," I said.

"No apologies are necessary," Balthazar said. "This staircase is awfully steep, isn't it?"

"It is," I said.

As we started moving, I realized where I'd seen the hurrying man before. He was part of the tweed brigade I'd seen the previous day in Sky's office.

*Yesterday. I just took this case yesterday.*

Once we finally reached the top of the stars, Balthazar led me down a hallway festooned with pine garlands and wreathes and bunches of holly and into the type of space they used to call a solarium—pale green furniture, potted orchids and hibiscus, the entire far wall and ceiling comprising large, courtyard-facing windows.

Directly beneath the windows was an elegantly set table, with one Welch at either end. Lydia wore a burgundy suit in a subtle pattern that I immediately recognized as Hermès. Bill wore a forest-green cashmere sweater over a white polo shirt,

tailored wool slacks, and a Bulgari watch—the epitome of multimillionaire casual. When I walked in, the two of them were
silently sipping their glasses of iced tea with sour expressions
on their faces—as if they were auditioning for a remake of
*Citizen Kane*. If Mr. Tweed had come to deliver news to the
Welches, it looked as though that news hadn't been great. And
here I was, about to crush them even more.

"Ms. Randall has arrived," Balthazar said.

They both looked up at me with tired eyes.

It occurred to me how much of a butler's job involved stat-
ing the obvious.

# TWENTY-SIX

S unny. You're right on time!" Lydia said. Bill just sat there scowling at me. I greeted both of them with a smile. Lydia directed me to the place setting facing the window, and I sat down. We all drank our iced tea.

"Sky said she'd be a bit late," Lydia said. "Something at work that she had to take care of. She said to go ahead and start without her."

"You know, I'm happy about that," I said, "because there's something I wanted to discuss with the two of you, alone."

"Sky can hear anything you have to tell us," Lydia said. "She's like a second child to us."

"All the same," I said.

"A second child who isn't ruining our lives like the first child does continuously," Bill said.

"Bill," Lydia said.

I drank my iced tea. Balthazar pushed a cart into the room. He placed bowls of consommé in front of us and set a basket of bread on the table. We all picked up our spoons. I took a sip of my consommé and waited for the butler to leave. Once he did, I launched into the speech I'd been dreading. "Okay, so . . . the good news is, your son is definitely alive."

"That's splendid. Splendid," Lydia said.

"Where the hell is he, and why is he hiding?" Bill asked.

"I'm not sure where he is. But he's got a lot of reasons to be hiding."

"You can say that again," Bill said. "I already know of one."

"Bill," Lydia said. "Let Sunny speak."

I then launched into the bad news, which started with the fact that Dylan had basically admitted to killing Trevor Weiss in an audio message to Elspeth.

"Good God, why?" Lydia said.

I then moved on, flashback-style, to the first time he contacted Elspeth after his disappearance, how he'd threatened to ruin and/or end her life if she didn't fetch him his gun. I told them about the stalking, the photo taken through Elspeth's bathroom window, the many times he'd called and texted her—right up through last night.

As I spoke, Bill's face got redder and redder, while the color drained from Lydia's, her cheeks sinking in, as if she were slowly deflating. I felt awful for her. I really did. As a woman, I couldn't imagine what it would be like to have a son like that. "It's not your fault," I told her.

Bill spoke through his teeth. "What exactly were the files he asked the receptionist to delete?" he said.

"Elspeth didn't know," I said. "She was frightened. She said she just wanted to get out of there as soon as possible and so she deleted them without opening them."

"I know what files they were," Bill said.

Lydia gave him a withering look, then turned to me. "Any other news about Dylan, Sunny?" she said. "Or is that all?"

"Is that all?" Bill said. "Did you honestly just ask that when this woman has just told us that our son is both a psychopath and a murderer?"

"He is alive," I said. "So . . . there's also that."

"Oh, yes, we're well aware of *that*," Bill said.

I cleared my throat. "To answer your question," I said to Lydia. "There's only one more thing."

"Yes?"

"Well . . . He apparently owes a good deal of money."

"To whom?" Lydia said.

"A man by the name of Moon Monaghan," I said. "He's thought to be within the Burke crime syndicate."

Bill was close to purple now. "What does he owe the money for?"

I stared down at my consommé. Balthazar returned with his cart. I was grateful for the interruption, as it was an excuse to stay silent, even for a few minutes. Balthazar removed our bowls and placed dishes in front of us. Salad Nicoise with seared rare tuna and the welcome addition of fresh crab. The hard-boiled eggs were perfectly done. It all looked incredible. But sadly, at this point, I'd completely lost my appetite.

Once Balthazar left, I turned to Bill. "As I understand," I said quietly, "it's for some designer drugs that he purchased."

Bill slammed his hand on the table. His salad shivered from the impact. "I told you, Lydia," he said. "I told you."

"You do not know it was him," Lydia said.

"Of course it was him," Bill said. "Who else could it possibly be?"

"Mistake," Lydia said. "Clerical error. Why must you always assume the worst of Dylan?"

"Excuse me?" he said. "Did you happen to hear what this woman has just told us?"

It was the second time over the course of five minutes that he'd referred to me as "this woman," as though I was some stranger on an elevator. It annoyed me. But I wasn't about to say anything about it.

"I heard what she told us, Bill," Lydia said. "But have you not heard of the phrase *innocent until proven guilty*? What if Dylan has been kidnapped and he's being forced to make these audio recordings and send them to this young girl? What if it was one of his kidnappers who killed the chemist—perhaps just to make our son look bad? To prove correct all the awful things you've always believed about him?"

"You're delusional, Lydia," Bill said.

"I am not," Lydia said. "Sunny. Isn't what I said possible?"

"Yes," I said. "It's possible." I turned my attention to my salad.

I took a small forkful of the crab and put it in my mouth. I chewed and swallowed. It was heavenly. I topped it off with a swallow of iced tea. "Mr. Welch," I said. "You mentioned a reason you knew of, as to why Dylan might go into hiding."

"He doesn't know of anything," Lydia said.

I kept looking at Bill.

"I don't know if you passed him on your way in, but Gonzo's chief financial officer was just here," Bill said. "His name is Martin Jennings."

"Yes, I saw him."

"Martin is a good man, but he's been known to jump to conclusions," Lydia said.

"No, he hasn't been known to do anything of the sort," Bill said.

"Why did he come to your home?" I said.

"Apparently," Bill said, "someone has been siphoning money from the company's payroll fund for the past several weeks. Our son and Martin are the only ones able to access that money. At first, it was done in small increments and went unnoticed, but lately the sums removed have been much larger. And now that you tell us that Dylan is definitely alive and owes money—"

"He could have been pressured to do it," Lydia said. "I'm telling you, Bill. He could have been forced—"

"To steal money from his employees? To finance his drug habit? And . . . And pay off the Mafia?"

His face was changing color again.

"Look, Mr. and Mrs. Welch—"

"Lydia."

"Mr. Welch and Lydia," I said. "You guys hired me to find your son."

"*She* hired you," Bill said.

"I was hired to find your son. And that's what I'm going to try my best to do. When I bring him back, you'll have the answers to all your questions. But until then—and I'm saying this for your own good as well as mine—it's best not to speculate."

They both stared down at their plates. Lydia took a bite of her salad. Bill drank his iced tea. I ate some of the tuna. It was very good. I wished I was hungrier.

"A few times, at our house in Nantucket, I took Dylan and his cousins fishing," Bill said quietly.

"That was sweet of you, Bill," Lydia said. "I know Dylan so loved the attention."

"I enjoyed those times, too," Bill said. "Until I found out that Dylan was stealing his cousins' fish, claiming he was the one who had caught them."

Lydia pushed her food around on her plate, then set her fork down. She lifted her napkin and dabbed at her cheek so subtly, it took me a while to realize she was crying.

"He has always been an embarrassment," Bill said.

"Because you never approved of him," Lydia said.

"He never gave me any reason to approve of him."

"You're his *father*," Lydia said. "That should be a *good enough reason!*"

I cleared my throat loudly.

The two of them went silent, as though they just remembered I was still there.

"Maybe he was just trying to impress you, Mr. Welch," I said.

"Excuse me?"

"I was just thinking," I said. "Maybe Dylan knew that he wasn't a fisherman. But he also knew you liked fishing. And he wanted to make you think that he was good at something that you liked. He wanted that bad enough to . . . uh . . . steal his cousins' fish on a family vacation."

No one said anything for several seconds, my own words hanging in the air. Why had I just said all of that? Maybe I'd been in analysis for too long.

Bill turned to me, a pained look on his face, as though he'd just been punched in the stomach but was trying to be strong about it. "Who knows why Dylan does anything?" He said it very quietly.

"It was just a thought," I said. "And anyway, it's none of my business."

Lydia dabbed at her eyes and folded up her napkin. There were still mascara smears on her face, but she was no longer crying. And when she spoke, her tone was calm and measured. "The police haven't called us, you know," she told me. "You said they'd call and they haven't yet, and so I just assumed they'd found another suspect."

"I'm sorry," I said.

"Why?" she said. "It isn't your fault."

I heard hard-soled shoes clacking down the hallway. We all turned toward the sound.

"What now?" Bill said.

"I don't want to know," Lydia whispered.

Balthazar stood in the doorway. He was holding up a phone. "I hate to interrupt, but you have a call, Mrs. Welch. They said it was very important."

Lydia nodded. She took the phone and said "yes" several times. Then she ended the call and closed her eyes and brought her hands to her face. Her hands were trembling. Her body began to heave.

"What is it, Liddie?" Bill said quietly. He rose from his seat and went over to put his arms around his wife. He pulled Lydia to him. She leaned in to his shoulder. "What happened? It's okay. I'm here. You can tell me."

Lydia looked up at Bill, her eyes big and helpless, her face shining from fresh tears. "That was Maurice Dupree," she said. "Sky has been shot."

# TWENTY-SEVEN

Sky had been found on the floor of her office, unable to speak and bleeding profusely. And poor Elspeth had been the one to find her.

According to Maurice, who had been contacted by Elspeth after she called 911 and promptly began to hyperventilate, the entire corporate staff had been out of the office for the holiday brunch. The metal detector was unmanned, the key-code lock enabled on the front door to the offices. Elspeth had returned to fetch the Secret Santa present she'd accidentally left in her desk. She'd punched in the code. But instead of just taking the gift and leaving, she'd made the fateful choice of checking on the company's COO—who'd begged off the party because of Lydia and Bill's luncheon. And that's when she'd made her shocking discovery.

Elspeth, Maurice told us, had suffered a panic attack and was currently in the ER. "Her mom came to be with her," Maurice said. "She'll be fine."

Knowing everything Elspeth had been through over the past few weeks, I wasn't so sure.

"The sad part is, Sky was the one who came up with the brunch idea," Maurice said. "She thought it would be less time-consuming and more cost-effective than a nighttime holiday party with alcohol and plus-ones. Dylan hated everything about the idea, of course, but he wasn't around, so she went full speed ahead with it." He looked at Bill and Lydia and winced. "I, uh, didn't mean to cause offense."

"None taken," Bill said tightly. "We know that our son doesn't think much of cost-effective ideas."

"At any rate, the doctors are working on her."

"This is all our fault," Lydia said.

"What do you mean?" I said.

"If we hadn't invited her to the luncheon, Sky would have been at the Christmas party when that shooter broke in," she said. "She would be safe."

"Oh, for heaven's sake. Who gets shot in their own office at eleven a.m. on a workday?" Bill huffed.

"You're making this sound like this is Sky's fault," Lydia said.

"I'm doing nothing of the sort," Bill said.

"With all due respect," I said, "you sort of are."

We were standing in the waiting area at Mass General's

ICU. We'd just arrived. Maurice had waited long enough to tell us what happened in person, but I could tell he was eager to get back to the Winthrop Center. The Gonzo offices were besieged by police, who would no doubt want surveillance footage and any other assistance the head of security could provide.

He started to say goodbye when Lydia put a hand on his arm. "Is Sky going to be all right?"

"I think so." He said it like he meant it. "I haven't talked to the doctors or anything. But Sky Farley is tougher than she looks."

"That's true," Lydia said.

"Besides," Maurice continued, "there's a whole lot of people who'd be upset if she didn't get better quick. Dylan included, right?"

Lydia nodded emphatically. Bill just stood there.

"Well, if there's one thing I know about Sky," Maurice said, "it's that she doesn't like to disappoint anybody."

Maurice was carrying his coat. As he stretched to put it on, I saw a bulge in his shirt pocket—a hexagonal shape. He noticed me staring and slipped it out. Sky's compact. Her one family heirloom. "She dropped this—or maybe one of the EMTs did when they grabbed her purse," he said. "I found it on the floor. I'm keeping it for her."

"You're keeping it safe," Lydia said.

"Yes," Maurice said.

"That's . . . That's very kind of you." Lydia's mouth twitched into a smile. Most of her makeup had rubbed off, and it made her look younger. Less intimidating. Bill put his arm around her. Maurice looked a little embarrassed. He said goodbye and headed out.

"He's so caring for a security guard," Lydia said. "Or maybe it's just Sky. She seems to have that effect on people."

I waited till Maurice was gone to excuse myself, and told Bill and Lydia I was going to look for a bathroom, but I was really headed to the ICU. I didn't want to insult Maurice, but he himself had admitted that he hadn't spoken to the doctors working on Sky. And I was willing to bet that he hadn't spoken to the two uniformed police officers whom I'd noticed stationed just outside the ICU door.

When it came to Sky's prognosis—and who might have shot her—I felt like I needed a second opinion.

# TWENTY-EIGHT

It was sad, but at this point in my life, I knew better than to drop my dad's name on the two uniformed officers standing guard in front of the ICU. They were simply too young to have heard of him, their combined ages roughly adding up to the number of years it had been since Phil Randall made captain.

It was a better tack to bring them coffees from the little place I'd seen in the lobby, and so that was what I did. "Thought you guys might need these," I said. And I'd thought right. Up close, the two of them looked as though they were falling asleep on their feet. They took the coffees and thanked me, then dumped in the packets of cream and sugar I'd also generously provided. "You know, there's no such thing as free coffee from a PI, right?" I flashed my private investigator's license and gave them both a smile. The twelve-year-old on the left rolled his eyes. The one on the right sort of giggled and blushed. Maybe he thought I was a MILF? I had no idea. But at any rate, I decided to focus my attention on him.

"You have any idea how she's doing?"

"Were you hired to protect her?" the eye-roller asked.

"If I was, I wouldn't be very good at my job, would I?" I grinned.

Boy on the right giggled again.

"Actually, I've been hired to find her best friend," I said. "Do you guys know anything about how she's doing?"

"Pretty sure they've got her stabilized," Right Boy said. "There's a lot of them working on her now."

A few guys in scrubs hurried past us, pushing through the double doors. When they did, I caught a flash of the scene in intensive care. A curtained-off area, the men in scrubs barreling toward it. There were at least ten people in there, clustered around a patient—one of the few patients in the suite. From their urgency alone, I knew it was Sky.

One of the people working on her had said something. I couldn't make it out. But I thought I heard "blood loss." And also "transfusion."

"I mean, these types of situations are always touch-and-go," my friend on the right was saying. "But one of the docs said they're cautiously optimistic."

I wasn't listening anymore. Not really. Even now, long after the doors had swung shut, my head was still in the ICU suite.

*What would Dylan think if he knew about this? After all he's done and as awful as he is, would he come out of hiding to be by his best friend's side?*

"I hope she pulls through," I said.

The two of them said nothing.

"Have you guys heard anything about the shooter?"

"Just that he acted alone," said Right Boy.

"Are we sure it was a he?" I asked.

"When they brought her in, she was saying *he* and *him*. 'He shot me.' She was barely conscious, though."

"We don't know anything," Left Boy said.

"Where did the info about him acting alone come from?" I asked. "Were there any eyewitnesses?"

"I don't think so," said the boy on the right.

"We don't know anything," his eye-rolling partner said again.

"I wasn't talking to you," I said.

Right Boy started to speak, but the eye-roller gave him a nasty look. Then he turned to me, his face like granite. *"We don't know anything,"* he said.

*He's just saying what his higher-ups told him to say,* I thought. Still, he didn't have to be such a bitch about it.

I glared at him. "I'm friends with Lee Farrell, you know."

"Well, maybe ask him, then."

I was this close to taking his coffee back.

"Thanks for your help." I said it to Right Boy alone. "Have a nice day."

---

kept thinking about Sky as I walked back to the waiting room. Between Maurice's hopeful account and that chaotic scene in the ICU, I didn't know what to believe about her prognosis. At this point, I was leaning toward *not good*. It made me sad—especially for Lydia.

It also made me think about the shooter. *He shot me,* Sky had allegedly said in her delirium. So it was a man, who had gotten past lobby security and into Gonzo's locked-up offices with apparent ease. Could Dylan Welch have shot his best friend for knowing too much? Was he capable of something that craven?

When I returned to the waiting room, the Welches were still standing where I'd left them. "Long bathroom trip," Bill said curtly. Apparently, he'd missed me.

"Bill," Lydia said.

"Actually, I stopped by the ICU," I said. "I tried to get an update from the cops."

"And?" Lydia said.

I considered telling her what I'd seen, and what I'd been thinking. But not for long. "They know nothing," I said. "At least, that's what one of them told me."

I looked around the waiting room. There were three other visitors standing awkwardly in the corner: a woman and two men, all of them in their late twenties or early thirties, all fashionably but unimaginatively dressed, all gawking at us, as though we were the season finale of their favorite reality show. I wondered when they'd shown up, or if they'd been there the entire time and I just hadn't noticed them. When the trio saw me looking at them, they offered shy waves to Bill and Lydia.

Lydia waved back.

"Who are they?" I asked quietly.

"I have no idea," Bill said.

"That's Kaitlyn, Timothy, and Henry," Lydia whispered.

"Who?" Bill said.

Lydia let out an exasperated sigh. "Kaitlyn is head of Marketing. Timothy and Henry do focus groups and brainstorming and whatnot," she said.

The three of them walked up to us in a triangular formation, with Kaitlyn in front. She gave Lydia a quick, tight hug. "You remember Bill, of course," Lydia said.

"Of course," Kaitlyn said.

Bill nodded at the three of them.

Lydia introduced them to me. I shook their hands. "Sunny Randall is a private investigator," Lydia said. "I've hired her to find Dylan."

"He's missing?" Timothy asked. Lydia responded with a death glare. I could tell that he wished he could suck the words back into his mouth.

"Yes," Lydia said. "He is."

"I'm sorry," Timothy said. "I didn't mean any disrespect. I just . . . I assumed he was on vacation."

"Dylan goes on vacation a lot," Henry said helpfully.

"No offense taken," Bill said.

It was a lie. Plenty of offense had been taken, if only on Lydia's part.

Lydia put her back to the two young men and spoke directly to Kaitlyn. "Who on earth could have done something like this?" she asked. "A shooting in the Winthrop Center in broad daylight?"

"I know, Mrs. Welch. We were talking about it, and the only thing we can think is that maybe someone knew we'd all be gone and tried to rob the place?"

"Of what?" I said. "Office equipment?"

"Yes."

"Really?"

"Ours is top-of-the-line," Kaitlyn said. "But also Gonzo. Gonzo merch. You'd be amazed at how popular it is right now. It's got that early-Nike vibe."

That sounded like an exaggeration. But then I remembered Blake back at my office, guzzling the rest of that thug Charlie's can. "People do like the stuff," I said.

"And Sky tried to stop the robbers," Lydia said.

"Yes," Kaitlyn said. "That's what we were thinking."

"That sounds like her."

"First that lab tech and now Sky," Kaitlyn said. "You think maybe it's the same person?"

Lydia cringed. I knew what she was thinking because it was the same thing I'd been thinking "Not Sky," Lydia said. "He would never."

"Who would never?" Kaitlyn said.

Lydia's face flushed. "Nobody."

"I think the shock is getting to all of us," I said quickly. "You really think it was a failed robbery?"

Kaitlyn looked at me. "It makes the most sense."

As they spoke, a question popped into my mind. But I'd have to wait to ask it until the marketers were out of earshot.

"She was such a brave person," Kaitlyn said.

Lydia swayed on her feet. Bill caught her.

"Is," I said. "She's still in that ICU, fighting away." I put on a smile. It actually hurt.

"Of course," Kaitlyn said. "Is." She looked at Lydia and Bill. "You know, we wouldn't have half the success we've had without Sky . . . and, uh, Dylan, of course."

"Totally," Timothy said.

"Sales took a big hit in the first quarter after the whole thing with the girl," Henry said. "But Sky hopped in the driver's seat and brought us back on track." He coughed. "Dylan, too."

Bill rolled his eyes. "Typically," he said, "there is only one driver's seat."

I watched the three of them. Their eager, pained smiles. It took me several seconds to figure out that by "the whole thing with the girl," Henry was referring to the death of Rhonda Lewis's daughter, Daisy. For marketing people, these three weren't particularly good with words.

"Anyhoo," Henry said, "we should probably head out, right? We . . . um . . . don't want to take up space in the waiting room, and we should get back to the office. The police might have questions."

"Good thinking," Bill said.

"Thank you for being here," Lydia said.

"It's our pleasure," Timothy said.

"That's not what he means," Kaitlyn said. "He doesn't mean 'pleasure.'"

"Just a figure of speech," Henry said.

*Jesus.* I caught Bill rolling his eyes again. I couldn't say I blamed him.

"It was just terrific meeting you guys," I said and nodded.

It was the prompt they needed. That one last kick in the butt to send them out the door. They said their goodbyes and left.

*Finally.* I looked at Lydia. "Didn't you say that Sky was going to be late for lunch because there was something at work that she had to take care of?"

"Yes," Lydia said. "Yes, that's right. She called me after Bill and I seated ourselves. Balthazar had our phones, of course. So he spoke to her and relayed the message." She smiled a little. "Balthazar likes Sky very much."

"What's not to like?" I turned to Bill. "When Martin Jennings was at your house, did he mention telling anyone else about the missing payroll money?"

Bill said nothing. He stared at Lydia.

"Stop it," she said. "She's Dylan's best friend in the world. Stop it."

"Sky knew," Bill said.

"Stop it," said Lydia.

"She knew. Martin told us. He let her in on it first, but she didn't believe it. She said there had to be a mistake."

"Stop."

"He said she was very upset." Bill looked at me. "Martin told us that. And he said that Sky couldn't believe Dylan would betray his own employees. She was able to go into the system and change passwords, work with the coding. She cut off Dylan's access to the fund this morning. She did it to prove her point."

Lydia didn't say anything.

"Think about it," Bill said. "If our son contacted Sky, just like he contacted the receptionist . . . But nicer, Lydia. Because as you said, she's his best friend in the world. If Dylan told Sky he was alive and well and wanted to come by the office and discuss some things . . ."

He kept looking at her, as though he expected her to finish his sentence. But Lydia wouldn't move. She wouldn't speak.

"Mrs. Welch?" I said.

*"Lydia!"* she shrieked. *"My name is Lydia!"*

I stepped back. A group of nurses in the hallway stopped and stared at us through the open door. Bill asked his wife what had gotten into her. But I understood. We all knew that old adage, *When someone shows you who they are, believe them.* But that's easier said than done when it comes to one's child.

"I didn't mean to shout." Lydia's shoulders slumped, her arms crossed over her stomach, as though she'd just taken a blow.

"It's all right," I told her. "I get it." I looked at the nurses in the hallway. "Everything's fine!" I called out. They nodded.

Mumbled a few things I couldn't quite hear. I watched them walk away. "We both get it, don't we, Mr. Welch?"

He ignored me. "Liddie," he said. "It breaks my heart, too. But at some point, we're going to have to face reality."

Lydia stared straight ahead, her expression unchanging. Her face looked as though it was made out of stone. "I just want to focus on Sky's recovery right now," she said.

"That's right. One crisis at a time," I said. "Isn't that right, Mr. Welch?"

"Let's sit down." He said it to Lydia. "My legs are getting tired."

My phone vibrated. I pulled it out of my pocket and glanced at the screen—a text from an unfamiliar number. And when I read it, I knew I couldn't tell the Welches who it was from.

"I'm sorry, but I'm going to have to leave," I said. "Please let me know as soon as you hear anything about Sky."

"Of course," Lydia said. They moved toward the bank of chairs against the far wall, Bill holding Lydia's arm, helping her to get there.

I was out of the room before they sat down.

Once I was in the elevator, I looked at the text again, just to make sure I'd read it correctly.

*This is Rhonda Lewis*, it read. *I'd like to meet.*

I replied quickly: *Tell me where and when.*

# TWENTY-NINE

Rhonda Lewis said she wanted to meet at the South Street Diner—a place I'd been to many times, especially during my college years. It was fun and atmospheric and something of a landmark, having stood in the same spot since 1947— crowned by a big coffee cup–shaped neon sign that everybody loved to take pictures in front of. Plus, it served good comfort food at reasonable (for Boston) prices. And it was open twenty-four hours. It was no mystery why the South Street Diner was largely responsible for my freshman fifteen.

Even though it had been decades since I'd devoured a bacon cheeseburger and fries at the South Street Diner at four in the morning after a few too many turns at the beer bong, I couldn't stave off the sense memories as I walked through the door. It happened every time I came here. I guess you could say the place made me feel young again—though, in this case, "young" meant unsteady on my feet and desperate for carbs.

The diner was packed, as usual, with a distinctly midday crowd: families and groups of tourists, a few contractor types tossing back beers, their workday having ended at two p.m.

I scanned the room for Rhonda, though I barely knew what she looked like. All I had to go on was the blurry image from the security footage. I'd been meaning to see if she had a Facebook or Instagram account last night, but with the shooting in the factory, the car chase with Moon's henchman, and Elspeth's unexpected arrival at my apartment, it had somehow slipped my mind. Go figure.

Fortunately, I was able to recognize Steve, the medical receptionist from Optima Urgent Care. He was sitting at a booth by the window, and he was waving at me. It looked as though he was wearing his scrubs and, from where I was standing, I could see his TARDIS tattoo.

I was glad Steve was here. A meeting like this one tended to benefit from an introduction. I waved back and walked over to the booth.

Steve stood up as I got closer. "Sunny Randall, I'd like you to meet Rhonda Lewis," he said.

Rhonda was sitting across from him. She wore a pale blue fleece pullover. She didn't stand up, but she smiled at me, which was encouraging. Her eyes matched the pullover.

In person, Rhonda looked a lot smaller and saner than she had on the surveillance video, but still there was a sadness to her, a tiredness I would have noticed even if I didn't know about her background. As a cop, I'd been tasked with consoling family members of murder victims numerous times—an especially tough assignment that almost always went to woman officers. I'd noticed in so many of them this same hollowed-out look—as though an essential part of them had been ripped away.

"Thank you for getting in touch," I said to her.

"Thanks for coming," she said.

It was the first time I'd ever heard Rhonda Lewis's voice, and it wasn't what I'd expected. It was soft and measured—a nurse's voice. Steve stepped to the side and I slid into the booth across from Rhonda. I said hi to Steve and made room for him next to me, but he stayed where he was.

"I actually have to get out of here," Steve said as he pulled on his parka. "My shift starts soon."

I felt a little disappointed. "I'm really glad you were able to make this happen," I said.

"It was no big deal," he said. "All I did was give Rhonda your card."

"He also walked here with me," she said.

Steve shrugged. "Again, no big deal," he said. "I'll leave you guys to talk."

I cleared my throat. "You never fail to be kind," I said to him. It was a butchered version of a *Doctor Who* quote. Thankfully, Steve recognized it as such. His face broke into a smile. "Not bad for a New-vian."

"I told you I wasn't faking," I said.

"I'm impressed," he said.

"Allons-y," I said.

He laughed. "Okay, now you're just showing off."

Rhonda was looking at us with a mixture of confusion and mild annoyance, like we were a couple kids speaking pig latin. If I were her, my tolerance would have been running thin. I said goodbye to Steve.

"I hope you find this asshole, so you can move on to a more enjoyable assignment," he said.

"Thanks," I said. Though the thing was, I wasn't *not* enjoying myself. I did want to find that asshole—not so much for his own sake as for Lydia's. Whether or not he was guilty of the shootings, she wanted to be with her son again. For Bill's sake, too, even if he pretended not to care. And for Sky's. I wanted Sky Farley to have her best friend back. And if he'd betrayed and shot her, I wanted her to live to see him brought to justice. *She'll live. She has to.*

It surprised me how much I'd grown to care for these people in just twenty-four hours. And it was why I loved working cases like this one. The higher the stakes, the greater the reward—and more often than not, that reward was an emotional one. I wished I could explain this feeling to Richie . . . Steve was staring at me. Apparently, he'd said goodbye and I hadn't responded.

I forced a laugh. "Sorry," I said. "Just time-traveling."

After Steve left, a server came to take my order. I glanced at Rhonda. There was a cup of tea in front of her, along with two pieces of rye toast she'd yet to touch. I ordered coffee and a blueberry muffin.

When the server left, Rhonda opened her purse and took out her wallet. She removed a picture and slid it across the table to me. I looked at it. It was a class photo of a girl in a cheerleading outfit. She had wavy brown hair, rosy cheeks, a dimpled smile. Blue eyes identical to Rhonda's. "This is Daisy," she said.

"Beautiful girl."

"Does she look frail or unhealthy to you?"

I cleared my throat. "No," I said. "Not at all."

"She doesn't look that way to me, either," she said. "But that's how those lawyers talked about her. They made it seem like she was hooked up to an iron lung and I should have been watching her at all times. Not letting her see friends. They made it seem like it was my fault she died."

"That isn't fair," I said.

"Daisy wasn't aware of it, and neither was I," she said. "We had no idea she had a heart condition. How would we know to check for that? She was active in sports. She was a *kid*."

The waitress returned with my coffee and blueberry muffin. I wasn't hungry anymore. "I assumed you knew," I said.

She shook her head.

"Even if you did know about her condition, it wouldn't make any difference," I said. "No one should lose a child like that. I'm so sorry."

She cringed. "That's what they said. The lawyers. That little COO. 'We're so sorry for your loss, ma'am,' but they're not sorry. They're liars. I could burn their offices to the ground. They still wouldn't be sorry."

She said it all in that same measured tone, but there was a

different look in her eyes—a hardness when she'd said *that little COO.* It nearly made me ask Rhonda where she'd been today between eleven and noon, when Sky had been shot. But instead I sipped my coffee and bided my time. When all was said and done, Sky's shooting was police business. I was here to find out what Rhonda might know about what happened to Dylan Welch.

She carefully put the photo back in her wallet. Then she drank her tea, that hardness in her eyes slowly dissipating.

"So," I said, "what questions do you have for me?"

She placed her cup back on the saucer. "Okay, first of all," she said, "who hired you to find Dylan Welch? Was it anyone involved with Gonzo?"

"Sort of." I picked at my blueberry muffin.

"What do you mean?"

"It was his mother who hired me," I said. "She's a primary shareholder in the company and I believe she's chairman of the board of directors. But she didn't hire me in . . . um . . . that capacity."

"She wants her child back."

"Yes."

"I understand that feeling."

"I'm sure you do," I said. It was, after all, why I'd relayed that information about Lydia.

She sipped more tea. "Do you know where he is and if he is alive?"

"Those are the questions I wanted to ask you."

"So you don't know," she said.

"Not yet." I swallowed my coffee. I wasn't going to tell her about the audio messages and texts he'd sent Elspeth—though, thinking about them now, I felt a little sick. In a way, Dylan was like Gonzo—there were good people who loved him, but that still didn't mean he wasn't disgusting.

"I hope he's alive," Rhonda said.

I blinked at her. "What?"

"Dylan Welch," she said. "I hope he's alive and well."

"Why?" I asked. "I mean, I know you saved his life once. But I figured that was just like me looking for him."

"How so?"

"It's the job. It isn't you."

"Well, it *wasn't* me." Rhonda opened her purse again and removed a piece of paper—a printed-out email, dated three weeks ago, from Dylan Welch to her. The subject line read DAISY. "My feelings about him changed when I got this."

I read it.

*Dear Ms. Lewis,*

*I hope you don't mind, but I got your email address from a mutual friend. I know I shouldn't be writing you, and no one knows I am. (Please don't tell!) But I just want to say how deeply sorry I am about your daughter's death. To be honest, I've been spiraling ever since Daisy passed— drinking too much, using drugs. Hurting people. Over the summer, I even stalked an old girlfriend like a psychopath. I'm not looking for excuses. That was wrong. It was one of a metric ton of fucked-up things I've done in my life. But of*

*all of them, Daisy's death is the worst. Or it feels the worst*
*to me, at least. I wish I could make it up to you, but there's*
*no way to make up for a loss like that. I am hoping I might*
*be able to do something to make sure that it doesn't*
*happen again.*

*I'm so sorry.*

*Dylan*


"He's the only one to apologize," she said. "I don't mean that
'I'm sorry for your loss' bullshit. I mean an honest, sincere
apology. So many people involved in that fucking company,
and he was the only one."

I looked at her. "You got this email after you saved his life."

"Yes," Rhonda said.

"But he doesn't mention it," I said.

"Honestly," she said. "I don't think he recognized me that
night. He was a mess, and so was the girl who brought him in."

"So he didn't know you had helped him."

"Nope. There was no quid pro quo. He just felt bad," she
said. "He wanted to share that with me. And it's funny, because
of all the higher-ups at Gonzo, I probably blamed him least for
Daisy's death."

"But he's the CEO."

She shrugged. "In name only. He was never in court, sticking
up for their warning labels. And as far as I know, he didn't have
much to do with the branding of the drink or the formula or
anything like that."

"He's a figurehead."

"Exactly," she said. "And you know . . . when he was at Optima and we were reviving him, he seemed like kind of an idiot."

"He is."

"Yeah, well. Leave it to the idiot to be the only one with a conscience."

"Is it okay if I keep this printout?"

She nodded. "That's why I brought it."

"Because you wanted me to see . . . what?"

"That he's worth looking for."

I folded it up and put it in my purse. "Thank you," I said. "I needed that." I meant it sincerely.

She drank her tea. I drank my coffee. This conversation was going in a very different direction than I'd assumed it would go. "Who was the mutual friend?" I asked.

"The one who gave him my email address? I have no idea. Obviously, we travel in very different circles. I figure he just went through whatever channels he had to track me down."

I found myself thinking again about how complicated people were, how contradictory. Even the shallow ones. Even the ones I had long believed to be wholly disgusting.

"I really do hope he's all right," Rhonda said.

And for whatever reason, that made me remember Dylan's phone, what I'd seen on it. "Can I ask you one more thing?"

"Sure."

"If you don't blame Dylan for Daisy's death, and you never really did blame him," I said, "why did you call him a murderer?"

Rhonda looked at me as if I'd just sprouted horns. "I never called him that."

"I saw his phone," I said. "There were five or six texts from you, calling him a murderer. They were sent right before he went missing."

Her eyes grew even wider. "I've never texted him in my life," she said. "Why would I even have his personal phone number?"

I stared back at her. "You're right," I said.

I knew she was being truthful. This was a woman who had defaced property in front of security cameras. She'd yelled at Sky and pounded on the walls until she was forcibly removed from Gonzo's corporate offices. She clearly saw herself as someone with nothing to lose—and so she had no reason to lie about sending a few texts. Plus, her shock was the type that couldn't be faked. "These text messages you saw," she said. "They were from my phone number?"

"They were from an anonymous number," I said. "I was told they were probably from you."

Her shoulders relaxed. "Ah," she said. "I get it."

My cheeks flushed. "I'm sorry," I said.

"It's all right," she said. "I'm just relieved my phone didn't get hacked."

I was angry with myself. Disappointed. It was always wrong to assume things. It ruined investigations. Got innocent people in trouble and set the guilty ones free.

Still, a lot of people in law enforcement and ex–law enforcement were prone to assumption—and Maurice, I realized, was one of them. I remembered the contempt in his eyes when he spoke about how Dylan wanted Rhonda "roughed up." *What he said was he wanted us to track her down so he could send her a message.* He'd programmed his mind to believe the worst, when, in reality, Dylan had literally wanted to *send Rhonda a message*—an apology email, in fact.

*He went through whatever channels he had . . .*

I sighed. "The problem is, I'm now stuck with even bigger questions."

"Such as?"

"Somebody out there sent anonymous texts to Dylan Welch, calling him a murderer," I said. "If it wasn't you, then who sent them?"

"It wasn't me," she said. "I swear. I don't think of him as a murderer."

"I believe you," I said. "Which leads me to my other big question: Who *does* think of him as a murderer . . . and why?"

She broke off a piece of rye toast and put it in her mouth, chewing it slowly. When she was done she picked up her napkin and dabbed at her mouth and looked at me with those lost, sad, powder-blue eyes. "Maybe he's done something really bad," she said. "Something that has nothing to do with me."

# THIRTY

C ould Dylan Welch have murdered someone before he disappeared? Had Trevor Weiss found out about it, sent those anonymous texts, and threatened to tell more people—forcing Dylan to come out of hiding and kill Trevor, too? And if Dylan's best friend, Sky, had somehow learned the truth . . . was he cold-blooded enough to make it a trifecta? I had answers to none of these questions, yet they wandered through my mind as I left the South Street Diner and headed toward my car.

It made me realize something important: I needed to tell the cops what I knew.

Several blocks away from the diner, I unlocked my car, got in, and headed back to my office. I'd been planning on calling Lee Farrell once I got there, but it was close to rush hour and the roads were already clogged, so, after about ten minutes, during which I'd moved maybe three inches, I told Siri to call him instead.

Lee answered quickly—and, if I was going to be honest, rudely.

"What is it now, Sunny?"

I gawked at my mounted phone as though it owed me an explanation. Lee had never snapped at me like that before. Either he was pulling my chain or something was going on with him. And Lee wasn't much of a chain-puller.

"Is there a problem?" I asked.

"Yes." He sighed heavily. "It's not your problem, though. It's mine. Sorry."

"That's okay. You want to call me back, or . . ."

"No, no. I'm fine. What's going on?"

I exhaled. "I'm assuming you know that Sky Farley was shot."

"Yes," he said.

"Okay, well, I'm afraid that Dylan Welch may have done it. I think he may have shot Trevor Weiss, too."

"What? Wait. Have you found him?"

"No, I haven't," I said.

"Damn," he said.

"Why *damn*?"

He sighed again. "Tell me why you think he shot Sky Farley and Trevor Weiss."

I told him about Elspeth, how she'd shown up at my apartment terrified. I told him about the phone calls, the texts, the audio messages she'd received over the past few days—all from a blocked number. I told him how he'd ordered her to go to his apartment and fetch his gun. How he'd forced her to call someone and tell that person he was dead. I told him how he'd made threatening comments, how he'd sent images of her, taken though windows, letting her know that he could kill her at any moment—and that he was capable of doing so. "In one of the messages," I said, "he all but confesses to killing Trevor."

"Uh-huh," Lee said.

I frowned. That wasn't the reaction I'd been expecting. I told him about the money stolen from payroll, and how the CFO suspected Dylan and how a sizable amount of those funds had gone missing following his disappearance. I even told Lee how the Mob was after Dylan for drug money and how I nearly got run off the road by some goon, just because I'd been in possession of Dylan's phone.

"Uh-huh," Lee said.

I pressed on. "I don't know if you saw this on the phone, but right before he left, he got a bunch of texts from an anonymous number."

"Murderer," he said dully. "Yeah, I saw those."

"Lee, I've gotta tell you," I said. "Considering the information I'm giving you, you're sounding pretty underwhelmed."

"Sorry," he said.

"What's going on?"

"Sky Farley came out of surgery," he said. "The bullet missed her vital organs. She lost some blood, but she's going to be fine."

"*Yes,*" I whispered, thinking of Lydia, how much she'd been through already. "That's wonderful news."

"Uh-huh," he said. "It would be more wonderful, though, if she would give us any information about who shot her."

Traffic started to speed up, the way it so often did around here—suddenly and inexplicably. Several cars honked. I moved forward. "What do you mean? She won't talk?"

"Oh, she's talking. But she's not *saying* anything."

"Why not?"

"Apparently, she's traumatized. She doesn't remember the shooting. She'd turned off the lights in her office when he came in, so she couldn't get a good look at him, or if she did, she honestly can't recall anything about him. Other than he's male and taller than her. Which means he's over five feet tall. And she's not even entirely sure he was male."

"She said all of that?" I asked.

"Yes," he said. "She did."

"To you directly?"

"Yes," he said. "I'm just leaving the hospital. I'm hoping she remembers more after she's had some rest. Security can't seem to get any good footage from the CCTV at Gonzo. Cameras were down all morning. Some computer fritz."

"How about the elevators?"

"Nothing yet, and it's a pretty narrow window of time," he said.

"Maybe he took the stairs."

"Very funny," he said.

"I try."

"Oh, and FYI, we did talk to Elspeth Wasserman. She gave us a statement about finding Sky."

"Did she tell you about Dylan's calls?"

"After we dragged it out of her," he said.

"Yeah, he warned her not to tell the cops."

"Well, that doesn't matter much."

"Why not?"

"Her phone was stolen."

"Ugh."

"Yep," he said. "She called 911 from Sky's office phone and didn't notice it was missing till she was in the ER, so it could have happened at the party, or any time after she left it."

"Big window of time."

"Enormous."

"Is she still at the hospital?"

"She was waiting to get discharged when I went to see Sky."

I exhaled. "He told her not to say anything to the police," I said. "He threatened her." I pulled up to the traffic light, which had just changed from yellow to red. An acid-yellow Porsche swerved around me to run the light, nearly hitting me in the process. It took me a few seconds to catch my breath. I flipped off the driver. He reminded me of Dylan.

"Thank you for the info," Lee was saying. "I didn't mean to sound ungrateful, and I'm sure you're right. That creep Welch is out there somewhere, and he's been stalking that poor girl, trying to make her believe he's something to be afraid of."

I drove for a few moments, my pulse still racing from the near crash, thinking about what Lee just said. "It's circumstantial," I said, finally. "Even if Elspeth's phone is recovered and you can hear the messages and see the texts, it doesn't tie

Dylan to the murders in any meaningful way. He could have been lying. He could have been messing with Elspeth's mind, some stupid Batman-villain fantasy playing out in his head. Anyone could have told him about Trevor's shooting. He could have been high and delusional, pissed off because maybe Elspeth rejected him at Bottle Poppin' Friday. He just wanted to scare her. Wouldn't stand up in court. Blah, blah, blah."

"Yes. All of that. Except what the fuck is Bottle Poppin' Friday?"

I ignored the question. "On top of all that, Dylan's still missing, so you can't question him."

"Right again," he said. "So far, we have two shootings that appear to be connected—one murder, one attempted murder. We are running ballistic tests. But we have no DNA, no murder weapon, no eyewitnesses that we know of—and one surviving victim who remembers nothing. I hate to minimize anybody's trauma, but, man, it would be good for us if Sky Farley recovered her memory."

"I hear you," I said.

"Maybe with time, she'll find some clarity," he said.

*Or maybe she already has clarity but doesn't want to point the finger at her best friend.* I thought it but kept quiet. I took my next available right, heading back to where I came from. "I'm going to try and talk to her," I told Lee. "I'll let you know if I find out anything."

"Thanks, Sunny." Over the Bluetooth, I heard a beeping sound, a car door opening and closing. "I owe you one."

# THIRTY-ONE

O nce I finally arrived back at Mass General, I noticed I had
three texts from Blake, two of which asked when I was
coming back to the office. The third one just said: *Helloooooo?*

It was odd, considering he almost never texted me. He also
knew I was busy—I'd let him know about both the shooting
and my meeting with Rhonda as they were happening. From
the front seat of my car, I called my office. Blake picked up
quickly.

"Hey," I said. "What's going on?"

"So you had four new client queries," Blake said. "Two calls
and two emails to the website. You want to hear about them?"
He sounded strange, his words running together. It was like
someone had pressed his fast-forward button.

"Is that why you texted me?"

"I texted you?" He stopped talking for a brief moment. "Oh, right. I did."

"Any replies to the emails you sent?"

"To the people on the list that Mrs. Welch gave you?"

"Yes."

"No. Not a one. That's kind of sad, isn't it? You'd think more of them would care."

I sighed. "So . . . can the queries wait, then? I'm back at the hospital. Sky pulled through. She's going to make it, and—"

"She did? Oh, that is great. *Amazing! Fuckin' awesome!*"

"Uh, yeah," I said. "Anyway, I'm going in to see her, so I won't be back at the office for at least an hour."

"Okay. I'll be here. Guess what? I waxed the floors. They look *sick*. Shit, I shouldn't have told you. It was going to be a surprise."

"Blake?"

"Yeah?"

"Are you okay?"

"Huh? What do you mean? I'm like . . . better than okay."

"Can you do me a huge favor?"

"Anything," he said. "Oh, wait. Oh, no. Do you need me to drive somewhere? Because I don't have a car. I took the T to work today. I'm sor—"

"Blake, listen to me." I said it slowly and, I hoped, soothingly. "I don't need you to drive anywhere."

"Good," he said. "Awesome sauce."

"All I need for you to do is this," I said. "You listening?"

"Yep."

"Take a deep breath—in for five counts. Then out for five counts."

He did. I listened. He exhaled so loudly it was like sticking my ear in a wind tunnel.

"Okay," I said when he was done. "The next thing I need for you to do is lay off the Gonzo."

"Bruuuuh."

"For the rest of the day," I said. "Please. Promise me."

He said nothing. I heard swallowing sounds, another outpouring of breath. I was pretty sure he'd just finished off another can.

"How about this, Blake?" I said. "I promise I'll bring Rosie tomorrow. But only if you don't touch another one of those drinks. If you do, she's staying home for a month."

"That's not fair."

"Life's not fair."

He sighed. "Fine," he said. "I promise."

"What do you promise? Say it to me."

"No more Gonzo," he said. "For the rest of the day."

"Thank you."

I ended the call and checked my email. There was a new one, from Lee, with a photo attachment. The subject line was *Because I owe you one.*

One of the best things about Lee was that he always made good on his word. It was a rare quality, and it made me feel guilty for keeping information from him, even if it was only on occasion.

I opened the photo—a gloved hand holding a baggie that was half filled with a white powder that sparkled slightly. It was Lee's hand. I recognized the Cartier Tank watch. The email itself read: *Call me when you see this.*

I called Lee.

"You opened the email," he said.

"Yes," I said. "What is the powder and where did you find it?"

"First question: We don't know yet. They're testing it in the lab," he said. "Second question: We found it sewn into the lining of Trevor Weiss's jacket."

"The one he was wearing when he was shot?"

"Yes."

"So . . . if someone murdered him and searched his body for the stuff—whatever it is—they wouldn't find it right away."

"That's true."

"But if the meeting had gone the way Trevor had wanted it to, he could have simply given this person his coat, and the powder would be hidden."

"True as well," Lee said. "But at this point, it's all conjecture."

"A dead man can't tell you his motivations for sewing a baggie full of mystery powder into his coat," I said. "Or even if he'd been the one to sew it in there."

"Exactly."

I thanked Lee—not just for the information, but for

reminding me again not to make assumptions during an investigation.

"I'll let you know what the lab says," he told me.

"I'll let you know what Sky says," I told him.

"Hopefully between the two of us," Lee said, "we'll come up with some real answers."

# THIRTY-TWO

S unny," Sky said, raising her good arm to greet me. "I'm so happy to see you." She'd been moved to a hospital room—a very nice one. Private, on a high floor. I wondered if the Welches had pulled a few strings to secure it. They were both in the room with Sky, Lydia hovering around her like an attentive mother, Bill sitting in a chair against the wall, where he was quietly taking phone calls when I came in.

Sky wore a hospital gown, her bloody clothes with police for testing. She was very pale, but otherwise she looked good, considering. The bullet had apparently struck her just below her right collarbone. A few inches to the left and she'd have died as quickly as Trevor, but as it stood, she was in good shape. She was hooked up to IVs, her right shoulder and arm were wrapped in thick gauze, and she was scheduled to be released later in the day—the following morning at the latest.

"Our driver is ready to take her home, whenever she's discharged." Lydia looked at Sky. "I bought you a suit at Saks to wear home. Gucci. I know it's not quite your style, but I couldn't resist."

"Thank you, Lydia," Sky said. "You really didn't have to do that." She sounded exhausted, and I felt for her—in more ways than one. I'd been shot before. I'd also been in the hospital before, repeatedly. And I couldn't imagine having to force an immobile, heavily bandaged shoulder and traumatized body into a Gucci suit.

Bill was talking on his phone, saying something about rescheduling an annual shareholders' meeting. Lydia shushed him. He stood up and turned away from us, speaking more quietly.

"Have you guys been here the whole time?" I asked.

"Since she's been conscious, yes," Lydia said.

I nodded. That explained a lot. "You were here when the police questioned Sky."

"Yes. They asked us to leave so they could speak to her privately, but she didn't want us to. She insisted. She was quite emphatic, weren't you? I was concerned about your heart rate."

"Sky didn't want privacy?"

"No," Sky said. "I didn't."

I turned to her. "Would you be able to speak with me alone?"

Sky glanced at Lydia.

"We all trust you, Sunny," Lydia said. "But why do you want to speak with her without us in the room?"

"It's all in the interest of getting Dylan home safe and sound," I said.

Lydia opened her mouth, then closed it again. I could almost read her thoughts—wanting me to elaborate and, at the same time, absolutely *not* wanting me to. "Okay," Lydia said. "Whatever Sky wants."

Sky's gaze was on me. She seemed calm. "Sure," she said. "I'll talk to you, Sunny."

Bill ended his call and turned around. "Ms. Randall, did I hear you say you'd like us out of the room?"

"Just for a little while," I said. "That okay?"

"Better than okay. I'm dying to get out of here." He turned to Sky, a sheepish look on his face. "You know I didn't mean that the way it sounded."

"No worries," Sky said, but then a shadow seemed to pass over her. Her features tightened. *Dread,* I thought. Or it could have been a wave of pain from her injury. "Should I get a nurse?" I asked. "Do you need meds?"

Sky shook her head. "I'm fine," she said. "I'll be fine. Go ahead, you guys."

Lydia and Bill left the room. I pulled the chair up to Sky's bed. There was a pitcher of water on the bedside table, along with an empty plastic cup. I took the liberty of refilling it for her. She picked it up and drank.

Before I spoke, I waited for Sky to put down the empty cup. Then I leaned in and gave her a smile.

"A Gucci suit?" I said. "Is she serious?"

Sky let out a laugh. "Yeah, I like to think I can handle any challenge, but come on."

"What about the shoes?"

"She brought me these pumps with three-inch stiletto heels," Sky said.

"Ouch."

"I couldn't even walk in those things on a *good* day."

"I can go to your apartment if you want," I said. "Pick up some sweats and sneakers?"

"God, I'd love that," Sky said. "But I don't want to . . . you know. Offend Lydia."

"We can tell her that you want to leave the hospital incognito," I said. "There's probably press out there by now, and you'd turn a lot more heads in a Gucci suit and heels."

Sky's face brightened. "That's a genius idea."

I smiled. "I have them sometimes."

Sky asked if I could pour her some more water. I did. She took a few sips, her shoulders relaxing. "Okay," she said. "What do you want to know?"

I gave her a look. "I think that's pretty obvious."

"What do I remember about getting shot?"

"Bingo."

"I already went over this with the police," she said.

"I know," I said. "Tell me, though. As a friend—a friend who is not law enforcement, and who just asked Bill and Lydia to leave the room so you can speak freely."

She nodded. "I understand," she said. "I just . . . I need to think."

"There's no hurry," I said. "Try and remember everything you can. Don't stop yourself from saying anything."

She took a deep breath. "Okay," she said. "Do I start with when I got shot?"

"Maybe start with when you told the Welches' butler that you were going to be late for lunch."

She blinked a few times. "Oh, right," she said. "I almost forgot about that."

"Tell me what was going on."

She stared up at the ceiling for a long while. Then, finally, she began to speak. "So everybody had left for the office Christmas party. I'd planned on going, too—just to put in an appearance before heading over to Bill and Lydia's. But I'd . . . I'd gotten a phone call."

"From who?" I asked.

"A reporter," she said. "She wanted to ask me about the death of that lab tech."

"Trevor Weiss."

"Yeah," she said quietly. "Trevor."

"I didn't realize the press knew about that so soon."

"Yeah, I was surprised, too," she said. "I'd only heard about it myself last night. The police asked me about him."

"Yes. Me too."

"Anyway, I told Balthazar it was just office business because I didn't want to upset the Welches. You know?"

I nodded.

"So I talked to the reporter for a little while, and by the time I was done, I knew I wasn't going to be able to drop by the party," she said. "I started turning off lights and shutting down my computer. Getting ready to leave for the Welches'."

"So the lights in your office were off, like you told the police."

"Yes. They were . . ." She took another swallow of her water. "I . . . I heard the door to my office open wider, and I turned around and he was standing in the doorway . . . this person. He was wearing a hoodie, I think."

"You couldn't see his face?"

"No," she said quietly. "I couldn't. It was dark. The hood was basically covering his face . . . It was scary."

She stared up at the ceiling, her eyes starting to glisten. Sky seemed broken—bandaged on one side, hooked up to IVs on the other. She looked tired, too. Frail, just from the act of remembering.

I noticed something on the bed then, resting against Sky's bad side, her bandaged side. A hint of jade green, bordered in gold. I recognized it immediately. Her mother's compact. Maurice must have brought it to her. *She's had a lot of visitors.*

"Sky," I said. "I'm going to ask you a question. It isn't an easy one. It will probably hurt. But for your sake, and ultimately for Dylan's, I need you to answer honestly."

Sky closed her eyes. "All right. Shoot." She winced. "God, talk about a poor choice of words."

"You're ready?

"Yes."

"Okay," I said. "Is there any reason why Dylan Welch would want you dead?"

Sky shut her eyes tighter. Tears seeped out of the corners. She stretched her good arm across her body and plucked the compact off the bed, clutching it like a rosary in that one small hand, twirling it in her fingers, bringing it to her cheek. "I don't know," she said. I glanced at the monitor. Her heart rate was steady.

"Do you think he's capable of trying to kill you?"

"I don't know." Her voice was so soft I could barely hear her. I hated doing this, but I had to.

"Remember, Sky," I said. "This is me you're talking to. The Welches aren't here. I won't tell them."

Her jaw tightened; the fist of her good hand clenched. "You promise?"

"Yes," I said.

She exhaled shakily, opening her eyes again. They were thick with tears now, a few slipping down the sides of her face. Again, I told her it was okay, that I wouldn't tell Dylan's parents.

And then, finally, she spoke. "I told you about that fight we had before he left," she said. "When he locked himself in his office? Remember?"

"Yes."

"I told you it was because he was using. And he was. But that was only part of it. He'd stolen from the company. I know the

Welches told you, but I saw the discrepancy in the numbers before Martin did, and it was a lot more than he knew. For weeks, I kept quiet. I was moving money around, trying to fix it. I was even putting some of my own personal savings into payroll, just to make up for the loss, but it was getting out of control. And I knew it was going to drugs. Weapons of self-destruction. That's what Dylan used to call the stuff he did, back when we were in college. I wonder if he remembers that . . . I mean, he really did want to destroy himself. He was aware of it."

I remembered Dylan's letter to Rhonda. The way he'd spiraled following Daisy's death, taking his guilt out on himself, on other people like Teresa.

Sky cleared her throat, clutching the compact tighter. "Anyway, I brought it up to Dylan and . . . I've never seen him like that. He can be awful when he's backed into a corner."

"I know."

"I didn't, though . . . not really . . . Not until that day. He got this look on his face . . . like a wild animal . . ."

More tears spilled down her cheeks. I went looking around the room for Kleenex. I didn't see any, so I ducked into the bathroom and grabbed a wad of toilet paper. Sky accepted it gratefully, holding the pile of tissue up to her eyes for several seconds before finally she was able to speak again. I looked at the monitor. Her heart rate sped up slightly. "For the first time, I was . . . I was scared of him, Sunny. I realized, I mean . . . I honestly have no idea what he's capable of."

I thought of the *Murderer* texts Dylan had received, the idea that he might have killed someone else before Trevor. Before he tried to kill Sky. *Not to make assumptions. We never make assumptions.* But still, it was compelling. "Sky," I said carefully. "Are you sure you didn't see his face? The man who shot you?"

She shook her head. And then she started to cry again. Harder now, her body quaking from the sobs, the compact clutched in her hands. Her heart rate grew faster. I told her to relax, to breathe. She held the toilet paper up to her face and I ran to grab more for her—a giant wad of tissue, practically the rest of the roll—and she sobbed into it, her shoulders heaving, as though what she was feeling, this grief, this horror, had suddenly grown big enough to consume her. I moved closer to her bed and she buckled onto me, her good arm around my back. I stroked her hair and told her it was okay, because I didn't know what else to do. She cried more and I kept trying to comfort her, horrified at the thought of anyone walking in—a nurse or, worse yet, the Welches, Lydia shrieking at me, *What have you done to her?*

Again, I told Sky to breathe deeply, and she did. I gave her water and sat back down on the chair, Sky holding my hand along with the Bakelite compact—so tightly, I was afraid she'd break it. Or my hand. Or both.

At long last, she calmed down. She closed her eyes. Her heart rate slowed. I watched her for a while, unsure of how to phrase the next question. I was worried she'd start sobbing again, but I had to say it. I needed to know. "Sky," I said. "If you didn't see his face, why that response? What was it that you remembered to make you cry like that?"

"His voice," she whispered. "I heard his voice." She took a deep breath and looked straight at me, her eyes now dry as stones. "Right before he shot me, I heard Dylan's voice."

# THIRTY-THREE

Sky agreed to talk to the police, but she wanted to tell Bill and Lydia first. Alone.

And so, after the nurses took her vitals, I left the room and let the Welches know that Sky wanted to see them. "She has something important that she wants to share with you," I said, adding, "It isn't good news."

They both nodded solemnly, neither one of them asking what the news was exactly. Heading back to her hospital room, they walked slowly, hand in hand, their heads bowed. Neither one of them said a word. It felt as though they were both about to receive the same grim prognosis, but it was an expected one. And so they were in no hurry to hear it.

I didn't envy them. What Sky had told me had been difficult to hear. It had been surprisingly hard for me to grapple with the idea that Dylan was capable of shooting his best friend—and I didn't even like him. I tried imagining what this news would be like for someone who *did* like Dylan—who loved him, even.

These were Dylan's parents. He was their only child. At some point in their lives, they'd pinned hopes on him. How could this not be a horrible shock?

Lydia and Bill had left me in the waiting room on this not-very-busy floor, and now, save for me, the room was empty. I took advantage of this newfound privacy and called my office.

The number rang several times. Nobody picked up, and my call went to after-hours voicemail.

I tried again, but this time my call was answered right away. "Sunny Randall Investigations," said a male voice. But it wasn't Blake's voice. It was Spike's.

"What the hell?" I said.

"Sunny?" Spike said. "I was just going to call you."

"What's going on? Why are you in my office, doing Blake's job?"

"Okay, first of all, Blake's fine," Spike said.

"That's good to know," I said. "Is he taking a break?"

"In a way."

"Pardon?"

"When we showed up, he was asleep at his desk," Spike said. "Not just nodding off. Like . . . deeply asleep."

"I . . . I find that hard to believe. Honestly. Blake's the most awake person I know."

Spike sighed. "Not that I have any skin in this game, but I'm looking at him right now," he said. "He's sleeping like a newborn on the floor of your new breakroom. He's even snoring."

"Weird," I said, but then the situation started to dawn on me. *Gonzo.* Blake followed a keto diet. No carbs. No drinking. Very little caffeine and sugar. One energy drink would probably send his brain over Niagara Falls in a barrel. And Blake had certainly consumed more than one. When I'd spoken to him, he'd sounded high as a kite.

I'd forced him to make me that promise. *No more Gonzo. For the rest of the day.* That was a couple hours ago.

Welcome to the crash.

"I suggested he try sleeping in one of your leather chairs, but he says he likes to stretch out," Spike was saying. "You should buy an office couch. You know that? You've got room for one. And if this kid likes to take naps, at least he won't mess up his back."

"Spike, can you do me a favor?" I asked.

"Sure."

"Can you look in the breakroom fridge? Tell me how many cans of Gonzo are in there?"

"You bet. Hold on."

Spike returned less than a minute later. "None," he said.

"Shit. I'm pretty sure we had a case yesterday."

"Wow," he said. "Did you drink any of them?"

I cringed. "I'd just as soon drink bleach."

"Well," Spike said, "I suppose he's sleeping it all off now."

"So, anyway," I said. "What are you doing at my office? And didn't you say 'we' came in? Who is 'we'?"

"I was wondering when you'd get around to asking. 'We' is me and Elspeth. Or should that be 'We *are* me and Elspeth'?" he said. "I suck at grammar."

"Elspeth's with you?"

"Yep. She came to my restaurant right after she got out of the hospital. Had her mother drop her off. Elspeth thinks I'm the only one who can protect her."

"Protect her?" I said. "From what?"

"That's what she wants to talk to you about." Spike put his hand over the receiver for a few seconds. I heard muffled conversation, then he returned to the line. "She wants to tell you privately in person," he said. "And knowing what she has to tell you, I've gotta say . . . she's right."

A fter I hung up with Spike, I waited for Bill and Lydia to get out of Sky's room. I told them I had a slight work emergency and that I'd call them later. They both seemed shaken up— Lydia especially. I understood. It was one thing to expect bad news about someone you loved. It was quite another to have it confirmed.

"You guys going to be okay here?" I asked. "You need me for anything else?"

Lydia shook her head. "That's fine, dear. You take care of your work issue," she said. "Sky has called the police, and I imagine that when they're done interviewing the poor girl, they'll want to speak with us as well."

"All right," I said. "If you're sure."

"You enjoy the rest of your day, Sunny," Bill said. An odd thing to come out of his mouth, especially now. It made me feel sorry for him, and *feeling sorry for Bill Welch* wasn't something that had been on my 2024 bingo card.

As I was leaving the waiting room, Lydia called out my name. When I turned to her, she gave me a pained smile that tore at my heart. "At least we know Dylan's close by."

On my way out, I poked my head into Sky's room. I told her I was leaving and asked if she still wanted me to pick up her sweats and sneakers.

"Oh, yes, please!" She smiled, her whole face lighting up. "I live in the Back Bay. I'll text you everything you need to know, and I'll call the doorman and tell him to let you in. Cool?"

It was strange how different Sky was acting, in less than twenty minutes' time—as though the memory of being shot had been a weight lifted from her and then placed squarely on the shoulders of the shooter's parents. Sky seemed less frail, more energetic, Lydia and Bill having taken on all of her suffering.

"I may be a little while because of work stuff," I said. "Is that okay?"

"No worries. They haven't even given me an ETA as far as discharging me goes," she said. "Plus, I've got the police coming." She opened her compact, examined her face in the mirror, checked her teeth, and smoothed her eyebrows, as though she was getting ready for a date. We said goodbye. Sky glanced up from her mirror and beamed at me again. "Thank you for helping me remember," she said. "It's weird. I feel so much better now."

*It is weird*, I thought. *We're in agreement on that.*

I had a hinky feeling as I walked toward the elevator. I didn't like being suspicious of Sky, but I couldn't help it. There was something about her mood shift that bothered me. It seemed extreme to the point of callousness—especially considering how distraught the Welches clearly were. On the other hand, Sky was also recovering from major blood loss, she was on a hell of a lot of pain meds, and she'd just remembered that her best friend had tried to kill her. Where was the reaction guidebook for that?

I decided to lay off Sky. She was an orphan who grew up with nothing but liked everybody nonetheless. Meanwhile, I grew up in a solid and fairly privileged family, and most people annoyed me. Clearly, we reacted to the world in very different ways.

I was just at the elevator when I remembered one more question. I jogged back to Sky's room and knocked softly on the door, and when I heard her say, "Come in," I poked my head in again.

Sky was smoothing her hair with her good arm as a nurse checked her monitor. She turned toward me, smiling. "Did you forget something?"

"Yes," I said. "Sorry. I'm usually a better questioner."

Some of her smile slipped away. "What's up?"

"I was just wondering," I said. "Who was the reporter?"

"Huh?"

"You said a reporter called you back in the office before Dylan shot you. They interviewed you about Trevor."

Her face relaxed. "Oh, right."

"Do you remember their name?"

She winced. "Crap. I don't."

"How about the newspaper? Or was it a website?"

Sky exhaled. "It's a blur, Sunny, I swear," she said. "But I'll call you if the name comes to me. I promise."

"No worries." I slapped on a smile. "You remembered what's important. That's what counts."

She smiled back. "True," she said. "Listen, Sunny . . . Does my hair look okay?"

# THIRTY-FOUR

By the time I got back to my office, Blake had woken up—barely. He was sitting at his desk, slack-jawed and bleary-eyed, with the worst case of bedhead I'd ever seen.

"Wow," I said once I got a good look at him. "For the very first time, I can honestly say that you look how I feel."

"Did you find Dylan yet?"

"Nope."

"Dang."

"Trust me, Blake, if I solve a case, you'll always be the first to know."

"Awesome." His eyelids fluttered. His head started to droop, but he jerked it back up quickly, then slapped both sides of his face.

"You . . . uh . . . feeling okay?" I asked.

"Not really."

"I'm sorry."

"It's my fault," Blake said. "I usually know my limits."

"I'm sure you'll be good as new in the morning," I said.

"I'd better be. I feel so . . . so *old*. Like I'm forty or some-thing."

I cringed. *Time for a change of subject.* "You hear back from any of those Dylan Welch contacts you emailed?"

"Not yet." He gave me a tired grin. "Trust me, you'll always be the first to know."

I smiled. "Good one."

"You wanna know what?" He picked at a fingernail. "You were right."

"About what?"

"Gonzo," he said. "I don't know why I got so into it like I did. It fuckin' sucks, man. Always has, always will."

"Live and learn," I said, taking off my coat. "You won't be able to drink it anymore. Just like I can't drink Ouzo because of this bad Greektown experience I had back in college. Your body will remember. You won't make the same mistake again."

"I hope not," Blake said.

I hung my coat on the hook near the door. "Your body always remembers," I said. For some reason, it made me think of Richie. I pushed the thought out of my head.

"I'm assuming Spike and Elspeth are in my office," I said.

Blake nodded.

"You make any of that good coffee?"

His face brightened a little. "No, but I can. You want some?"

"I could use a cup." I peered at him. "You probably could, too."

He made for the breakroom. I made for my office, where Spike and Elspeth sat on my leather chairs, deep in conversation.

They didn't look up until I closed the door behind me.

I stared at Elspeth—the purplish circles under her eyes, the smeared mascara. She looked exhausted, as though she hadn't slept in weeks. She was still wearing my white suit, dried blood caked on the sleeves and smears of it across the lapels. *Poor thing.* That was all I could think. *All she's been through in these past few days . . .* Elspeth was keyed up, her whole body tensed, that eyelid of hers twitching.

"Is Sky going to be okay?" she asked. She was gripping the arms of my chair so tightly, I was worried she might hurt herself.

"Yes," I said. "I just saw her. She's going to be fine."

Elspeth deflated, some of the tension draining out of her. "Oh, thank God," she said. "Thank God."

Spike looked at her, then at me. "Did she say who shot her?"

I nodded. "Dylan Welch."

"I don't get it," Elspeth said. "Sky was so nice to him. She was his friend."

I shook my head. "She knew about some bad stuff he was doing—financial stuff," I said. "But from what she told me, she'd been trying to protect him, so I don't get it, either."

Elspeth tensed up again. "What's wrong with him?" she whispered.

"What isn't?" Spike said.

I nodded. "Good point." I thought about Sky again. "It took her a little while to remember who shot her," I said. "She told Lee Farrell she didn't know at first. I thought she might be covering for Dylan. But she seemed to have this breakthrough with me . . ."

"Trauma," Spike said. "It can mess with your head."

Which made me remember Sky's interview again. That phantom reporter she'd spoken to just prior to it. "She lost some of her memories before the shooting, too," I said, which made me think of something else. If she'd spoken to a reporter about Trevor this morning, the interview was almost assuredly online by now. It was time-sensitive information, after all— and very newsworthy, since Sky's own shooting had taken place moments later.

I quickly excused myself, opened the door, and shouted out to Blake, "When you get a chance, can you google Sky Farley, Trevor Weiss, and shooting? See if anything was posted today that has quotes from Sky?"

He shouted back, "Can I finish making the coffee first?"

I told him there was no hurry, whenever. Then I shut the door and apologized to Elspeth and Spike. "I would have forgotten if I didn't say it right then," I said. "Too many things in my head at once."

"Well, we're about to squeeze something else in there," Spike said.

"Oh, yeah?"

Spike leaned forward in his chair, his thick fingers laced

together. "Elspeth needs to tell you something," he said. "But the thing is, you can't tell the police. Not now, at least."

"Why not?"

"You'll put me in danger," Elspeth said. "For real."

"Who told you that?"

"Dylan," she said.

I stared at her. "What's happened now?"

"Okay." She took a deep, trembling breath. "I don't know if I can do this."

"You can," Spike said. "You just have to trust us. Your secret's safe. Right, Sunny?"

I exhaled, thinking of Lee. His case versus the safety of a young woman who was putting all her trust in Spike and me. It didn't take me that long to make a decision. After all, I'd already gotten Sky for him . . . "Right," I said.

"Here you go, guys." Blake walked in with a tray. On it were three cups of coffee, a pitcher of cream, and some packets of sugar. "Don't mind me."

Still trembling, Elspeth smiled at Blake as he set down the tray. He smiled back. "It's really good coffee," he said. "Nutmeg and cinnamon. That's what does it."

"I saw that on TikTok," Elspeth said.

"Me too!" Blake said. "What are the odds of that?"

Elspeth laughed a little.

Blake did, too. He still looked rough, but it was good to see he was getting his people skills back. In better circumstances, he might have asked her for her number. She'd have given it to him, too. I could tell these things. It was kind of a sixth sense.

After Blake closed the door, Elspeth sipped her coffee. She closed her eyes. "Okay," she whispered. "Okay."

"You got this," Spike said encouragingly.

"I know," she said, opening her eyes again. "I know I do." She put her cup down at the edge of my desk and took a few deep breaths. "So . . . first of all," she said, "most of what I told the cops is right."

"Meaning?" I asked.

"Meaning I *was* at the Loews at the office Christmas party. I *had* left my Secret Santa present in my desk. I *did* go back to get it . . . And that *is* when I found Sky."

"All that's true?" I asked.

"Yes," she said. "I just left one thing out."

I looked at her, then at Spike, who was stirring cream into his coffee.

Elspeth cleared her throat. The eyelid twitched again. "What I left out was that I was *told* to leave my Secret Santa present in my desk," she said. "I was *told* to go back and get it, as well as exactly what time I was supposed to go back."

"Dylan gave you those instructions?" I said.

"Yes."

"In an audio message?"

"No. On the phone. He called from a blocked number."

"When?"

"This morning. Before everybody left for the party. He made

me go somewhere private to receive my 'latest assignment,' he called it. I went into the bathroom."

Elspeth clutched her coffee mug with both hands, as though the gesture would keep them from shaking.

"I didn't know Dylan was going to shoot Sky," she said quickly. "I tried to ask him why he wanted me to go back to the office, but he wouldn't answer. He just kept repeating the instructions. Then he hung up."

Spike nodded. "He wanted you to find the body."

"Yes," she said. "You know, when I got that call, I felt like I always do when he contacts me. Like I was going to throw up. But I still had this little bit of hope. I mean . . . if you want to call it that." She drew a frail, trembling breath. "I know this sounds kind of morbid," she said. "But I was thinking, *At least if something happens to me, there's evidence of what he's been doing on my phone. The texts, the audio messages.* You know? If he killed me, all that stuff would point right to him."

"But then," I said, "your phone got stolen."

"Yeah. It did. How did you know?"

"Lee Farrell told me," I said.

Spike put his coffee cup down and looked at me. "You think Welch took it?"

"Or someone else," I said, the idea crystalizing in my mind. "You know . . . it would be pretty hard for him to shoot Sky, clean up, escape from a skyscraper unseen . . . and then, at some point during all that, steal someone's phone."

"You think he's been threatening other people besides me?" Elspeth said.

"Either that or he's got someone on the inside at Gonzo," I said. "Someone who's working with him willingly."

Spike picked up his coffee and took another sip. "Any ideas about who that might be?"

"None whatsoever," I said.

There was a knock on the door, and then Blake opened it slightly. "I googled what you asked me to and found a bunch of articles about the two shootings," he said. "But nothing quoting Sky Farley."

# THIRTY-FIVE

Elspeth went with Spike to his restaurant, where she'd stay under his watch and, as he put it, "eat some of the best lobster mac and cheese in Boston," until closing time. From there, she'd go to his place, mine, Spike's boyfriend, Flynn Tipton's, or Elspeth's mom's in Newton (in which case Elspeth would probably have to let her in on exactly what was going on). We weren't sure which home would be safest, so we all decided to play that one by ear. I agreed not to tell the cops—Dylan was already on their radar because of Sky's account of her shooting, so this new information wasn't vital. Not now. But if we or the police couldn't find him within the next twenty-four hours, I warned, I was ready to go back on my word. The police could work with Elspeth's phone company to trace that blocked call. Even if it turned out to be some discarded burner phone, I told them, it was worth a shot.

After the two of them left my office, Sky texted me her address with instructions on where I'd find her sneakers and sweats, telling me she was going to be discharged soon. I thumbs-up'd the text but sent no reply beyond that. I didn't want to ask her about the reporter again. At this point, I wasn't even sure if she was lying about the interview—or what the significance was, if that was indeed the case. What if she had, in fact, been communicating with Dylan rather than a reporter? And due to either her faulty memory or her simply wanting to keep that a secret, she'd chosen to tell me otherwise. It didn't change the fact that moments later, Dylan had nearly killed her.

The only option, it seemed, was to wait on it, see what else Sky remembered about that vague period before she was shot. As my dad once told me, *The truth is like a splinter. It has a way of working itself out, in time.*

I sighed heavily. My dad, the ever-patient and dogged Phil Randall, had apparently never heard of tweezers.

Just in case anyone needed further proof that my beloved town was too small for its own good, Sky's apartment was in the exact same Back Bay high-rise that Blake used to live in, when he was a macro-influencer and I was hired by his then manager, Bethany Rose, to protect him from a stalker.

Walking toward the security station, I was practically woozy from déjà vu. Save for the massive Christmas tree with its bulbous gold and silver ornaments, the lobby looked the same—like Donald Judd had spent some time renovating a jet hangar and then threw in a boatload of mirrors at the last minute to appease the building's appearance-obsessed tenants.

The new doorman/security guard was named Roger. While he was suitably large and terrifying in appearance, Roger's personality was a lot more pleasant than that of his predecessor, Eddie Voltaire. You might even say he was respectful. When I let him know I was a friend of Sky's, Roger said, "Oh, you must be Sunny," and shook my hand. He told me Sky's apartment number and that he knew I'd be coming, as Sky had called in advance. "It's just awful, what happened to her," Roger said. "Heavens to Betsy. You can't be safe anywhere these days."

He was the first person I'd ever met under the age of eighty to say "heavens to Betsy," and I had to say, I found it impressive.

I shook my head. "It's a dangerous world."

"Ain't it the truth, sister," Roger said.

Another bonus: During this entire hospitable exchange, Roger didn't once use his height advantage to sneak a peek down my blouse. It was a distinct improvement from what I'd come to expect from security at this place. And I was here for it. As he rode the elevator with me, he praised Sky for her friendliness, her generosity around the holidays, and how, unlike so many of her neighbors, "Sky Farley has never, not once, thrown one of those noisy GD parties."

It wasn't until he was walking me to Sky's apartment that I

realized "GD" wasn't some sort of drug or sexual activity I was too uncool to know about—it was just Roger's G-rated way of saying "goddamn."

Sky's place was on the eleventh floor—one floor down from Blake's old digs. At Mass General, Sky had mentioned she'd lived here for nearly two years—which meant she was a resident six months ago, when the building became a crime scene. I tried to remember if I'd seen Sky back then—she easily could have been one of the terrified young tenants clustered in the lobby, whispering to one another, asking the uniforms when it would be safe to return to their homes.

And now Sky was a crime victim herself, the perp her best friend. Dangerous world, indeed.

As Roger unlocked Sky's apartment for me, I kept thinking about what Lydia had said back at the hospital: *At least we know Dylan's close by.* As poignant as I found it at the time, the statement was, more important, true.

Even if, as I'd speculated, Dylan did have an accomplice who had been able to steal Elspeth's phone at the Loews party and was somehow slipping him cash and food, there were the stalker pics, taken outside Elspeth's apartment and mine, there was Sky's admission that Dylan had been the one to shoot her this morning—and the audio message he'd sent Elspeth, in which he basically confessed to killing Trevor Weiss.

If Dylan had done any single one of those things, then he *was* close by. Yet the police couldn't find him. I couldn't find him. Not even the Mob could find him. He hadn't been caught on surveillance cameras. No one in the Winthrop Center had seen him take an elevator to one of the top floors. No one had spotted him entering or leaving the Gonzo manufacturing plant, before or after Trevor's murder.

No one had witnessed Dylan anywhere, doing anything, in two weeks.

It was baffling to me. When I last saw Dylan, he hadn't even been able to figure out how to pull the trigger on his own gun while remaining upright. And yet somehow, within the past six months, he'd transformed into "the Fugitive."

Once Roger left, I looked around Sky's apartment, which was yet another surprise. Judging from her personality and appearance, I'd have expected her home to be sweet and welcoming—maybe even a little messy. But this lair—and I would have absolutely called it a *lair*—was none of those things. At first glance, it seemed similar to her office, in that it was a minimalist space built around a stunning view. But somehow it wasn't quite as tasteful or warm as Sky's office, or even Blake's old place—which wasn't saying much at all. *Hell's waiting room.* That was one way to describe it—spotless and sterile and slightly torturous, with an intimidating vibe and a rigidly enforced color scheme.

Against the wall on the left, there was a white leather couch I was terrified of going anywhere near for fear of staining it, set alongside a red enamel coffee table with matching chairs that looked incredibly uncomfortable. Parked close to the floor-to-ceiling window was a white enamel dining room set, a gleaming chrome bowl at the center filled with fake red roses, and beyond that stood a small open-air kitchen, all in white, save the red knobs on the cupboards, the scarlet stovetop, and the crimson fridge, which sported silver handles. On the living room walls hung a smallish wide-screen TV betwixt a series of rather generic-looking abstract paintings—all of them in (you guessed it!) white and red. And don't even get me started on the red-and-white polka-dot curtains.

*Gonzo colors.*

Except for the view, I found it all pretty vomitrocious. And it hit me that, serious and brilliant as she clearly was, it most likely *was* Sky who had chosen Gonzo's corporate office décor.

*People are complicated. And they keep proving it again and again and again.*

I moved from the living and dining room area into the bedroom, which was much easier on the eyes, if plastered in pastel. For Sky's sake, I hoped she spent most of her time here, and when I saw the desk in the corner—which housed a computer that made the one in her office look antiquated—it was clear she did.

I noticed two framed pictures on the desk—one that looked to be taken in the nineties, of a pregnant woman in a sundress with a smile identical to Sky's. Obviously, this was her late mother.

The other framed picture was the same Gonzo staff photo that I'd seen on Dylan's phone. I picked it up and gave it a closer look. The happy group picnicking in the Common, toasting the camera with their then-brand-new product. Besides Sky and Dylan, I now recognized Elspeth, Kaitlyn and Henry from Marketing, Maurice Dupree, and even Martin Jennings, the dour CFO.

It was always interesting to me—which pictures people chose to go that extra mile for, framing and displaying them in their offices and homes. In Sky's case, her most cherished images were of a mother she'd barely known, and her work friends. It was a little sad.

I gazed at Dylan. He looked so different in the staff pic. Healthy and happy, with Sky to his right, Elspeth to his left, all of them relaxed, Dylan's blond curls gleaming in the sun. It made me think: Maybe it wasn't these people that Sky cherished. Maybe it was the day—that long-ago springlike day in the Common, when Dylan appeared to be sober and everyone was in good spirits, Maurice's arm around Sky, Sky's arm around Dylan. A photo taken before Rhonda's daughter had died, back when Gonzo was a brand-new start-up and no one could imagine a metal detector in the corporate offices or a young chemist found dead on the factory floor, when these disparate people shared the same silly dream and the only thing anyone was guilty of was being overly optimistic about that dream's chances at becoming real.

I put the photo down. I was giving Sky's life way too much thought. She wasn't the one I was looking for, after all. It was Dylan. Where was Dylan? Would I be able to find him before he destroyed more lives?

# THIRTY-SIX

I moved quickly to Sky's dresser to gather her things, placing them in the duffel bag she said I'd find on her closet shelf. From a shoe rack in the same roomy and well-organized closet, I took the pair of Chucks she requested—the red ones she'd been wearing yesterday, when we met. Next, I grabbed her toiletry bag out of the primary bathroom.

As I was about to leave the bedroom, my phone dinged. It was a text from Lee.

*Thanks for talking to Sky. We have her on tape now, identifying Welch as the shooter.*

*No problem*, I responded. *You hear back from the lab about that baggie Trevor Weiss was carrying?*

ALISON GAYLIN

His text arrived quickly, crossing paths with mine: *Lab thinks the substance in the bag is a designer drug that contains a very powerful distilled alkaloid.*

I replied: *Like cocaine?*

*More like a much stronger nicotine,* he wrote. *Not much of a high. Whole point is that it's highly addictive.*

I typed: *Why would Dylan want that?*

Lee responded: *Your guess is as good as mine.*

I stared at my phone, thinking about, of all things, what Lydia had told me the other evening. When I was talking to her over my Bluetooth, just before I got into that high-speed chase with Moon's baseball cap–wearing flunky, she told me about Dylan's phone conversation with the "research scientist," how skeptical she'd been about it—and how she'd overheard Dylan saying, *What's the point if there's no buzz?*

I had a thought. It was a compelling one that had come to me quickly, Lydia's voice in my mind and that staff picture right in front of me, those raised cans of a then-harmless new product. Things were adding up a little too quickly.

*Thx*, I texted Lee.

I put down the duffel bag and moved over to Sky's computer. I turned it on, thinking of Blake, his sudden love for Gonzo, how strange he'd been acting over the past few days, and of the awful crash once I forced him to quit cold turkey. Blake—who normally thought of sugary soda as poison—had downed an entire case . . .

*The whole point is that it's highly addictive.*

I started to scan the desktop. I felt bad for doing this. Sky had been through so much already. Yet Rand Carlson, that fetus-faced lab supervisor, had said it himself: *Mr. Welch isn't the kind of person who likes seeing how the sausage gets made.*

Sky was, though. Sky—the ultimate pleaser, who lived and breathed Gonzo to the point of turning her living room into an eyesore, just to match the cans—was more than willing to make the sausage herself. After seeing the company take a hit following the death of Rhonda's daughter, Sky, Carlson told me, had asked for his "best and brightest" to come up with a new formula. Which brought us straight to the doomed Trevor Weiss, the baggie of this "highly addictive" substance sewn into his jacket.

According to Rand Carlson, Trevor Weiss had worked closely with Sky and other corporate people on that formula, this tiny brain trust, devoted to the same project for weeks, if not months. Who wouldn't grow close in a situation like that? Yet one day after his tragic death, Sky—kind, empathetic Sky—had referred to Trevor as simply "that lab tech."

I remembered the text on Dylan's phone: *WHERE R U?* Somehow, on some device somewhere, the two of them had arranged a meeting. Maybe it wasn't because Trevor was trying to extort money from Dylan or sell him drugs. Maybe he was trying to alert him as to what his COO had done to the formula— without knowing Dylan was in on it. And maybe that's why Dylan had shot him, later bragging about it in that audio message to Elspeth.

Was Sky Dylan's accomplice—or was it the other way around? And if that was the case, why had he tried to kill her?

I scanned Sky's desktop. I wasn't sure what I was looking for—research papers on the addictive effects of certain alkaloids when mixed with carbonated water and caffeine, maybe. Or a nondisclosure agreement regarding all scientific work on Gonzo's new formula, made out to and signed by Trevor Weiss.

Of course, I had no such luck. There were no documents in sight. The screen was filled with audio and video files, which made sense, I supposed, for someone who had double-majored in data sciences.

I was probably barking up the wrong tree. All Lee had said was "highly addictive" substance, and here I was, turning Sky into the Griselda Blanco of energy drinks, with Dylan her disgruntled partner in crime.

I was about to shut the computer down when I noticed one video file. Sky had named it Gonzo Marilyn. I had no idea what that could possibly mean—and I was curious enough to want to sneak a look.

The video file was only one and a half minutes long. I tapped the PLAY button.

It was black-and-white footage of Marilyn Monroe in that famous glittering dress she wore to celebrate JFK's birthday. I would have thought for sure it was archival—save for the fact that Marilyn was holding a can of Gonzo. "Happy birthday, Mr. President," Marilyn crooned in her whispery voice, before toasting the camera with the anachronistic can and then kissing it, as though it were an Academy Award. "Have a Gonzo with me."

I actually gasped. It was the creepiest thing I'd ever seen: a perfect deep-fake video, in which Marilyn's every gesture looked real and natural, the lips synched expertly with the voice. And the voice . . . The voice was perfect.

My phone buzzed. I nearly jumped out of my skin. I pulled it out of my bag and looked at the screen. Sky's name was on it. My stomach tightened. I shut down the computer fast, as though she could see me through the screen—and for all I knew, she may have developed that technology, too. I took a deep breath, put on a smile, and answered, forcing myself to sound normal. "Hey, Sky."

"Hey, Sunny," she said. "I was just wondering if you were able to find everything okay."

"Yeah," I said. "I, uh, couldn't find the Chucks at first, but now I've got them, and I'm on my way back."

"It turns out the doctors and I were a little over-optimistic," she said. "They want to keep me overnight for observation, so no need to rush. But whenever you get a chance, I'd love to have my stuff anyway. I'm hoping they let me out first thing tomorrow."

"Sure," I said. "I'll be there before visiting hours are over."

"Thank you so much," she said. "The pain is really starting to set in, and the thought of my having to wear that Gucci suit . . ."

I forced a laugh. "Say no more."

I ended the call. *Don't assume.* I said it out loud. "Don't assume. You don't know anything yet. Stop creating narratives in your head until you have the facts to back them up."

*Don't assume. Think. Doubt. Ask questions. Learn the truth.*

I grabbed the duffel bag and left her apartment quickly. Once I was outside in the cold, late-afternoon air, I found Elspeth's number on my phone and called it.

"Oh, hi, Sunny," she said. "Spike just made me lobster mac and cheese and he's mixing me a margarita."

"Lucky you."

"Right?"

"I'll let you get back to it, but I wanted to ask you one question."

"Yeah?"

"That phone call you got from Dylan this morning, when he told you to go back to the office."

"Yeah?"

"You said you kept trying to ask him why he wanted you to do all these things, but he wouldn't tell you."

"That's right," she said. "It was scary. But also pretty annoying."

"I get that," I said. "Can you tell me, though, if he ever spoke to you directly during this conversation?"

"What do you mean?"

"Did he respond to or repeat anything you said? Did he answer any of your questions? It can be as minor as his saying 'Yeah' or 'No.' Or getting angry with you. Telling you to shut up."

"No, he didn't."

"Did he say anything to you at all that didn't sound like he was reading from a script?"

"No," she said. "I'm telling you. He just kept repeating the same things, over and over and over."

"Thank you," I said—the idea I had, the suspicion, solidifying in my mind. *Of course he did. Of course he just kept repeating himself.* I thought about Lydia, all her hopes hinging on the concept that, no matter what he'd done, her son was close by and that we had proof he was alive. I didn't want to have to tell her what I'd been thinking—not until I was absolutely sure.

"Sunny?"

"Yeah?"

"Why are you asking me this?"

"Just a theory I'm working on," I said quickly. "I'll tell you about it later."

I hung up before Elspeth could say anything more.

There was a sweet little park outside this hulking new building, with a wrought-iron fence and a few benches, planted with delicate pink cyclamen and waxy bromeliads. The park may have been new, or, like so many things in this world, it could have been there all along and I'd just never noticed it.

I sat down on one of the benches and took deep breaths and tried my best to collect my thoughts. *Don't jump to conclusions,*

I told myself. *Keep asking questions. The truth will work itself out like a splinter.*

All the while, though, I kept thinking about Sky, of her dual major in biotechnology and data sciences—and of her shocking ability to re-create voices.

# THIRTY-SEVEN

S ince Sky had told me I didn't have to rush to bring her
the clothes, I figured I'd do what I'd planned to when I
first took the case: talk to Dylan Welch's girlfriend-turned-
stalking-victim, Teresa Leone. Only now that my focus had
shifted to Sky, I had an entirely different set of questions.

I knew where Teresa worked—a PR firm near Copley Square
called Nichols and Associates. It was walking distance from
Sky's apartment building, and when I called her direct line and
asked if I could come by, Teresa said, "Sure," adding, "Is this
about you-know-who?"

"Partly," I said.

"Well, now I'm intrigued."

"I am, too." Though there was probably a better word for
what I was feeling.

"There's a Starbucks in my lobby, with places to sit," she said. "If you get there before me, grab us a table. I'll buy us a couple of lattes."

"Decaf for me. And you don't have to buy."

"I insist," she said. "It's the least I can do."

With my purse over one shoulder and Sky's duffel bag over the other, I reached the building within ten minutes. It was a mirrored high-rise that managed to dwarf the Public Library without being obtrusive—a building designed to reflect the beauty of its neighbors. There were many architectural juxtapositions like this in Boston—the new and historic coexisting harmoniously. It wasn't like that down the Shore, where the historic district was its own separate entity. Yet one more thing to get used to, I supposed, if I decided to relocate. *If.*

After I found the Starbucks, I started to phone Teresa to tell her I'd arrived, but she was already sitting at a table, our two lattes in front of her, waving at me as though we were old friends. I was a little confused by all this enthusiasm, as I'd been by her insistence on buying.

I'd spoken to her only once—and it wasn't as though our conversation had been particularly enjoyable, centered, as it was, around Dylan.

Yet when I sat down, the first thing she said to me was, "I've been meaning to send you flowers or something."

She slid the decaf to me. I took a sip. "Why?"

"You scared Dylan Welch away."

"I *did*?"

"One chat with you, he's never spied on me, texted me,

called me, or purposefully run into me again. I'm free. I can go out with my new boyfriend without worrying about him showing up wasted and threatening to cut him." Teresa smiled. "I don't have to wear disguises anymore."

I'd thought she looked different. The last time I saw her, Teresa had on a face full of makeup, a lacquered updo, and heels—aging herself by at least a decade—all so she wouldn't be recognized by Dylan. Today she was wearing a pink T-shirt, a charcoal blazer, jeans, and boots, her hair loose. Minimal makeup. Younger, more comfortable, and, I imagined, more like herself.

"I wouldn't quite call it a chat," I said. "How did you find out about that, though?"

"Lydia called me," she said. "She said he was in rehab, he wouldn't be bothering me anymore, and that you had taught him a lesson. She apologized for him." Teresa grinned. "I don't know how you did it, but thank you."

"Well, my dog helped."

"I remember that dog."

"Everybody does."

She sipped her latte. "So what can I help *you* with?" she said. "Like I said, I haven't heard a word from Dylan."

"Well, he's actually been missing for the past couple of weeks."

She frowned. "Really?"

"I was hired by his mother to try and find him."

Teresa put her cup down. "Wow," she said quietly. "Poor Lydia. She must be hurting."

"She is," I said.

"I'm sorry," Teresa said. "I couldn't have imagined saying this six months ago, but I really do hope he's okay."

"I hope so, too," I said, thinking of Lydia. That pained smile. *At least we know Dylan's close by . . .*

"So you met Dylan at Harvard," I said.

"Yep."

"I'm assuming that when you were there you had a similar circle of friends."

"Well, mine was a little wider," she said. "But more or less, yes."

"I wanted to ask you about Dylan's friend, Sky Farley."

"Oh, Sky," she said. "She was everybody's friend."

"Really?"

"Yeah, we all loved her," she said. "What do you want to know?"

"I'm interested in her hobbies," I said.

"She had a ton of hobbies," she said. "That brilliant, restless mind of hers. I never quite got why she hung out with Dylan. I mean, don't get me wrong. *I* hung out with Dylan back then, but she was so far ahead of us in terms of intellect."

"She was a science major, right?"

"Yeah, but she was also very creative," Teresa said.

"How so?"

"I mean . . . Dylan kept talking about film school, right? But I always thought Sky would be the one to make it big in Hollywood."

"As a sound designer?" I asked. "Or creating CGI?"

Teresa blinked at me. "No, as an actress," she said. "She was in all the plays, and she was amazing. She could do everything from Shakespearean tragedies to sketch comedy—and she could burst into tears at the drop of a hat."

My eyes widened. *"Really?"*

She sipped her latte. "Why do you ask?"

"Well, she works with Dylan at Gonzo now," I said.

"Yeah, I'd heard that."

"I don't know if you saw this, but there was a shooting today . . ."

"Oh my God. The female employee?"

I nodded slowly.

"That was Sky?"

"Yes," I said.

"Oh, no . . ."

"She's going to be okay." I drank some of my latte. It was very hot. "They're releasing her from the hospital in the morning."

"Thank God. I saw that story on my newsfeed today. Terrifying. I can't believe it was *her.*"

"I know," I said. "It seemed touch and go for a little while there. She was very lucky."

Teresa shook her head, both hands resting on the cardboard cup as though it were a crystal ball. "You're looking for Dylan, though."

"Yes," I said.

"So . . . does that mean you think that Dylan's disappearance and Sky's shooting might be related?"

I almost started to explain the entire situation to her but

stopped myself. People like Teresa—they had an ability to make you feel as though you knew them better than you did. Like you could trust them before that trust was earned. I'm sure it was helpful in PR. It certainly was in my line of work, and I was able to recognize this because I had a similar skill set. I made sure not to take the bait.

"I'm just looking into everything at this point," I said.

She drank her latte. I drank mine.

"Why did you say 'sound design'?" Teresa asked.

"Just . . . venturing a guess," I said.

"And why were you asking about Sky's hobbies? Do you think Sky's hobbies had something to do with her shooting—or with Dylan's disappearance?"

"Hey." I said it as lightly as I could. "Who's doing the investigating here—you or me?" I brought the cup to my lips and gulped down too much latte. My throat burned.

She put her cup down and laughed a little. "Sorry," she said. "I mean . . . I'm obviously jumping to conclusions. But I was wondering if maybe she might have pranked the wrong person."

My back stiffened. "What do you mean, 'pranked'?"

Teresa shifted in her chair. She ran her hands through her shiny hair, pulling it back into a ponytail and letting it go. "Okay, so when we were in college," she said, "Sky used to record people and play with their voices. I think it all started for a class project, but then it just became something she liked doing. Deep-fake audio and video. You know what that is?"

I coughed. "Yes," I said. "I know what it is."

"A lot of people don't, even now. And Sky was doing it seven years ago. Just for fun."

"Was she good?" I asked.

Teresa snorted, which I took for a yes. "The one time I can ever remember her getting into trouble at school was when she created this video of one of our professors—a jerk of a guy named Dr. Stiffly."

"That was his real name?"

She nodded. "And God help you if you ever cracked a smile over it," she said.

I shook my head. "I'd have changed it if I were him."

"Same," she said. "Anyway, Sky made a video of Dr. Stiffly singing 'I'm a Little Teapot,' with all the gestures and everything. She posted it on Instagram, and the Dean was furious. Sky wound up in front of a faculty tribunal. Nearly got kicked out of school. It was so funny, though. We all thought it was worth it."

She laughed. I tried to laugh along, waiting for the right moment to ask my next question. It took a while.

"Teresa?" I asked finally.

"Yeah?"

"Did Sky ever do prank phone calls using recorded voices?" I held my breath, waiting for the answer.

Her smile evaporated. "Not with me." She said it slowly, carefully, her entire posture changing—until I caught a hint of the frightened girl I'd met back in July.

"Okay, not with you," I said. "But with somebody else?"

"It wasn't what you'd call a prank."

"What would you call it?"

"I think Sky called it a favor," she said. "But Dylan didn't feel that way."

I looked at her. "What happened?"

"Dylan had gotten into a fight with his father. I don't even remember what it was about—there were so many. But this one was really bad. Bill threatened to cut him off completely. Dylan claimed he didn't care. Lydia was begging him to apologize, asking me if I could get to him, but I couldn't. Dylan was adamant. Plus, he was abusing Adderall, I think, which made him even more stubborn."

"So Sky came to the rescue?"

"Yep," Teresa said. "Sky patched together audio of Dylan making this eloquent apology, telling his dad how much he appreciated him, all kinds of stuff Dylan would never have dreamed of saying in real life," she said. "Then she called Bill from Dylan's phone, played him this Franken-apology. Bill was touched. All was forgiven. He even back-paid Dylan for the weeks he withheld his allowance."

"Did Dylan ever find out why?"

"Yeah, and he was furious," Teresa said. "He didn't talk to Sky for months."

"I can't really say I blame him," I said.

"I guess I can't, either," she said. "But at the time . . . I don't know. I felt so sorry for Sky. She was only trying to help out a friend."

"That always seems to be her motivation," I said. "But in this case, she also made sure that the friend kept his fortune."

Teresa didn't seem to be listening. "I was scared for her," she said.

"Why?"

"Sky told me that when he found out what she'd done, Dylan got this look on his face, like a wild animal. I mean . . . She played the apology for me, and it was beautiful. She'd actually worked really hard on it, and, I don't know . . . for Dylan to react that harshly, to not even take into account her motivations . . ."

I gaped at her. "She used those words?"

"Huh?"

"You said Sky told you that Dylan got a look on his face, 'like a wild animal,'" I said. "Were those the exact words she used?"

She narrowed her eyes. "Yes," Teresa said. "I'll never forget it. Years later, I saw that look and I finally knew what she was talking about. And the way she cried when she said it, you know? Sky's tough. I'd never seen her cry before that."

"Except onstage," I said. "You told me yourself. She could burst into tears at the drop of a hat."

"Well, yeah, Sunny. But that's obviously not the same thing."

An image of Sky sobbing in her hospital bed flashed through my mind, remembering the fight they'd had before Dylan's disappearance over the missing funds—the first time, according to her, that she'd ever seen him shift gears like that. The very first time. *He got this look on his face . . . like a wild animal . . .*

"No, it's not the same thing," I echoed back to Teresa.

I didn't mean it, though.

We talked some more, finishing up our lattes. Then I thanked Teresa for meeting with me.

"Was what I said helpful?" she asked.

"Very."

"Really?" she said. "Is this info about Sky going to help bring you closer to Dylan?"

I exhaled. "Further, actually," I said. "But that's okay."

Teresa squinted at me for several seconds, as though I was some ancient text she was trying to decipher. "You work in mysterious ways, Sunny Randall."

I gave her a smile. "I try," I said.

We said goodbye, Teresa wishing me luck in finding Dylan and me wishing her luck in staying away from him.

After she was gone, I glanced at Sky's duffel, sitting so innocently next to my chair, and then I thought about Lydia, that shred of hope in her eyes—the thought that, even if he did need to be brought to justice, at least her only son was still alive. I couldn't guarantee her that now, though. I couldn't guarantee her anything. Sky had deep-faked Dylan's voice on a phone call seven years ago, with the technology available back then—and it was so good that his own father hadn't known the difference.

Who's to say she hadn't been doing it again with Elspeth?

I put in a quick call to Blake, who reminded me that at six-thirty tonight was my standing drinks-and-catch-up with my dad at The Street Bar. "He called to remind you," Blake said. "He didn't want to bother you during the workday on your phone." Blake told me that if I was too busy, he could reschedule for me, but I said no. I needed someone to talk to about all this—someone who I knew could help me put it all together. "It actually couldn't happen at a better time," I said.

After I ended the call, I picked up the duffel and walked back to my car. I'd be going to the hospital next—not because I had any desire to see Sky Farley right now, but because her things were giving me a serious case of the heebie-jeebies.

# THIRTY-EIGHT

S ky was in a meeting when I arrived at her hospital room.
That was the only way to describe the scene I walked into.
Her IVs appeared to have been removed, and she was sitting up
in bed, her arm in a sling, her shoulder bandaged, and the
jacket from the Gucci suit Lydia had given her wrapped around
her shoulders. Clustered around the bed were Kaitlyn from
Marketing and three young women with sleek buns and center
parts, all of them wearing pant suits in primary colors. If it
wasn't for the bed, the bandages, and the hospital gown Sky
wore under the fitted jacket, they could have easily been in a
boardroom, strategizing a campaign. Which, as it turned out,
was exactly what they were doing.

"Sunny! Thank God!" Sky said. She told me to set the duffel
bag next to her bed. "I can't wait to get those clothes on, once

we're through. I mean, even if I have to stick around here, at least I don't have to be freezing my tush off."

I was going to ask her what it was they were going to be through with, but Lydia went ahead and answered. She was sitting in a chair against the wall. I hadn't even noticed she was there until she spoke. "They're crafting a statement for the press about the shooting," she said.

My eyebrows went up. "Do the police know about that?"

"I'm not sure," Lydia said.

"Normally, they don't like people talking to reporters about an active investigation," I said.

"It's just a statement," Sky said. "To get the media off our backs. It's about me, my recovery. Not Dylan. He won't even be mentioned."

"But *you* haven't been mentioned," I said. "The only thing the police have revealed to the press is that the shooting victim was female."

"Oh, I checked with Detective Farrell," she said. "He told me if I wanted to out myself as the victim, that's fine. I just can't give any details about Dylan or the investigation."

Sky didn't wait for my response. Instead, she turned to Kaitlyn and her backup dancers. "I think the release reads great as is. But down the line—and I know this is going to sound weird—this shooting might wind up being good PR for us."

"Oh my God," Kaitlyn said. "I was thinking the same thing."

"Like . . . Gonzo. The gangster brand," Sky said.

Kaitlyn grinned. "*Very* that," she said.

"Or even. Wait . . . You ready?" one of the pantsuits, the red one, said.

The rest of them nodded enthusiastically.

"Gonzo can help you survive anything—even getting shot. We can do outreach on TikTok."

"Oh, that's *good*," Kaitlyn said.

"Just as long as we don't encourage anyone to test that theory out," Sky said. "It would be worse than the cinnamon challenge. Remember that?"

Kaitlyn and the pantsuits all laughed in unison.

I looked at Lydia. She was alone now, still sitting in that chair, staring at her shoes. "Where's Bill?" I asked her.

"He had to get back to work," she said softly. "He asked if I needed him to stay, but I told him I don't mind. The truth is, at this point, I prefer being alone."

Kaitlyn was saying something to Sky about a photo shoot for *Boston* magazine. "I'm thinking you in some skimpy, sexy Versace number, showing off your bullet wound."

"I don't know, Kaitlyn," Sky said. "Versace? Really?"

Lydia stood up. "I need a breath of fresh air," she said.

Sky was suggesting Balenciaga instead, "or some other brand that's not associated with a shooting death," when I decided I needed fresh air, too.

I started to follow Lydia, but then Sky asked me if it would be too much trouble to put her duffel in the small standing closet against the wall, and then Blue Pantsuit recognized me from the *Globe* article and asked, "What's it like to be a PI?"

"Every day it's different," I answered. "Sometimes it's boring as hell; other times, it's chaotic." The others joined in: "What's the most dangerous case you've ever taken?" "Do you carry a gun?" "Have you ever met Spenser?" Blah, blah, blah.

I tried to answer them as succinctly as I could without being rude or calling attention to my newfound distrust of Sky. By the time I finally managed to pull myself out of the room and into the hallway, Lydia was slumped against the wall in her Hermès suit, her knees against her chest, her arms clasped around them, and her head bowed. I couldn't imagine seeing Lydia Welch in this position, ever. And yet here she was, curled into a ball on a hospital floor.

"Lydia?" I said. "Are you all right?"

She looked up at me. Her face was red, her eyes bloodshot. "What's wrong?" I asked.

"My son," she said quietly. "My son is what's wrong."

I just looked at her.

"He murdered a young man. He tried to kill his best friend," she said. "I knew he'd done some bad things in the past, but nothing like this. And I can't help but think . . . if Bill and I had seen the warning signs. If we'd forced him to get real help instead of these ridiculous rehab stays . . ."

I moved closer to her. "You don't necessarily know that he shot either of them."

"Sunny, his Rolex was found in the factory, not far from where that poor young scientist was killed."

"It was?"

"Yes."

"When?"

"Last night."

"Who told you?"

"Detective Farrell."

Apparently, Lee kept information from me, too . . .

"He questioned Bill and me after Sky," Lydia was saying. "He brought the watch in an evidence bag and asked if it looked familiar. Of course it did. We gave it to him. It was Dylan's high school graduation present. It's a very rare pearlescent gold, and it's engraved. *We're so proud! Love, Mommy and Dad,* it says."

I thought of Sky. I was now 95 percent sure that she'd been the source of the audio messages and phone calls that had been sent to Elspeth—the only "proof" that Dylan had committed either shooting, other than Sky's masterly acted eyewitness account. So now there was also the Rolex. Conveniently placed near the dead body of the man who knew of a highly addictive substance that I now believed Sky had sneaked into Gonzo's new formula.

I heard myself say, "Doesn't the Rolex seem a little obvious to you?"

Lydia blinked at me. "What do you mean?"

"Why would Dylan leave the watch behind, on a night when he was clearly so careful about everything else? Why is he leaving no fingerprints or footprints or shell casings or DNA— only to conveniently lose a big, clunky, unusual-looking timepiece, with an engraving that makes it extremely identifiable?"

She said nothing.

"Lydia," I said. "Do you understand the meaning behind these questions?"

"I don't know, Sunny," she said. "I feel like a more important question is: Why is my son shooting people?"

I exhaled. "What I'm saying is, I think it might have been someone else who left Dylan's watch at the crime scene."

"And I think you're grasping at straws," Lydia said. "Believe me, I appreciate the effort. But Dylan has not taken off that watch since we gave it to him."

I remembered the picture Lydia had posted on Facebook and tagged her son in—that long-ago weekend in Nantucket, Dylan posing with his parents, his cousins, Teresa at his side, Dylan the dictionary definition of *privilege*, that pearly Rolex glinting in the sun as proof. I'd seen it in the family pictures on Dylan's computer, in that happy Gonzo staff shot in the Common, announcing its owner's wealth from behind Sky's glass frame.

But I'd also seen it somewhere else . . . My brain could have been playing tricks on me, recalling things I hadn't seen, just to fit into this freshly forming narrative. But still, it was worth checking, because, if it was true, Dylan most assuredly did take off the watch from time to time. I pulled my phone out of my purse and opened my photographs.

"What are you doing?" Lydia said.

I found it before I needed to answer: the close-up of Bella (*Some influencer*, according to Sky). I gazed at that perfectly manicured hand against the side of her face. Those coral fingernails.

That unusual pearlescent watch. I showed it to Lydia. Tapped Bella's wrist. "Isn't this Dylan's Rolex?"

Lydia's eyes widened. "Yes," she said, very quietly. "That's it."

"See?" I said. "He doesn't always keep track of the watch. He might have given it to someone. It might have been stolen from him and planted at the crime scene." I thought about Sky again, but I didn't want to say her name. Not now, with Lydia's emotions at this pitch, knowing how deeply she cared for Sky. *Like a second child.* I couldn't do that to her now. "More and more, Lydia," I said, "I feel like someone might be trying to frame your son."

I reached for my phone, but she held on to it. She was staring at the image. "Where did you get this picture?" she asked.

"It was on Dylan's work computer," I said. He had four photos of this girl, including his screensaver. So I figured it was worth saving."

I looked at Lydia. She was still staring at my phone. "I didn't know they were still in touch," she said.

"Who?"

"The girl in this picture is Anna Horton," she said. "Dylan's prom date from Exeter. She's changed a lot. But I'd know her anywhere. She and Dylan were quite close back then."

"She was on your list," I said. "The one that you gave me."

"I put down everyone I could think of, but I certainly didn't think Anna's contact info would help you. The last I heard, she was in a very bad way—like Dylan. Maybe worse."

"Really?"

She nodded. "After graduation, her father left her mother

for a twenty-two-year-old actress. He moved out to Hollywood. Her mother was hospitalized for mental health issues. Anna dropped out of college and just . . . disappeared for a while."

"And resurfaced in Boston, apparently," I said.

"Apparently." She touched the picture on my screen. "You know, I always hoped that Anna and Dylan would find each other again," she said. "Two lost souls. I thought maybe they could heal together."

My gaze shifted from Lydia's face to the photograph on my phone. "I thought her name was Bella," I said. "That's what Dylan named the photo files."

Lydia looked up at me, her eyes wistful and sad. "Her full name is Annabella," she said. "She must have changed what she calls herself. Who could blame her, really?"

# THIRTY-NINE

Y ou're holding back on me," I told Lee Farrell. I was in my
car, in heavy traffic again, on my way home to walk and
feed Rosie before meeting my dad at The Street Bar. Blake had
reminded me about our standing drinks date—again—when I
went back to the office to answer emails, shut down my computer, and listen to Blake's updates. Sadly, none of the contacts
on Lydia's list had returned our phone calls, and there had
been no replies to Blake's emails, either. I couldn't even share
in Blake's disappointment because I could hardly speak. I was
that tired. One thing was certain: I planned on taking an Uber
to The Newbury. After all the time I'd spent in my car over the
past few days, I really needed a break from driving.

"What do you mean, I'm holding back on you?" Lee said.

"Hello? Dylan's Rolex. Found near Trevor Weiss's body. I had to find out from Lydia Welch."

Lee let out an enormous sigh. "I needed a positive identification on the watch before I could even consider it evidence. It would have been pointless to tell you about it this early," he said. "And anyway, you're holding back on me, too."

"What do you mean?"

There was a long pause. I waited. The only thing I was holding back on was that final call from "Dylan" to Elspeth—and I'd promised her I wouldn't come forward with that . . . for now.

"Seriously, Lee," I said finally. "What do you mean?"

Lee chuckled. "Okay, okay," he said. "I was just trying to fake you out."

"Good one," I said—which beat the hell out of *Whew.*

"I try," he said.

"It's actually kind of ironic," I said. "Because the reason why I called is sort of the opposite of holding back."

"Oh, really?"

"Yes," I said. "I've gathered a lot of information within the past few hours. And if you have time, I'm just going to lay it all out, and you and your team can use it however you want."

"I have time," he said.

"Okay," I said. "Here goes . . ."

I was about ten blocks away from my loft, but the streets were congested to the point where the rest of the trip home would last at least fifteen minutes. And so I took up a good percentage of that time telling Lee everything I'd learned—starting with Sky's surprising skill at deep-fake audio recordings, and the fact that close to ten years ago, she'd made one of Dylan's voice that was accurate enough to fool his own father. From there, I moved on to Sky's much-lauded acting talent when she was at Harvard, and Teresa's recollection of her being able to "burst into tears at the drop of a hat," making her sudden "recollection" of Dylan shooting her more suspect—to me, anyway—than it had been at the time.

I spoke then about the "highly addictive" alkaloid substance that Lee already knew about—placed into a baggie and sewn into the lining of Trevor Weiss's jacket. The doomed Trevor Weiss, who was recruited by Sky to work on Gonzo's new formula and had seemed unusually "intense" in recent weeks, according to his supervisor, spending a lot more time than usual on the phone. At least one of those calls may very well have been to Dylan, whose mother had overheard him say, *What's the point if there's no buzz?*

"Can you guess what the point was?" I said it to Lee as though I were a grade-school teacher.

And Lee answered like the conscientious young honors student that he'd undoubtedly been. "They put the alkaloid blend in the new Gonzo formula without listing it in the ingredients—even though it's technically as legal as those crazy mushroom tinctures they advertise online as 'immunity boosters.' The alkaloid gets customers hooked. Sales go up. Everybody's happy."

"Except Trevor, who felt guilty and contacted the one higher-up he knew of who had no idea what the hell was going on."

"Let me get this straight," he said. "You don't think Dylan Welch is responsible for either of the shootings."

"No."

"You think Sky pieced together fake audio messages with Dylan's voice and convincingly scared Elspeth into getting Dylan's gun for her, as well as deleting files. Stuff like that."

"I think that was one of three things she accomplished," I said.

"What were two and three?"

"Well, she also made sure that Elspeth kept quiet about anything Trevor might have told her—which is why I think she targeted her in the first place."

"Because Elspeth went out with Trevor a few times."

"Yep," I said. "And the third thing this plan did was, if Elspeth were to get fed up and go to the police, she'd give them the audio messages as evidence that Dylan killed Trevor—which, in my opinion, would be much more convincing than some stupid watch."

"Interesting," Lee said.

"Isn't it?"

"There's only one problem," he said. "Somebody shot Sky. She didn't do it herself. Not from that distance or that angle. If it wasn't Dylan who shot her, who was it?"

I winced. "Shit," I said, immediately thinking of Elspeth—the panic attack that sent her to the emergency room, those last instructions from "Dylan"—which were issued not via audio message, but on an unrecorded phone call. Did Sky finally come clean with Elspeth . . . only to threaten her even more severely into shooting her in a nonlethal spot?

*If Sky trusted Elspeth enough to believe she could do that, she's crazier than I thought. Luckier, too.*

"We never tested Elspeth for gunpowder residue," Lee said. It was as though he'd been reading my mind.

"Jesus," I said. "The poor kid."

"Yeah," Lee said. "But only if this theory of yours turns out to be true."

I sighed heavily. "Come on."

"Look, don't get me wrong. Everything you've said makes sense," he said, "but an overheard phone call, a bag of turbo-nicotine, and info about Sky's hobbies back in college couldn't indict a ham sandwich."

I frowned. "I don't think that's the saying," I said.

"Whatever," he said.

"Fine. You're right. A prosecutor wouldn't like any of this," I said. "There's no solid evidence. Yet."

"You know it's true," he said. "Intriguing though it is."

"Think about it, okay?"

"I'll do more than that."

"That said, can you do me a little favor?"

"I suppose you're going to tell me I owe you one."

"If you don't now," I said, "you will later."

Lee chuckled. "Can't argue with that," he said.

"I'm looking for an old friend of Dylan's, but all I have is a phone number that doesn't work and an email address from Lydia that's probably ten years old," I said. "I think Dylan's been with her recently, though. I saw photos . . . She may know where he is."

"Have you tried checking her social media?"

"My assistant, Blake, did, but it's private," I said. "Here's the thing, though. Lydia Welch says this girl's been in a bad way with drugs, so I'm thinking she may have been arrested at least once."

"Worth a try," Lee said.

"Okay," I said. "So her name is Annabella Horton. Probably five-six, white, with dark hair, brown eyes, tan or spray-tanned. Dylan's age, so twenty-seven, twenty-eight—"

"Say her name again."

"Annabella Horton? I think she's been going by Bella recently."

"Hold on a sec."

I heard Lee talking to someone, but I couldn't make out the words. I waited, inching ever closer to my home. *At this rate,* I thought, *I may not even have time to change clothes before drinks.*

I was about five blocks away from my building and debating parking here, despite the cold, when Lee came back to the phone. "Well, I've got good news and bad news about Annabella Horton," he said.

"Good news first."

"I know who she is," he said. "I recognized the name right away."

"Who is she?"

"That's the bad news," he said. "I knew the name because it belongs to a body we just identified."

My heart sank. "Oh . . ."

"She was found in the Charles a few weeks ago. Floating. Cause of death probable opiate overdose."

I gripped the steering wheel, thinking of Lydia, what she'd said about two lost souls. "When you say a few weeks ago," I said, "when exactly do you mean?"

"Well, the ME estimated that when she was found as a Jane Doe, she'd been dead for less than twenty-four hours," he said. "And that was a week before Thanksgiving."

I didn't say anything for a long while. It wasn't until Lee asked me if I was still there and the breath exited my lungs in a whoosh that I realized I'd stopped breathing.

"That's it," I said, those texts on Dylan's phone blazing through my brain: *MURDERER, MURDERER, MURDERER . . .* All dated around Thanksgiving, when Dylan left his phone in his messy desk drawer—and, in the dead of night on a holiday weekend, escaped his office and his day-to-day life. "He blames himself for Annabella's death," I said. "And whoever sent those texts scared him into hiding."

"I think you lost me," Lee said.

"It's okay," I said. "I'm just theorizing again."

# FORTY

**D**o you think he's still alive?" my dad asked, sipping his
Hendrick's martini. He was talking about Dylan Welch.

"I do," I said. "But I'll admit I don't have a logical reason for
feeling that way."

We were sitting at our favorite table at The Street Bar, the
two of us in comfy chairs under low lighting. I sipped a very
dry Chablis, snacking on potato chips, mixed nuts, and green
olives. I'd just given Dad the full update on this increasingly
bizarre case.

I'd found it a lot easier than talking to Lee. One, because I
didn't have to worry about keeping any information from
my father. And two, because The Street Bar was so damn atmospheric. It reminded me, in a way, of Susan Silverman's
office—not so much in terms of décor but in its sense of calm.

How strange was it that, just twenty-four hours earlier, I'd been there, in Susan's office, complaining about Richie, his suggestion that I ease up on "dangerous" cases like this one fresh in my mind and stinging? *One day ago.* It felt like a year . . . Regardless, this place did make me realize how much more enjoyable therapy would be if booze and snacks were provided.

"Think about it," Dad was saying. "Welch may have supplied the drugs that led to this girl's overdose, when he'd nearly died himself just a couple weeks earlier. If he has a conscience, that might have been enough to send him over the edge. If he's conscience-free, he had plenty of practical reasons: The Mob was after him, and maybe he'd been made aware, maybe not . . . he was the prime suspect in a murder and in the attempted murder of his best friend." My dad took a sip. "Not much to live for."

"I've thought about all that," I said. "It's true. But my intuition says otherwise."

"What exactly does it say?"

I took a sip of my Chablis and ate a few more potato chips. I was hogging all the snacks, but I couldn't help it. I was starving. I'd barely eaten since the bagels this morning. "I guess I just keep thinking about what Lydia Welch said when she first hired me," I said. "She told me she has a connection with Dylan. She knows he's alive and he needs her help . . . Jeez, saying it out loud . . . I know it sounds like a bunch of woo-woo crap."

"*Woo-woo?*" Dad said.

"Mumbo jumbo," I said.

"Ah. Well, actually, no, it doesn't," he said. "Parents can sense these things. It's not mumbo jumbo. It's a part of nature." He smiled.

I smiled back. "Oh, I almost forgot," I said. "The head of security at Gonzo is a former cop, and he remembers you fondly."

"Who doesn't—I mean, who isn't dead or in jail?"

I shrugged. "I can't think of anybody." I sipped more of my Chablis.

"So what was the fellow's name?" he said.

"Maurice Dupree."

"Hmm . . ." He stared off into space for a moment, then started to laugh. "I remember Maurice," he said. "I liked him a lot."

I drank more wine. "Well, the feeling's mutual."

"Not the greatest cop, but a sweet, sweet guy."

"Not the greatest cop?"

Dad sighed. He drank his martini. His hand trembled a bit as he raised the glass, but we both pretended not to notice. I popped more olives into my mouth and waited for him to speak.

"That wasn't very fair of me," he said. "He was a perfectly fine cop, but he had a very, very messy personal life. Married with three kids and a very demanding mistress that we all knew about. It's a wonder his wife didn't."

I stopped chewing and stared at him. This genuinely surprised me. Maurice did not seem like a cheater—this man who apologized for saying the f-word. Though, when I thought about it, I wasn't sure what one thing had to do with the other.

"The mistress wanted presents, but his wife did all their bills, right?" Dad was saying. "If he spent a dime, the jig was up. So what Maurice did . . . He swiped a few items for her out of the evidence locker."

I drank more of my wine and stared at him. "Are you kidding me?"

"Trust me, it sounds a lot worse than it was. It was never anything really material. I remember there was a fake fur. Some costume jewelry. All cold-case stuff," he said. "In fact, nobody could even prove it was Maurice who was doing it, but a bunch of us had our suspicions. Then he takes this one item . . . Damn. It's so long ago, I can't remember what it was . . ."

He raised his glass with a shaking hand, then put it down again without drinking, as though this were a battle and the tremor had won. "Anyway, this thing Maurice took was so obvious, no one could ignore it. Sergeant had to let him go." He pushed his drink away, his smile fading. "It was such a good story. And now it's . . . it's gone." An emotion passed through his eyes—a type of melancholy. I'd seen it before. It happened when he lost memories, but it looked as though he was losing dear friends. And these days, it was happening more and more frequently.

I put my hand over his and gave it a squeeze. "It's okay," I said. "You can call me when you remember."

He nodded. I sipped my wine. He ate a few potato chips. I ate some nuts.

"Anyway," I said. "I feel like Dylan's out there. And if anybody knows where he is, it's Sky."

"So talk to her," he said.

"In the hospital?"

"Visiting hours are up until eight or nine," he said. "Go over there and sit at her bedside and act like you're concerned. Chat her up. You know how it goes. The truth works itself out like a splinter. You just have to wait and be patient. She'll slip."

"But, Dad," I said, "she's really smart."

"You're smarter." He said it as though it was the absolute truth.

My throat tightened up. I drank more wine and watched my father raise his glass to his lips, successfully this time. He drank his martini and smiled at me, and I thought, *What would I ever do without him?* The question didn't feel as rhetorical as it used to, and I didn't like that. I didn't like this train of thought at all.

"One of the things I like about Richie," Dad said. "He's always known how smart you are."

I sighed. Finished the rest of my glass. "And here I thought we'd go for a whole evening without talking about Richie."

"He's a good kid. You're good together. I can't help it."

I finished the potato chips. "We had an argument yesterday. Kind of," I said. "I don't think he knew it was an argument, because the arguing part happened in my head."

"What was it about?"

"He wants me to semi-retire."

Dad looked at me. "Richie said that?"

"Well . . . no."

"What did he say, then?"

"He wants me to stop taking dangerous cases."

Dad shrugged. "Sounds like he cares about you."

I looked at him. "I know you retired because of Mom."

He smiled and shook his head. "I retired because it was time."

"But Mom was the one who started making noises about it."

"It's so long ago," he said quietly. "I can barely remember."

"Do you ever resent her for that, Dad?" I said.

He started to say no, but I held up a hand. "Please," I said. "Be honest with me. I know it's your passion because it's my passion, too. You retired for Mom. Because you love her and she wanted you out of harm's way and so she insisted. I love Richie, and so I need to know . . . If I do what he wants—and what he wants is for me to live, I understand that—will I ever regret getting back together with him?"

I swallowed the rest of my Chablis. I hadn't intended to say any of that. It had been weighing on my mind more than I thought it had, this whole thing with Richie, how it felt like an ultimatum. But was that an excuse to ambush my father like that—to make him dig up emotions he'd no doubt conveniently buried? "You don't have to answer that, Dad," I said. "Honestly, I'm so caught up in this case, I don't know what I'm talking about."

It was his turn to hold a hand up. He took a sip of his martini and set the glass down and gave me a slight smile—a mixture of bemusement and concern. "Mom was the one who started making noises about me retiring. You're right about that," he said. "But she made them for seven years before I did anything about it."

I stared at him. "Seven years?"

"Maybe seven and a half."

"But . . . I thought—"

"Nope. You two girls know a lot about Mom and me. But you don't know us in our entirety." He finished his martini, that wry smile still on his face.

"She waited for you," I said.

"Yes," he said. "And I bet Richie will wait for you, too. It's what you do when you love someone."

I drank some water. Put the glass down carefully. I was at a loss for words—the way I always was when I realized I'd been wrong about something. And this particular something was huge. *My mother, making an actual compromise. Out of love.* "What do I do, Dad?" I said finally.

My father waved to the server and asked for the check, handing her his credit card the way he always did, without letting me look at it. "I already told you what to do," he said once she left.

"You did?"

"Yes," he said. "Go to the hospital."

# FORTY-ONE

I didn't think Sky would take kindly to an ambush, so I texted her from The Street Bar and asked if I could stop by the hospital to ask her a few questions. She replied right away with a chipper *Sure!* And so I grabbed my purse and said a quick goodbye to my dad, determined to make it there before visiting hours ended.

On my way to Mass General, I called Spike from the Uber and told him everything I'd figured out today. The driver kept glancing at me in the rearview, until I explained to him that I was brainstorming a screenplay idea.

"So where are you off to now?" Spike asked.

"Mass General," I said. "I'm going to see what I can get out of Sky." The driver glanced at me again. "You know . . . for screenplay research."

"Whatever," Spike said. "You want me to come?"

"I think it's best if you stay with Elspeth," I said. "We don't know who . . . the other characters are going to be and if they might . . . surface in the third act."

"I hate it when you speak in code," he said flatly.

"I can't help it," I said. "You have to admit, this is a very scary-sounding script, and we don't need people telling others . . . about our idea."

He gave me an exasperated sigh. "Look, Greta Gerwig, I really don't think Elspeth shot Sky."

"Tell me why," I said.

"Okay, I'm not being sexist. But she's very small, especially in the shoulders. Even if it was just a .22—and I'm guessing it was a higher caliber if it did the damage you said it did to Sky's shoulder—the kickback alone would probably take her arm out of its socket."

"If you say so."

"I do. Plus, she'd be more traumatized than she is."

"Yeah?" I said. "How is she?"

"Pretty good, considering. Calling friends. Working her way through my menu. I gave her one of Flynn's tracksuits to wear so she didn't have to be in that bloodstained Armani anymore. Fits her pretty good. Which concerns me about Flynn."

"Okay, so I tend to agree with you. But that means someone else had to have shot her."

"Don't forget to say 'in the screenplay.'"

"In the screenplay."

"God, that's annoying."

"It means there's more of them working with our villain. And so our supporting character needs to be protected."

"I know, I know," he said. "I'll take her to your place after work. How's that? It went pretty well before. Your building's secure. And you can update us on whatever you get out of Sky."

"Sounds good." I smiled. "For the screenplay."

Spike ended the call without saying goodbye.

F ive minutes later, we were at Mass General. I got out of the car quickly and headed for the elevators, checking my watch as I ran. I had about twenty minutes before visiting hours ended. I wondered if that was enough time for the truth to work itself out. I hoped so.

I arrived at Sky's floor and headed directly for her room, bumping squarely into Maurice from behind. He was still wearing his security guard uniform, along with a heavy coat, and he was talking to one of the nurses. He turned around when I bumped into him. "Sunny!" he said. "Good to see you." Sky's room was empty.

I looked around. "What's going on?" I said.

"That's what I'm trying to figure out," Maurice said, turning back to the nurse. "This young lady says Sky was discharged an hour ago. But I was told by Sky herself that she was being kept overnight for observation."

The nurse shook her head. "That was never the plan, though," she said. "She was never told that. She was probably just confused."

Maurice turned to me, his eyes widening slightly. "Probably," he said. The nurse left. I looked at him.

"She clearly told me tomorrow morning," he said.

"Me too," I said. "She even texted back 'Sure' when I asked if I could stop by the hospital tonight."

"Really?"

I nodded.

"It's almost like . . . I don't know . . . she didn't want anyone to find out when she was leaving."

Something passed between us—a knowledge that neither one of us seemed to want to voice.

I cleared my throat. "I told my dad about you, by the way," I said. "He told me to tell you hi."

"Phil's a great guy," he said.

"He feels the same about you."

"That's good to know," he said. "Because I was going through some things back then."

I gave him a smile that I hoped looked understanding. "We all go through things," I said.

"True story," he said.

"Maurice?"

"Yeah?"

"I think Sky may be up to something."

He breathed out loudly. "Oh, man, I'm so glad you said that."

"You are?"

"I've thought it for a while now," he said. "I think she's harboring Dylan."

*"What?"*

"That's not what you were thinking?"

"Well, it was part of what I was thinking," I said. "Kind of. Maybe."

"Okay, well, can I tell you what's going through my head first?" he said. "Because my, uh, theory has time constraints."

I looked at him. "I'm all ears," I said.

He spoke very quietly. "A bunch of times since he disappeared, I've seen her talking on her phone to someone in a very low voice. And when she sees me looking at her, she hangs up. Mid-sentence sometimes."

I nodded.

"Then I found this on her desk." He pulled a piece of paper out of his pocket—a list, written in neat block letters. I read it.

3 WARM SWEATERS, MEN'S LARGE

4 SETS LONG UNDERWEAR—MEN'S LARGE

1 JAR INSTANT COFFEE

5 CANS TUNA, PACKED IN WATER

6 BOXES POP-TARTS—FROSTED STRAWBERRY, CHOCOLATE (ANYTHING BUT CINNAMON)

1 BOTTLE MAKER'S MARK

1 BOTTLE JOHNNY WALKER BLACK

3 BOTTLES OXY (IN MEDICINE CABINET)

I looked at Maurice. "That's not for Sky," I said.

"I know," he said. "I brought it with me to the hospital because I wanted to confront her with it." He cleared his throat. "I found one like it a few days ago—you know, with different things on it," he said. "I was super-curious. I guess it's the cop in me. But I decided to stake her out. I followed her from work. She does all these errands, stops at the liquor store, the drugstore, Dylan's apartment building. Then she starts driving out of town. I follow her to this crappy stretch of beachfront, just outside of Marblehead. I think my dad took me to a carnival there once when I was a kid." He rolled his eyes. "Jesus, my dad was a cheap asshole. Anyway, Sky stops at this motel—The Dunes, it's called. It's a pit. Meth Addict City. And I watch her bring all these bags into this one room on the first floor."

I stared at him. "You didn't go in?"

He shook his head. "I felt like a stalker," he said. "Like it was none of my business, and I'd probably lose my job if I did anything more. I also thought, *What if it isn't Dylan? What if it's a crazy sister nobody knows about or a secret boyfriend or something, and I'm about to insinuate myself into someone's private business?*"

I nodded. "Do you still feel that way?"

"No," he said. "I mean, I don't think I do."

"Good," I said. "Because I think you should insinuate. I think it's the right thing to do."

"Really?" he said. "You don't think I'll look like some creepy stalker?"

"Okay, listen," I said. "There's a crime investigation going on, and even though I don't think Dylan had anything to do with these shootings, he's wanted for questioning. And if it goes much further and they think they've got enough on Dylan to make him a suspect, Sky is, at the very least, aiding and abetting a fugitive."

"Wait, hold up," he said. "You *don't* think Dylan did the shootings?"

"You want to go to The Dunes or not?"

"I'm not sure I—"

"Because you're right, it's time-sensitive. And if you're really going to talk to Sky and Dylan, convince them that what they're doing is wrong and that they should come back, you should do it now, before Sky leaves."

"I should, right?"

I took a breath. Said it as casually as I could. "If you think it would help, I can go with you."

His face brightened. "Okay, see, that wouldn't look anywhere near as creepy."

It was a special type of thrill, that feeling of everything coming together the way I wanted it to—a missing person about to be found, a criminal about to be brought to justice, all those questions roiling in my mind finally on the verge of being answered. It happened rarely during cases, but when it did, like right now, it was exhilarating. How could I give this feeling up for the man I loved? *Maybe I won't have to. Maybe he'll wait.*

Maurice was looking at me expectantly. I smiled and clapped his shoulder. "Come on, big guy," I said. "Let's hit the beach."

# FORTY-TWO

Maurice drove a cherry-red MINI Cooper, which was surprising. I guess I'd figured he'd have more of a macho ride, which was probably sexist of me. But practically speaking, I found it hard to believe this tiny car could contain his imposing frame. It couldn't have been comfortable for him. He had the driver's seat pushed back all the way, and even then he seemed bent at an odd angle. I wanted to ask if the car came with a chiropractor, but I didn't want to insult him.

As I got in the passenger seat, Maurice turned the radio on—a Willie Nelson station on Sirius. "This is my empty-nester car," he said, Willie's sweet voice enveloping us. He grabbed a bottle of water from a basket he had hanging from the door and took a big swig. "I bought it after my youngest moved

BUZZ KILL

out—she's in nursing school. I always wanted a MINI, so I figured what the hell."

"It's a great car," I said.

"I don't care if it's too small for me—it's got zip," he said. "Meanwhile, my wife is five-foot-nothing and she drives a Kia Carnival. It just goes to show . . . something, I guess."

"People don't always conform to one's expectations?"

"Sure, that works," he said. "Anyway, this MINI gets great mileage, so we can stop once on the way there and then we won't have to stop again the whole way home."

"Excellent," I said.

He offered me a bottle of water. I took it and leaned back, feeling the warmth of the seat heater and inhaling that new-car smell. There was a lot less traffic now, and before we knew it, we were out of town, the car humming along Route 114, Willie working his magic. I sipped my water, thinking about Sky in that motel room with Dylan. I wondered if she was holding him captive or if he was there willingly, whether he was blissfully unaware of the police investigation or devouring every news report. Did he miss his mother as much as she missed him? I wondered that, too, and then Maurice asked me a question I couldn't quite hear over the music.

Turning toward him, I asked him to repeat what he said. He switched the volume down and asked the question again. "Why do you think Dylan didn't do the shootings?"

"Because he didn't have the motive."

Maurice shrugged. "That jerk does a hell of a lot of things without a motive."

| 291 |

"Yeah, good point," I said, turning my body back to face the front. "But is he smart enough to pull off both shootings—or even one of them—without getting caught?"

"Could be luck," he said.

"I don't know," I said. "It's hard for me to go with that narrative when somebody with brains and motive is sitting right there in front of us."

"Who?"

I turned and looked at him, thinking about what my dad had said. Messy personal life, but a good cop. The thought must have crossed his mind already. "Sky," I said.

His face went still. "Come on," he said. "You're joking, right?"

*Guess it didn't.* "I'm dead serious, Maurice."

"Come on," he said again.

I told him about the powder found in Trevor Weiss's jacket—the highly addictive alkaloid I believed Sky had sneaked into Gonzo's new formula—then I told him about everything I believed she did to keep word of that formula from getting out, from the deep-faked audio messages, to killing Trevor and getting someone to shoot her, to her crying on cue when talking about her shooting, effectively removing her from suspicion. The whole time I offered up this theory, Maurice's features didn't move. He glared at the window like some humorless despot—to the point that I no longer felt like elaborating. "Anyway," I said. "I could be wrong."

"You are wrong." He said it through his teeth.

*Yikes,* I thought.

We were getting near the ocean now, and there was a storm

brewing, swirls of wet snowflakes in the air, a strong wind whipping the scrubby trees. At the side of the road there was a gas station, and Maurice pulled up. "Gotta fill 'er up," he said.

"Hey, Maurice?"

"Yeah?"

"I'm sorry if I offended you. It's just a theory."

His face softened. "I understand," he said. "I just know Sky better than you do."

"That's right," I said. "You do."

He got out of the car, moved to the tank. My phone rang. I looked at the screen. *Dad.* I answered it.

"I remembered!" he said.

"What?"

"You told me to call when I remembered what Maurice Dupree took from the evidence locker. The thing that got him kicked off the force."

"Right," I said quietly, my eyes on Maurice at the tank, sticking his card in the slot, then removing it. Plucking his phone out of his pocket and putting it to his ear. "What was it?"

"You're never going to believe this, because . . . Man, he's a good guy. But what a dumb thing to do."

Maurice ended whatever short call he'd made and dropped the phone back in his pocket. Then he began filling the tank.

"What was it, Dad?"

"It was a compact," he said. "A ladies' compact made from Bakelite, I think. It was some relic from the forties. But the thing about it was, it was monogrammed. Same initials as his mistress. *SF.* I even remember her name. Seraphina Farley.

Reminded me of a Dickens character. No one else would have taken it but Maurice. No one else had a girlfriend or a wife with those initials."

My mouth went dry. I stared at Maurice, leaning against the car.

"Of course, he got bumped off the force for that. But a lot of the guys were sad. They kept in touch with him. Last I'd heard, he'd gotten the mistress pregnant. He was offered a job in security at one of those casinos in Connecticut, so he relocated his family there. But sometimes he'd tell his wife he was going to a conference in Massachusetts, just so he could visit the mistress and the baby. Sweet guy. Tried to do right by people. But, boy, what a messy life." He chuckled. "I don't think his wife ever found out."

My heart pounded. I said, "Call Lee Farrell, Dad. The Dunes. Marblehead."

"Wait, what, Sunny?" he said.

But I couldn't answer. I could only stare at Maurice, who had opened the passenger-side door. He was holding a gun. I wasn't positive, but it looked a lot like the gun Dylan had held on me back in July. Dylan's gun, taken from his apartment by Elspeth. Picked up by either Sky or Maurice, used to kill Trevor and shoot Sky. Maurice looked so much more comfortable holding it than Dylan had looked.

Maurice, Sky's father.

I could hear my dad asking what was going on as I ended the call, but all I could think of were those two pictures on Sky's desk—the old one of her pregnant mother, and the one of her work friends in the Common. *She framed that photo because of Maurice. Those were framed pictures of her parents.* I put my hands up. Maurice grabbed my phone, turned off the power, and tossed it into the trash can that stood between the pumps. It came to me then—that last question, answered.

"She trusted you. You knew where to aim," I whispered. "You're the one who shot Sky."

Maurice raised the gun, pressing the cold barrel against my forehead. "Get out of the car," he said.

# FORTY-THREE

Maurice told me I would be driving the rest of the way there. I complied. It occurred to me that this was the first time during the whole ride that Maurice had told me what to do. From the initial plan to come here together to the bottle of water I'd been drinking from, he'd made me feel as though everything we did had been my idea. It was masterly, really. Manipulation skills clearly ran in that family.

My heart thudded against my ribs. I wanted to listen to Willie Nelson again, just to calm my jangling nerves, but I didn't want to anger Maurice with a request. He didn't seem to want the music on. He preferred talking instead.

"Sky was the one who looked me up. You know that?" he said. "I hadn't seen her since her mother died, and she was just a little kid then. I get this call from her, at the casino where I was working. About three years ago. She remembered this one day when I took her here. Well, not here. But Marblehead. She remembered walking along the beach with me. How I bought her a vanilla soft-serve ice cream with rainbow sprinkles, and I told her she was the brightest and toughest little girl in the world—bright and tough like a diamond. See, I don't remember that at all. But she did. Sky remembered it. She said she's aimed to be a diamond ever since."

He jabbed the gun into my ribs. "Make a left," he said.

I did as I was told. "You were a good father to her," I said. "She remembered."

"No, I wasn't," he said. "That isn't the point of the story at all. The point is, she's a good *daughter*. She's grateful and kind, and when she had a chance to call me, she did—even though I'm still married and my wife and other kids don't know about her, other than her being my boss. She worked around my life to bring me into hers, just because I gave her that one nice day a million years ago."

I nodded. Thinking about it, I was sure there were other, shrewder reasons—leverage, for instance. I was willing to bet that even if he hadn't bought an ice cream for his little diamond of a daughter, Sky knew that Maurice would do anything for her now—so long as she didn't tell his wife about their family ties. "My other kids, they're nowhere near as grateful as she is," Maurice said. He told me to take a right, and I did. We drove down a desolate beach road to The Dunes, which was just as Maurice had described it—a crumbling mess of a motel that almost looked abandoned, save for three beat-up cars in the lot. A light on in one of the dirty windows. *A pit.*

Maurice told me to park the car and forced me out of it, the barrel of the gun pressed to my neck. The storm was more forceful now, the wind biting at my cheeks, bits of ice flying into my hair, my eyes.

"I didn't mean to insult her," I said. "Sky is tough and bright. That's what I meant. Dylan couldn't have done what she did because he isn't either of those things."

He marched me toward a room on the first floor, shoving me ahead of him as he unlocked the door and pushed it open. "Let me tell you something. Shooting Sky. That was the hardest thing I've ever done in my life," he said. "I feel like I could shoot anybody after that, and it wouldn't even faze me."

"Great," I whispered.

Inside the room, the lights were off. It was pitch-black, except for a tiny, muted TV—news about the storm. I read the caption on the screen: *It's expected to get worse.*

"You brought her," Sky said. "The great, soon-to-be-late Sunny Randall."

Slowly my eyes began to adjust. Sky was on the bed with Dylan. He wasn't moving, and I could smell him more than I could see him—a rank, rancid odor. He clearly hadn't bathed in weeks. "Say hello to Sunny," Sky said. She reached over and yanked something from his face. A gag.

Dylan screamed. *"I thought I could trust you! I thought you were my friend!"*

Sky got up on her knees and pressed something to his throat. "You want to wake the neighbors? Is that what you want?" She flicked on the light on the nightstand. My eyes ached. It took a while for them to adjust, different things coming into focus. Empty pizza cartons. Liquor and pill bottles scattered on the floor. The antithesis of Sky's pristine apartment. I remembered that just yesterday Sky had called Dylan "kind of a slob," and all the while, she'd been coming to visit him here, in this pigsty, feeding him, giving him drugs, recording his voice, framing him.

And now he'd clearly outlived his usefulness. When my eyes adjusted, I could see everything. Sky in the sweats I'd brought to the hospital, one arm in a sling, a hunting knife in her good hand. She was holding it to Dylan's throat.

Dylan looked at me. "Sunny," he said. "Can you tell me how Bella is?"

I swallowed hard. For the first time, I actually felt sorry for him. "She's . . . she's gone, Dylan."

He started to shake, tears spilling down his cheeks. "Sky told me she was still alive. She said she could feel her pulse. She said she was bringing her to the hospital."

"She didn't make it," said Sky, who had apparently dumped her in the river.

"I called you for help," Dylan said. "I always called you for . . . for . . ."

"Maybe it's time you learned to help yourself." Sky said it without a hint of emotion. I remembered Trevor. The way she'd flatly referred to him as "that lab tech."

Dylan started to cough. Tears streamed down his cheeks. "I killed her," he said. "I gave her those drugs and I . . . Bella brought me to urgent care, and I didn't do that." He looked at Sky. "You . . . you said you were going to take her to the hospital."

"Enough talking," Sky snapped.

I looked around the room. Tried to collect my thoughts. My gun was in my purse. My purse was in the MINI. Maurice had Dylan's gun. But as far as I could tell, Sky's only weapon was the hunting knife. And that shoulder and arm were a serious liability. For some reason, I thought of Spike. *If only he'd taught me judo.*

"Sunny complicates our story," Sky said to Maurice. "If he just offs himself because he can't handle the guilt . . . hmm. Maybe he kills her first?"

"That's it," Maurice said.

"Explain it to me like I'm five," Sky said, the knife still at Dylan's throat.

"Okay, kid. Here's what we're telling the cops," Maurice said. "With my help and yours, Sunny here tracked Dylan down to this room. Rather than go back with her and face justice for the crimes he committed, he shot and killed Sunny, then he turned the gun on himself." He looked at his daughter. "We survived. But it was traumatic. We'll never be the same. But on the bright side, we're heroes."

"Good narrative," Sky said. "I mean, if I killed two people and tried to murder my best friend, I'd probably want to end things, too. It's believable."

"It's not what happened," I said. "You'll be living a lie."

"Truth is just a matter of perception," she said. "If you're dead, you can't perceive anything, so you don't really have a say."

"What about Dylan's parents?" I said. "What about Lydia? Don't you care about her at all?"

She gave me a sweet smile, the knife tight in her hand. "Lydia adores me," Sky said. "I'm the daughter she never had. I'll help her through this difficult time. I mean . . . if need be, I could even move in with them."

My heart sank. I'd been suspicious about Sky for so long—but I hadn't said a word about it to Lydia.

Sky glanced at Maurice. "I made Dylan's audio confession this morning," she said. "It's moving, I think."

"I have no doubt, kiddo," Maurice said. "You are a talent. We've got to get the show on the road, though. Cops will be coming soon."

"You called them?" Sky asked.

"Sunny did, back in the MINI," he said. "She told her dad to call them. She didn't have time to implicate us, though."

Sky helped Dylan to his feet. He was frighteningly compliant. She moved him to the dresser and leaned him up against it, Maurice holding the gun on me the entire time. "Hey, Sky?" Maurice said.

"Yeah?"

"No more murders after this, okay?" he said. "I mean . . . I do have a family to think of."

She gave him a long, probing look. "As long as I have

everything I want, Daddy," she said, "you've got nothing to worry about." She glanced at me. "You know, if you hadn't texted me to say you were coming by the hospital, Maurice wouldn't have known to head over there so he could run into you. You'd still be alive."

"What's your point?" I said.

She shrugged. "I dunno. Transparency is overrated?"

I glared at her. "I'll keep that in mind."

Sky started to untie Dylan's right arm. "You ready?"

"Bella's gone," Dylan said quietly, his whole body lax and useless. "I killed her. I may as well kill someone else. And I don't give a shit whether I live or die."

Maurice placed the gun in Dylan's hand. "You try anything," he said, "she'll cut you."

Dylan seemed to barely notice it. He was focused on Sky. "You were the one who sent me those texts," he said. "'Murderer.' Because you knew that's what I was."

Sky backed away from Dylan, Maurice holding his free arm, aiming the gun at my head.

"You've never been a very good person, Dylan," she said. "Even before you overdosed Bella."

His head lolled to one side, greasy hair flopping in his eyes, Maurice posing him like a mannequin.

I waved my arms at Dylan, trying to wake him up.

"People need you!" I shouted.

"No, they don't," he said.

"Your parents need you. Your mother needs you. Please don't

do this to Lydia. *She's* a good person. And you're her entire world."

For a moment, I thought I saw a spark in Dylan's eyes—as though a tiny part of him was coming to life.

Maurice wrapped both of his hands around Dylan's right one. He pulled back the trigger. I closed my eyes. I heard a loud *crack*—the bullet hitting the ceiling. And then I opened my eyes to see Dylan, his arm in the air, Maurice grappling with him, Dylan thrashing. I jumped at Sky, wrestled her to the floor, and sat on her. It was easy, what with that bad arm of hers. She cried out, "You're hurting me!"

"To be fully transparent," I said, "I don't give a damn."

The hunting knife was on the floor next to the bed. I grabbed it fast. Dylan freed himself of Maurice and shot the lamp. It exploded, bits of plaster flying everywhere.

"I've got your daughter, Maurice!" I called out. "I've got the hunting knife. Let go of Dylan's arm or I write a new fucking narrative."

Maurice jumped back, leaving Dylan with the gun. "You're a shitty person just like me," Dylan said to Sky, who whimpered beneath me like a child. "And just like me, you get to live with yourself for fifty, sixty, seventy more years. It will be just like living in this disgusting room. You'll never be able to escape."

Dylan shot through the windows, the bed, the cheap linoleum floor. Icy winds pushed into the room, sleet seeping through holes in the walls, everything cold and wet and brutal.

And Dylan kept firing, again and again. He shot the bathroom door, the mirror, the toilet. He kept shooting, the rest of us ducking, our heads down, our eyes shut tight. He murdered the motel room—a place he hated as much as himself—until he ran out of bullets and in the near distance, through the wind and rain, we finally heard the sirens.

# EPILOGUE

### One month later

If someone had told me a year ago that Rosie and I would be spending New Year's Eve on the Jersey Shore, listening to a Bruce Springsteen tribute band called the Wrecking Balls (*Go, Balls!*) and having the time of our lives, I'd have said they were crazy. If they'd told me Richie would be with us and we'd feel at peace and in love with him in a way we'd never thought possible (I should have said "I" rather than "we," as I couldn't speak for Rosie), I'd have insisted they shut the hell up. Because now they were making fools of themselves, creating scenarios that didn't exist.

Yet here I was, at a table in Candy's Room, toasting the New Year with Richie and Rosie—champagne for us, a super-sized dog biscuit for her—listening to a killer version of "Badlands" and feeling pretty damn glorious.

In a way, my elation was understandable. No one had been killed or even injured during that horrible night at The Dunes. A rarity for me, anywhere. And in another shocker, I had Dylan Welch to thank for it. A few weeks ago, before he'd checked in to a real, serious rehab for a minimum of two months, Dylan had sent me an email. *Thank you for saving my life*, it read. *And for reminding me what's really important.* I suspected Lydia had coached him on it. It sounded just like something she would say, after all. But I could have said the same thing to him. He showed *me* what was really important. When I mentioned Dylan's mother and how she needed him, I saw a change, a spark in his eyes. And just like that, he shifted from killing himself to killing the trap he'd found himself in. It was powerful. Symbolic. And very true. One of the most important reasons to go on living is because we're needed by others—others we love.

I thought about being needed the whole time Dylan shot up the room and I was lying there on the floor, avoiding shrapnel. *Who needs me in that reason-to-live way?*

The answer, of course, was Richie. It had been the reason he'd asked me to reconsider the cases I took on—but it wasn't an ultimatum. He'd explained that recently. Although he'd said he certainly wouldn't mind if I stopped taking on dangerous cases, he was really just telling me to try to stay safe. He was willing to wait. Just like my mom had been. Not that love couldn't make some people reckless—Maurice had stolen pieces of evidence for his sidepiece, but that was nothing compared to what he'd done for their daughter. And now they'd both been charged with a long list of crimes. Sky was in jail, awaiting trial for the murder of Trevor Weiss, as well as conspiring to kill Dylan and me, kidnapping Dylan, and a slew of other charges. Meanwhile, Maurice had been charged as an accessory to murder and with conspiracy and kidnapping—but far worse for him was that his wife had learned about Sky's parentage at long last and left him. His empty-nester years looked bleak, to say the least.

But situations like those were rare. Richie loved Richard Jr. and me fiercely, protectively—and never involving felony indictments. After all the years we'd been together, Richie loved me for who I was—and that included my flaws, my misgivings, and my ever-present fear of putting my foot on the gas. And in turn, I'd put aside all of those things and agreed to tie the knot with him again . . . someday. In the future.

We even decided to make it official. Last week, Richie had asked my parents for my hand in eventual marriage. And, liberated soul that I am, I'd done the same with Desmond Burke. *What the hell does "eventual marriage" mean?* Desmond had said when I went to see him. And I'd replied, *We'll see.*

Desmond was wearing a tailored black suit at the time, and for a few seconds, I thought he'd dressed specially for the occasion. But as it happened, he'd just come back from a funeral— Moon Monaghan's. *Poor Moon,* he'd said solemnly. *To live all those years only to step in front of a bullet. Such a pity. Hearty man like that. Wrong place, wrong time.* All debts to Moon had been cleared—including Dylan's, which Desmond had pointed out. *Moon should have consulted with me first,* he'd said to me in that lyrical yet ominous Irish brogue. *Were that the case—who knows? He might have chosen a safer path for his nightly walk.*

At any rate, Richie and I were on the same page at last, and that's what I was thinking about when the band stopped playing and everybody started the countdown. I was thinking about it all the way until Richie got down on one knee, a black box in his hand.

*10, 9, 8 . . .*

"What the actual hell, Richie?" I said.

He grinned. "Open it."

"I'm too scared."

Richie sighed. He opened the box. On the white satin pad stood a small gold key. I looked up at him. "It's the key to my heart," he said. "And it also happens to be the key to my apartment."

I laughed and teared up at the same time.

*7, 6, 5, 4 . . .*

"Sunny Randall, my partner in crime, co-parent to Rosie, love of my life," Richie said. "Will you cohabitate with me for at least half the year?"

*3, 2, 1 . . .*

*Happy New Year!*

I gazed into Richie's eyes and saw lifetimes within them—

the one we'd lived together, the one we'd lived apart, this exciting new one that stretched out into the future, unknown and familiar at the same time. Uncertain as everything else was in my life, I knew one thing for sure: I needed Richie in it. I always would. And so I said yes. Obviously.